**Praise for the Novels
of Joseph A. West**

"I look forward to many years of entertainment from Joseph West."

—Four-time Spur Award–winning
author Loren D. Estleman

"Original, imaginative."

—Max Evans, Spur Award–winning
author of *The Rounders*

"Wildly comic and darkly compelling."
—Robert Olen Butler, Pulitzer Prize–winning author
of *A Good Scent from a Strange Mountain*

"[A] rollicking big windy."   —Elmer Kelton

"Take a pair of pugnacious cowboys who never saw trouble they didn't like, mix them with a fiendish villain and his diabolical filibusters, and the result is comic delight. Joseph West [has] an encyclopedic knowledge of the West. He keeps the body count sufficient to satisfy gluttons, frosts his cake with bawds, throws a few wolfers, a boxer, and a patent medicine huckster into the pot, rings in all the Western legends worth recounting, and seasons the stew with smiles. . . . Western fiction will never be the same."

—Richard S. Wheeler, Spur Award–winning
author of *Sierra*

GUNSMOKE™
DODGE THE DEVIL

Joseph A. West

Foreword by
James Arness

A SIGNET BOOK

SIGNET
Published by New American Library, a division of
Penguin Group (USA) Inc., 375 Hudson Street,
New York, New York 10014, USA
Penguin Group (Canada), 90 Eglinton Avenue East, Suite 700, Toronto,
Ontario M4P 2Y3, Canada (a division of Pearson Penguin Canada Inc.)
Penguin Books Ltd., 80 Strand, London WC2R 0RL, England
Penguin Ireland, 25 St. Stephen's Green, Dublin 2,
Ireland (a division of Penguin Books Ltd.)
Penguin Group (Australia), 250 Camberwell Road, Camberwell, Victoria 3124,
Australia (a division of Pearson Australia Group Pty. Ltd.)
Penguin Books India Pvt. Ltd., 11 Community Centre, Panchsheel Park,
New Delhi - 110 017, India
Penguin Group (NZ), cnr Airborne and Rosedale Roads, Albany,
Auckland 1310, New Zealand (a division of Pearson New Zealand Ltd.)
Penguin Books (South Africa) (Pty.) Ltd., 24 Sturdee Avenue,
Rosebank, Johannesburg 2196, South Africa

Penguin Books Ltd., Registered Offices:
80 Strand, London WC2R 0RL, England

First published by Signet, an imprint of New American Library,
a division of Penguin Group (USA) Inc.

First Printing, October 2006
10 9 8 7 6 5 4 3 2 1

Foreword

These days I still receive many letters, e-mails, and cards from people thanking me for making a show that affected their lives. The show also affected the lives of all the actors on the show. We became like one big family and sometimes we acted like a family, having disagreements just like everyone has with their siblings. We did, however, respect each other's privacy too.

You know, my longtime set double, Ben Bates, was a lot like me both in personality and stature. My wife and his had a hard time telling us apart when we were at a distance. A little known fact is that we both had a real-life limp, though his was just on the other side from mine. Until we pointed that out, no one noticed. We spent a lot of time together over the years and sometimes it was spooky for me to look up and see myself coming down the street. I think we even started looking more alike as the years went on.

We have remained friends after all these years.

Along the way Ben sure saved me from some rough
scenes. I remember one scene we were filming up in
Utah at about 9000 feet. He had to run through knee-
level snow chasing a bad guy. Each time Ben would
get through the entire scene, the director yelled that
we had to do it all again. I think it took him two
days to recover. Another time, a scene was designed
for me to ride into town and have the horse rear
up—I was to slide off the saddle and run for cover
while being shot at. After the take, everyone kept
saying what a great stunt I did and I don't think Ben
or I ever told anyone it was him instead of me.

I recall a time prior to Ben joining the *Gunsmoke*
family—we were shooting up on the Rogue River in
Oregon. I was being chased by the bad guys because
I had a saddlebag full of money that they wanted to
take away from me. In the scene, I rode up to the
edge of cliff, and in order to get away, I had to jump
eighty or ninety feet into the river. Needless to say,
that required my stunt guy. It was getting late in the
afternoon, and as the shadows were creeping up the
canyon wall, the director kept yelling for him to
climb higher and higher. After the fact, we measured
and found out that he had jumped 120 feet and only
missed the cliff rocks by about two feet. I think it
scared both of us then, and we were glad we didn't
realize how far and how dangerous it was at the
time.

In another scene sometime later, the stunt double
had to swim the rapids and then climb up on the
bank over a large group of rocks. The crew was in a
hurry and told him not to bother with a wet suit.
But he insisted on using the wet suit and so they

waited. When he crawled up on the bank, a startled rattlesnake suddenly attacked him. The only thing that saved him was that the snake's fangs could not penetrate his wet suit. He and all the rest of us were really glad he had insisted on that suit. Maybe these scenes were the reason this guy wasn't my double for long

We had a regular group of extras that played the townspeople. Usually they were not in any danger. One time, however, we were shooting a scene in which we had a herd of stampeding cattle. We found out really quickly that a herd of cattle do pretty much whatever they want. The extras, my stunt double, and at least one cameraman had to scramble to get out of their way. Fortunately no one was injured in that scene. You can be sure that we were more careful with all of our cattle scenes in the future.

We were really lucky that in all twenty years of filming, no one was ever seriously hurt. I guess we can thank our directors and producers for keeping us all safe.

You know that everyone claims that the success of *Gunsmoke* was Matt Dillon, Doc, Kitty, Festus, Quint, and Newley. The truth is that this show would never have made it without all the stuntmen, the extras, the character actors, the cameramen, the scriptwriters, the grips, and everyone else who worked on the show. We would have been lost without our directors and producers. Most days it seemed like the main characters were the last ones on the set and the first ones to leave. I always tried to make sure that everyone working on the set knew that we appreciated all their hard work and dedication to making

the show a success. We truly would not have been
the long-running success we were without all of
them.

                            —James Arness
                             "Marshal Matt Dillon"

chapter I

Death Rides a Pale Horse

A tired gray mustang plodded into Dodge City, puffs of yellow dust rising from its dragging hooves. The horse's rider was young, his pleasant, sunburned face covered in freckles. That he was a Texas puncher there was no doubt, his origins betrayed by his wide sombrero, the stars on his boots and the spurs on his heels, the rowels as large as teacups. A holstered Colt with a bone handle rode at the cowboy's waist, and at first glance, the man's slump-shouldered posture in the saddle suggested that he had traveled fast and far and with little sleep.

Only when United States marshal Matt Dillon looked closer did he realize that the young puncher was dead.

The man's eyes were wide open, but they had the fixed, unblinking look of one who saw nothing of the dusty street but was intently gazing into a distant eternity.

Matt stepped off the boardwalk, caught the mustang's trailing reins and halted the exhausted animal. The gray's flanks were streaked with sweat, and a bullet had burned across its right shoulder, drawing blood, now brown and starting to crust.

The big marshal effortlessly lifted the dead cowboy from the saddle, gently laid him on his back on the ground, then got down on one knee at his side.

The puncher was very young, a kid no more than fourteen, and Matt guessed he'd recently made his first trip up the trail. Apart from that, there was little else to be learned about the boy, but the manner of his dying was much more obvious.

He had been shot in the back three times. Two of the wounds were close together at the top of his right shoulder blade and looked to have been made by the same rifle. A third bullet had crashed into the boy's spine, just above his gun belt, and then ranged upward, blowing a fist-sized hole as it exited at the base of his throat, where it met the left collarbone. A larger-caliber rifle had produced this wound—to Matt's experienced eye, a Sharps .50-70—and this had been the shot that had killed him.

The fact that the cowboy had managed to stay in the saddle after being hit so hard was a testimony to his pluck. Whoever he was, he'd had sand in plenty.

Matt slid the Colt from the puncher's holster. He'd thought the handle was bone, but now he saw that it was walnut crudely covered with white paint. The marshal thumbed open the loading gate and spun the cylinder. All five rounds had been fired, so the kid had made a fight of it, and he'd had the presence of mind to holster the gun, hoping for a chance to reload. The lathered pony suggested it had been a running fight, and the cowboy had been killed not long before his mount carried him into Dodge.

Matt rose to his feet and looked around him. Apart from a few curious onlookers, mostly women from the respectable side of town across the tracks and the bearded, profane drivers of the jostling freight and express wagons, Front Street was almost empty of people.

The sun was at its highest point in the sky, but still Dodge City slumbered. Worn-out from the night before, the fifteen hundred cowboys and ranchers in town were sleeping off their exertions with the saloon girls and their close association with the whiskey bottle. And so too were twice that many others, sharp businessmen, real estate agents, farmers, land seekers, Mexicans up from the border country, hungry lawyers, worn-out soiled doves who worked the line, pale gamblers and hundreds of ragged men without visible means of support who followed the herds and preyed on the free-spending Texans.

Only when the sun went down and the streetlamps were lit would Dodge bestir herself and, like a tired dove, paint her face and smile a welcome to another night of sin that came easy but never cheap.

To Matt's right, the door of the marshal's office swung wide and his deputy Festus Haggen stepped onto the boardwalk, blinking like an owl against the sudden glare of the noon light.

Festus scratched a hairy jaw, glanced over at the Long Branch and touched his tongue to a dry upper lip.

Matt, reading the signs, smiled inwardly. It seemed that last night Festus had again prevailed on Kitty

Russell's openhanded generosity and was suffering the consequences.

Only after a few moments' deep contemplation of the saloon did the deputy turn and see Matt with the dead cowboy at his feet. A few quick steps brought him to Matt's side. "Didn't see you there at first, Matthew," he said. "The light, you know."

The big marshal nodded, holding back his smile. "It will do that to a man—a man suffering from a hangover worst of all, I'm told."

Festus studied Matt's face, searching for the sting, but the big marshal kept his expression bland.

"I never could cotton to early risin'," Festus said finally, looking grouchy. "Seems to me fellers who get up before noon think the sun comes up just to hear them crow." His eyes dropped to the dead cowboy. "What happened, Matthew?"

Matt shrugged. "His horse brought him in a few minutes ago. He's been"—the marshal was about to say *shot* but changed his mind and said—"murdered."

Festus' knees cracked as he squatted beside the body. "Hell, Matthew, he's only a boy."

"I'd say he played the man's part, though," Matt said. "His gun is shot dry, so he made a fight of it."

"Doc Adams?" Festus asked, his eyes lifting to the marshal in a question.

Matt shook his head. "Way too late for Doc. Best you go fetch Percy Crump."

Festus rose to his feet. "I'll do that." After a last, lingering glance at the Long Branch, he hurried away in the direction of Crump's funeral parlor.

Out there on the street, away from any shade, the day was insufferably hot. Matt took off his hat, wiped the sweatband with his fingers, then drew the faded blue sleeve of his shirt across his forehead. He settled the hat back on his head and looked once again at the dead cowboy.

The kid was typical of the hundreds of Texas punchers who had crowded into Dodge in the past couple weeks, young men who had never lived where churches and schools stood and were as wild as the cattle they nursed.

Sitting a forty-pound saddle that galled even his tough hide, this kid had helped drive a herd through the mud and rain of storm-swept plains and into the mad symphony of the keening north wind. He had crossed waterless wastelands, endless miles of scorching heat and dust, and he'd known that at any time he could find himself in the middle of a prairie fire, quicksand or stampede.

For months he'd drunk alkali water that gave him running sores and beans that gave him the croup, and through it all, he'd dreamed of the bright lights of Dodge, where for a week or maybe even a day he'd squander his money and live like a king.

But all that had ended in a hail of gunfire that had snuffed out his young life.

For the first time Matt noticed a silver signet ring on the little finger of the cowboy's right hand. He got down on a knee, lifted the dead boy's hand and looked closer. The ring bore some kind of elaborate crest that the marshal did not recognize. If he were a gambling man, he'd bet the farm that someone had seen the ring and killed the cowboy to get it. Life was cheap on the frontier and there were those who would kill a dozen men, or women and children come to that, to own a piece of silver jewelry that fancy.

Matt rose to his feet and saw Percy Crump hurrying toward him in his strange crow-hop gait, the tails of his frockcoat flapping behind him like broken tail feathers. The marshal could never understand why Percy ran like that. Dead men weren't going anywhere.

The undertaker stopped beside Matt, followed shortly by his assistant, a sad man with brown hound dog eyes and a weak chin.

"Deputy Festus said we have a murder here, Marshal," Crump said. He looked down at the puncher. "My, my, and the deceased is only a boy."

Matt nodded. "That's already been noted, Percy."

The undertaker dropped to a knee and, as was his custom, riffled through the pockets of the dead youngster. After a few moments, he wordlessly handed Matt a thin wad of notes, a crumpled envelope, a rubber comb and a folding knife.

"That ring on his right hand, Percy," Matt said. "Let me have that."

Crump slipped the ring off the boy's finger. He studied the crest for a moment, shook his head and handed the ring to Matt.

"Lay him out decent in your parlor window, Percy," Matt said, shoving the cowboy's meager belongings into his pant's pocket. "I want the ranchers and the other punchers to see him. Somebody will know who he is."

Crump nodded. "It's always easier with the young ones," he said. "They make much better-looking corpses." The man studied Matt expectantly while a fly buzzed around his head. Crump batted at the fly, then said in a disappointed tone: "That was a little undertaker humor there, Marshal, only to lift the sad solemnity of the occasion, you understand."

Matt nodded, unsmiling. "Yeah, I understand, Percy. Now get this youngster off the street."

As Crump and his assistant bent to their task, Matt gathered the reins of the mustang and led the little gray toward the livery. He stopped when he saw Festus on the boardwalk. The deputy was still looking longingly across at the Long Branch, where even at this time of the day the beer was pouring cold.

"Seems like I never paid that dollar I owe you, Festus," Matt said.

The deputy shook his head, his face puzzled. "I don't recollect lendin' you a dollar, Matthew."

"It was a while back. I remember it plain as day." He reached into the pocket of his leather vest, found a dollar and spun the coin to Festus, who caught it deftly. "I always believe in paying my debts," Matt said. "Then, the next time I need a loan, you won't mind giving it to me."

Festus was still baffled, but he was not a man to study the teeth of a gift horse. "Well, thankee, Matthew, an' next time you need to borry a dollar or two, you surely know the feller to ask."

Matt nodded. "I never doubted that, Festus." As the marshal led the mustang to the stable, he glanced over his shoulder and saw his deputy hurrying across the street to the saloon. Matt smiled to himself. Thirsty as he was, it hadn't even dawned on Festus that he never had a spare dollar to lend anyone.

When he reached the livery, Matt decided the mus-

tang was now cool enough to be watered. He led the
horse to the zinc trough outside the door and let the
gray drink its fill. Then he led the animal inside to
a stall, stripped off the saddle and rubbed the horse
down with a piece of sacking. That done he forked
the little horse some hay and fed him a generous bait
of oats.

Squinting against the glare of the sun, Matt left the
stable and walked through the heat of the afternoon
to Percy Crump's funeral parlor. He stepped inside,
enjoying the coolness, though the odor of embalming
fluid hung in the air, the remembered smell of a
death in Dodge.

Crump had already washed the boy's body and
rouged his cheeks. As he greeted Matt, the undertaker was applying a bright red color to the young
puncher's pale lips.

"Almost done, Marshal." Crump smiled, revealing
teeth as long and yellow as piano keys. "As I told
you already, the young deceased don't take much in
the way of paint. Later I'll put a clean shirt on him
to cover that terrible bullet hole in his neck."

Fighting down sudden revulsion, Matt forced himself to remember that Percy Crump was as necessary
to Dodge as were buzzards to the plains. Both disposed of the dead and made their living in a place
of skulls.

"Remember to display him in the window, Percy,"
Matt said, the words hesitant, refusing to come easy.
"I want him to be seen."

"Will do, Marshal," Crump said cheerfully as he
applied more color to the boy's lips with the tip of
his little finger. "He'll be ready in an hour or so."

Matt walked out of the dim funeral parlor and into the sunlight. The air was hot and thick and smelled of the cattle pens by the railroad tracks. But he breathed deep and then walked quickly to his office, as though to rid himself of the smell of death that clung to him.

He recalled the dead boy's rouged face and made a solemn vow. He would hunt down the young puncher's killer. He'd find him and then hang him.

chapter 2

The Preacher's Brood

Matt stepped into the office and took his Winchester from the rack. The kid had come from the south. Matt would scout in that direction first.

He was about to leave when the door slammed open and Mayor James H. Kelley stormed inside, a glowing cigar clenched in his teeth, his blue eyes bright with a smile.

"Are you going somewhere, Matt?" the little Irishman asked, his gaze dropping to the rifle in the big marshal's hand.

Matt nodded. "A cowboy was murdered this morning. I'm heading out to see if I can track down his killers."

Kelley took the cigar from his mouth, his face aghast. "Jesus, Mary and Joseph preserve us. It didn't happen here in Dodge, did it?"

"No, Mayor, not in Dodge. Somewhere south of town, I reckon."

"Then it's none of your concern, Matt," Kelley said.

"It is my concern. I'm a United States marshal, Mayor. My jurisdiction doesn't stop at the city limits."

Kelley thought that through, finally accepted the logic of it and nodded. "I understand. Be careful out there, Matt." His eyes lifted to the marshal's face. "Murdered, you say?"

"Three bullets in the back." Matt reached into his pocket and passed the envelope and money to Kelley. "The kid was young, no more than fourteen. This was all he had on him. Well, that and a ring." Matt dug into his pocket again and dropped the ring into Kelley's palm. "It's got some kind of crest on it, but I don't know what it is."

The mayor held the ring closer to his eyes and studied it for a few moments, then said: "Three boar heads. That's the clan crest of the McDermotts. Whoever the boy was, he was the descendant of ancient Irish kings." Kelley hefted the ring. "Heavy, a goodly chunk of silver. It must have been a family heirloom passed down from father to son."

"I believe the kid was murdered for it," Matt said. "Some men will kill for a ring like that."

Kelley counted the money. "Ninety dollars. His wages for the drive." He opened the envelope and removed a scrap of paper torn from a tally book. In pencil the young puncher had written:

DEAR MA, I HOPE THIS LETTER
FINDS YOU WELL. I WILL BE HOME
BY THE LATE SUMMER AND WE WILL

"He never finished it," Kelley said. He glanced at the envelope. "It's addressed to Mrs. Sarah McDermott, El Paso, Texas." Kelley shoved the cowboy's money and ring into the pocket of his coat. "Matt, I'll see that the boy's effects are returned to his mother, God help her. It will break the poor woman's heart."

Matt was relieved that he did not have to write to the boy's mother. Kelley had an Irishman's way with words that might help soften the blow.

"I'll be on my way now, Mayor," Matt said, nodding toward the door. "If you'll give me the road?"

Kelley reread the address on the envelope and shoved it into his pocket. "Of course, Matt, of course," he said absently. Then his head snapped up and he said: "Wait! This sad business made me completely forget why I came here to talk to you." He touched Matt's forearm with his fingertips. "It will only take a minute."

"Mayor," the marshal said, impatience tugging at him, "if it's about stray dogs—"

"Not that, though heaven knows it's a problem we have to address. No, this is about a boxing booth." Kelley saw the puzzlement that crept into Matt's eyes, and said quickly: "A man who gave me his name as G. P. Proctor came to see me this morning. He manages a pugilist who has never been defeated in the ring. Proctor wants to set up his booth and have his boy take on all comers. He's offering a five-hundred-dollar purse to any man who can come up to scratch five times against his champeen."

Matt shook his head. "Mayor, every man I've ever known who operated a boxing booth has been a crook and his fighter a broken-down pug. I'd bet the farm that this Proctor feller is no exception.''

"Matt, it will be good for the town," Kelley said, unfazed by Matt's lack of enthusiasm. "His pugilist is a young black boy. Battling Ben Hillman they call him, and Proctor said he fought Gypsy Jem Mace to a draw over twenty-two rounds just a month ago in Bay St. Louis, Mississippi." The mayor shrugged and studiously observed the glowing end of his cigar. "Anyway, that's what Proctor says."

Despite himself, Matt was intrigued. "I was speaking to Bat Masterson a while back. He loves to talk about boxing and he mentioned that an Englishman called Jem Mace is currently the undisputed champion of the world."

Kelley beamed. "Indeed he is. Bat got it right as usual. But here's the clincher, Matt—Proctor is offering to pay the town fifty percent of his gate. That could add up to some real money because a pugilist as famous as Ben Hillman will draw folks from miles around. Hell, Matt, he could attract a bigger crowd than a double hanging."

The marshal thought it through for a few moments, then said: "All right, Mayor, let Proctor set up his booth. But at the first sign that's he's doing something crooked, and I mean anything, I'll shut him down."

"That's fair enough, I suppose," Kelley said. The little mayor had more than a touch of larceny in his soul, and in the past, he'd revealed a soft spot for men like Proctor who tiptoed along the ragged edge of dishonesty.

"Where will Proctor set up his booth?" Matt asked.

"In the vacant lot between the Dodge House and the New York Hat Shop," Kelley answered.

"I just want to know where to find him."

"That will be easy, Marshal," Kelley said, his smile wide. "Just follow the crowds, my boy. Follow the crowds."

A few minutes after leaving the mayor, Matt trotted his bay over the wooden bridge across the Arkansas, then swung to the east, following the river.

He rode across gently rolling country, once passing through grama grass that in places stood belly high to his horse. Wildflowers cast a purple haze across the prairie, and here and there were contrasting streaks of white and orange bouquets of butterfly milkweed. On the slopes of the shallow rises grew prickly pear and yucca, pink catclaw and yellow coneflowers scattered among them.

The sun rode high in a blue sky free of clouds, and in the distance toward Mulberry Creek, the land shimmered in the heat like a shifting lilac veil.

Matt let his bay drink at the creek in the shade of the cottonwoods, then splashed through the water and headed south, the unceasing prairie wind tugging at him.

Ahead of the marshal, the country seemed empty. Once he saw a herd of antelope emerge from the dancing heat waves ahead of him, looking strangely elongated until they cleared the shimmer and slowly resumed their normal size.

Matt figured the dead cowboy had been heading home when he was shot. But where in all that vast wilderness could he pick up a clue to the kid's murder? It was like looking for a needle in a haystack, and he knew his chances of stumbling on the killers were slim.

After an hour, the big marshal swung to the west and then north again toward the creek. He was in perfectly level country now and the soil was sandier, more cactus growing around him, even in the bottoms of the dusty dry washes made by the spring's rains.

He cut the horse tracks when he was still a mile south of the creek.

Matt swung out of the saddle and dropped to one knee, studying the sign. At least a half dozen horses had passed this way and not long before; the droppings of one of the animals were still moist.

Were these the tracks of the young cowboy's killer?

Matt got to his feet, his hand instinctively moving closer to his holstered Colt. His long-seeing blue eyes studied the land ahead of him, the cottonwoods and willows lining Mulberry Creek a smear of cool green in the distance.

There, he saw it! Matt caught a fleeting glimpse of a thin column of smoke rising from the creekbank before it was shredded by the wind.

The riders, whoever they were, had made camp.

Matt stepped back into the saddle and eased his Winchester into the scabbard under his knee. He kicked the bay into a walk, sitting high, every nerve in his body alert for any sign of trouble.

The men at the creek might be honest travelers, maybe punchers who had come late up the trail and made camp while others had pushed on with the herd into Dodge. But there was always the chance these were the men who had killed a half-grown boy for the silver ring on his finger.

As he rode closer to the creek, Matt saw several men sitting around a fire. There were women too, one of them carrying a heavy coffeepot. She bent over from the waist, her eyes fixed on Matt, and set the pot on the coals.

If these were honest citizens, it would be the height of bad manners to ride up on their camp unannounced, and downright dangerous if they were wary of strangers. The marshal drew rein, then stood in the stirrups and yelled: "Hello the camp!"

Immediately the men by the fire sprang to their feet. One of them, a small man wearing black pants and a woollen vest, which had once been red but was now faded to a dirty pink, scooped up the rifle that had been lying beside him. "Who are you and what do you want?" he hollered.

Matt rode closer, and when twenty yards separated him from the man, he again stopped the bay. "I'm United States marshal Matt Dillon," he said. "And I want nothing. I'm just passing through on my way to Dodge."

The three men at the fire were joined by three others, and after a hurried consultation, the man with the rifle said: "Come on ahead, Marshal. We're all honest folks here."

After Matt stopped the bay near the campfire, the man with the rifle propped the gun against a tree, close enough, Matt noted, that he could reach it in a hurry. The man bent and picked up a white clergyman's collar attached to a black bib. He fitted the collar around his neck and then looked up at the tall lawman. "Sorry about the unfriendly reception, Marshal. We are but poor travelers in a hostile land and much afraid of strangers."

The man took a step closer to Matt. "Please to step down, Marshal Dillon. We have little enough, but what we have we are willing to share."

When Matt swung out of the saddle and stood with the reins of the bay in his left hand, the man smiled, revealing broken teeth blackened by chewing tobacco. "I am the Reverend Barnabas Shaklee," he said. He waved a hand. "And these are my sons, from oldest to youngest, Joshua, Aaron, Micajah, Mordecai and Simeon." Shaklee's glance fell on the women, who looked dirty and unkempt but were regarding Matt with bold, measuring eyes. "The females belong to my sons, but their names don't matter."

For a few brief moments, Matt studied Shaklee. The man claimed to be a preacher, but an odd craziness was camped out in his sky blue eyes. Matt decided they were the eyes of a madman or a fanatic. Unwashed tangles of thin gray hair fell over his skinny shoulders, and his cheeks were covered in three day's growth of beard.

Shaklee's sons were all cut from the same mold, tall, lank men with black eyes that slid from Matt's like snails, leaving tracks of guilt, as though they feared he knew something about them that they thought was hidden.

All in all, the marshal decided, men and women,

they were a sorry-looking bunch, a ragtag outfit who had probably never done an honest day's work in their lives, yet toiled hard at living by their wits.

A smile touched Shaklee's lips. He knew he was under scrutiny by the marshal, and he was shrewd enough to read Matt's face and realize that the tall lawman's opinion of him and his brood was not high.

"Coffee's bilin', Marshal," Shaklee said, glancing behind him. "Can I get one of the women to bring you a cup?"

Matt shook his head. The sharp tang of wood smoke hung in the air, and a fish jumped in the creek, making a soft plop.

"Where you folks headed?" he asked.

"Dodge City, just like yourself," Shaklee said. Without warning, his voice rose in a harsh shriek. "Amen and amen, I will enter that painted dove of the plains to bring the gospel to the righteous and cast out the devil from the sinner."

"That's tellin' him, Paw," one of the sons said, and another guffawed.

"You'll have your work cut out for you, Reverend," Matt said.

Shaklee nodded, his eyes on fire. "Yea, but verily I say unto you, Marshal, that the work of the Lord is never easy."

"Hallelujah, Barnabas, you dirty old goat," one of the women jeered. She had hiked up her skirt, showing a deal of naked thigh, and was squatting by the fire checking on the coffee.

"Stella," Shaklee snapped without turning, "you shut your trap." Now he looked at one of his sons, a man in a ragged, collarless shirt and battered hat who was wearing a gun. "Mordecai, see to your woman."

The woman at the fire went pale to her lips as Mordecai strode toward her. He grabbed the woman by the arm, then roughly pushed her behind a wagon parked close to the picketed horses. Matt heard a hard slap, then another, followed by a muffled sob.

Mordecai reappeared and stepped beside his father. "Stella says she's sorry for what she done, Paw."

Shaklee nodded. "The serpent's bite is less sharp than the tongue of a dove." His eyes lifted to Matt. "Just a family squabble, Marshal. You understand."

Matt would not tolerate the abuse of women or children, but the Shaklee clan looked tense and ready, and he knew if he intervened now it could lead to shooting and there would be dead men on the ground.

He stepped into the stirrup, then swung into the saddle.

"Not staying for coffee, Marshal?" Shaklee asked, his pale eyes crafty and calculating.

"Maybe some other time," Matt said. He saw the woman called Stella emerge from behind the horses, her face buried in her hands. A thin trickle of blood ran between her fingers.

The big marshal backed up his bay, keeping his face to Shaklee and his sons.

The preacher took note and grinned. "Not a trusting man, are you, Marshal?"

"Live longer that way," Matt answered.

"Well, we'll see you in Dodge, then."

Matt stopped the horse when twenty yards separated him from Shaklee and the rest. "You can bet the farm on it," he said.

He wheeled the bay and spurred the horse into a trot, following the bank of the creek. He would cross at a point farther east, well away from the Shaklee clan.

That Barnabas planned to preach in Dodge didn't bother him in the least. Parsons hollering about fire and brimstone were not rare in town, and the cowboys generally tolerated them with good humor as just another sight to see at the end of the trail.

But what did trouble him was Barnabas Shaklee's rifle.

It was a Sharps .50-70.

chapter 3

The Man from El Paso

Matt Dillon was attending to paperwork in his office before first light the following morning when a young cowboy pushed his way through the door. Obviously uneasy at finding himself in a lawman's office, the puncher came to a stop inside, uncertain what to do next.

"Can I help you with something?" Matt asked. He smiled, trying to put his visitor at ease.

The man shrugged. "I come to tell you something, Marshal."

"Then tell away." Matt nodded to the chair on the other side of his desk. "Set a spell. Take a load off."

His spurs ringing, the cowboy crossed the room, then perched on the edge of the chair, looking around. His eyes rested briefly on the racked guns just inside the door before he turned to Matt, opened his mouth to speak, then closed it again.

The big lawman understood why the young puncher was on edge. He was a towheaded teenager, and this could have been his first time up the trail. He'd probably been warned by older and wiser hands to step wide around gun-handy cow town lawmen like Matt Dillon, whom talking men mentioned in the same breath as Hickok, Masterson and Earp.

"Can I get you a cup of coffee?" the marshal asked.

The kid shook his head. "No, thanks. Me, I drank a gallon o' that this morning, trying to get sober. I'm headed back to Texas just as soon as the sun comes up." The puncher managed a weak smile. "I'm flat broke and all I got to show for it is a mighty bad headache and I guess a few memories that I really don't entirely recollect." He shrugged. "Still, it's better than helping Pa on the farm. Working behind a plow all a man sees is a mule's hind end. Working from the back of a horse and he can see across the country as far as his eye is good."

Matt nodded. "I reckon that's the case."

The young cowboy hesitated a moment, reached into the pocket of his shirt with his left hand and unfolded a sheet of paper and slid it across the desk to Matt. "I seen this in the undertaker's window last night right next to a dead man in a coffin. I had him take it down for me."

For the first time, Matt noticed that the young man's right arm was short and withered, like it had been broken a while before and badly reset. He wore his gun high on his left hip. The rubber handle was worn, the result of constant practice on the draw and shoot. The kid had probably been right-handed and was training himself to use his left.

Now Matt's eyes shifted to the paper on which Percy Crump had scrawled in thick pencil:

DO YOU KNOW THIS
LATE DEPARTED?
IF SO, APPLY WITHIN.

"So did you know him?" Matt asked.

"I should say," the puncher answered. "His name is, or at least it was, Sam'l McDermott. Him and me came up the trail together. As soon as we drove the herd into Dodge and got paid off, Sam'l said he was heading right back for Texas. He said he wanted to save his wages so he and his ma could put together a small herd he could drive to the railhead next spring. He said they owned a two-by-twice spread that was mostly desert and rock, but he reckoned he and his ma could make a go of it."

"Did Sam'l McDermott have any enemies that you know of?" Matt asked.

The puncher shook his head. "Nary a one. He was real quiet, didn't say a lot. He wore a gun, but the only time I ever saw him shuck it was to use the barrel to string fence wire. Sam'l was a good hand, though, and he did his part on the drive. But he never seemed to take much interest when the camp-fire talk got around to women and whiskey." As if the very mention of two of Dodge's main attractions caused him pain, the young cowboy touched his forehead and groaned softly.

Finally he lifted bloodshot eyes to Matt's face. "Marshal, I liked Sam'l McDermott, liked him just fine. Me and him stuck together on the trail, being the two youngest hands on the drive an' all. Do you know who killed him? Can you give me a name?"

Matt shook his head. "No, I don't know who killed him, but I'm working on it." He smiled. "You head back for Texas, boy, and leave the tracking of Sam'l McDermott's killer to the law."

The puncher nodded and glanced out the office window. The night was shading into dawn, and the morning sky was on fire to the horizon. He stood and adjusted his hat so the brim shaded his eyes. "I got to be pulling my freight, Marshal," he said. "I'm heading home, back to the El Paso country."

Matt also got to his feet, reached into his pocket and counted out five silver dollars into his other palm. He extended the money to the puncher. "Take this. A man who's flat broke will get mighty hungry before he makes it back to Texas."

The cowboy shook his head. "That's real considerate of you, Marshal, and kindly meant. But I'll get by. I reckon I'll ride the grub line or shoot my chuck if I have to."

"Call it a loan," Matt urged. "Pay me back next time you're in Dodge."

"There won't be a next time," the puncher said. "I've had enough. I don't plan on coming up the trail again."

The boy had a stiff-necked pride and Matt didn't push him. He returned the coins to his pocket and said: "You never did give me your name."

"It's Hughes. John Hughes. I was born and raised in Illinois but headed for Texas when I was fourteen. Been punchin' cows ever since."

Matt stuck out his hand. "Then you ride easy, John Hughes."

The cowboy took the marshal's hand. "Find Sam'l McDermott's killer, Marshal," he said. "He deserved a whole heap better than he got."

Matt nodded. "I'll find him. Depend on it."

For the next few days, Matt pushed the murder of Sam'l McDermott to the back of his mind as he had his hands full with the routine affairs of Dodge.

Two doves got into it at the Lone Star Saloon over a stolen necklace and the catfight ended in a cutting. The guilty party, a buxom blonde who gave her name as Dolores LaGrange, was fined three dollars and costs for assault with a deadly weapon. She later claimed it had been worth every penny.

Rats from the feed sheds swarmed into one of the expensive homes across the tracks, and Festus rounded up a posse of small boys, armed them with clubs and hunted down the invaders.

Over to the Alamo, Doc Holliday pulled a gun on a whiskey drummer who had tried to mark the deck with his thumbnail. A shooting scrape was avoided when the drummer promptly fainted.

A cowboy reported seeing a band of hostile Indians out by the south fork of Buckner Creek. Matt investigated and found nothing. The puncher later admitted he had been drinking at the time and might have been seeing things.

Then Mayor Kelley, who was death on stray dogs, took a potshot at what he thought was a scavenging cur and killed the pet nanny goat of Nathan Burke, the freight agent. The whole thing was written off as

a misunderstanding, but Kelley had to pay Burke
two dollars for the dead goat and got a stern lecture
from Matt on the dangers of discharging firearms
within the town limits. The marshal added that from
now on he expected the city fathers to set a good
example, especially His Honor the Mayor.

Four days after his meeting with Shaklee, as night
crowded into Dodge, Matt walked over to G. P. Proctor's boxing booth, where a noisy crowd had already gathered.

Proctor stood on a raised dais in front of a large
blue-and-white-striped tent. He was flanked by two
kerosene torches, their naked flames guttering in the
wind, and beside him stood a young black man,
wearing only a pair of boxing tights, his chest bare.

Battling Ben Hillman and his manager were a
study in contrasts.

Proctor was short and stocky, very red in the face,
his restless gray eyes under the brim of his battered
plug hat constantly moving over the crowd, missing
nothing. Hillman was an inch or two above six feet,
lean and muscular as a gazelle, a fine tracing of
healed scars around his eyebrows and cheekbones.

There was little in Hillman's 180 pounds to suggest
raw strength and power, but Matt had seen his kind
before, though such men were rare. When he moved,
he'd be as fast as a striking rattler, his fists not swinging clubs but flashing rapiers that could cut a man
to shreds.

Ben Hillman would be hard to hit and harder still
to bring down.

Matt stood at the edge of the crowd and listened

to Proctor's spiel, as polished and persuasive as that of any freak show barker.

"My boy Ben here beat Gypsy Jem Mace to a pulp," he yelled. "He left the champion lying in the dust, begging for mercy." He turned to Hillman. "Show them, boy. Shake the fists that shook the world!"

Hillman raised his clenched fists above his head and danced on his toes. As the crowd enthusiastically roared its approval, Proctor beamed and held up his hands for silence.

"Look here, men," he yelled. He let gold double eagles trickle through his fingers and chink onto the palm of his other hand. "Here it is: five hundred dollars in hard Yankee gold to any man who can come up to scratch against Battling Ben five times." His eyes swept the sea of grinning faces. "Just five times, mark you. That's easy money by any standard. Come now. Is there such a man among you? Could it be there is a man standing before me that Ben privately fears—a man who knows his one secret weakness, a debilitation that he has kept hidden since he first entered the ring?"

"An' what secret is that, perfesser?" a puncher yelled.

"That's for you to find out, cowboy!" Proctor yelled as the crowd hooted and hollered. "Could it be a glass jaw? Might it be a weak gut? If you go toe-to-toe with Ben and discover his hidden frailty, the five hundred dollars in gold I hold in my hand could be yours before you even break a sweat."

Another cheer went up from the crowd, and Matt

found Festus at his elbow. "Is ol' G. P. getting any takers, Matthew?" the deputy asked.

Matt shook his head. "Not so far, but he's working on it." He turned his head. "Any more rat complaints from across the tracks?"

"Nary a one. Them boys o' mine done a good job. After we was through, I took them to the general store an' tole Wilbur Jonas to set them up with sody pop, cheese an' crackers an' peppermint candy sticks. I said for Wilbur to add the bill to your account."

"How many kids were there?" Matt asked, raising an eyebrow.

"Oh, nigh on a dozen. But I knowed you wouldn't mind, Matthew, on account of how dead set the mayor was on getting rid of them rats."

The big marshal stared hard at his deputy. "How much cheese and crackers did those boys eat?"

"A lot, Matthew, a whole lot. Rat catchin' is hungry work and them are growin' younkers. At that age they can eat their weight in groceries, you know." Festus' eyes lifted to the marshal. "Wilbur says you can come in an' settle your bill anytime, but he says the sooner the better."

Matt's gloomy calculations on the possible dollar amount rung up by the appetites of twelve hungry boys were interrupted by a yell from the crowd.

"Hey, you, I'll fight your champeen, an' be damned to ye."

The crowd was suddenly hushed as all eyes turned to the speaker—a tall, thick-shouldered man in dusty range clothes. He had a nose that looked as if it had been broken several times.

"Ah," Proctor said, "a challenger at last, a man among men. And what might your name be, brave sir?"

"I might be Bill Kennett. And I'm willing to put my money where my mouth is." He waved a handful of money in the air. "I'll ante up another five hundred if you're willing to match it. Winner take all."

Pretending a look of dismay, Proctor let his eyes sweep the crowd. "Does he know about Battling Ben's secret weakness?" he fretted. "I fear I may be undone. I implore you kind people out there: Dare I take this man's bet?"

"Secret weakness be damned," Kennett yelled. He raised huge, battle-scarred fists. "All I need are these!"

The crowd, now swollen to a couple hundred, roared and a saloon girl called out: "You can take him, Billy boy!"

Festus leaned closer to Matt and whispered in his ear, "Ol' Bill is a rancher down around McAllen way, and he's as good with a gun as he is with his dukes. I've heard tell he's a sore loser, be it over cards, women or business, an' that there are four or five men pushin' up daisies who can testify to that. They say Bill killed a couple o' them boys with his fists."

Matt's eyes moved to Kennett, taking his measure. The rancher was well over six feet with heavy, sloping shoulders, the muscles of his enormous arms bulging under his shirt. He was carrying a little weight around his belly, but this just added to his appearance of unmovable solidity. He had the look of a massive grizzly bear, and there would be no backup in him. His heavy, square jaw was made to take a pounding, and his own punches would hit almighty hard.

Kennett was six inches taller than Hillman and out-weighed him by at least fifty pounds. All in all, Matt decided the big rancher was not a man to mess with, and for the first time, he had doubts about Ben Hillman's chances of winning the fight.

Proctor was speaking again. "My boy, Ben, just told me he is willing to accept the gallant Mr. Kennett's challenge." His voice rose, soon joined by loud cheers from the crowd. "The fight is on! One thousand dollars at stake. Winner takes all!" He grinned. "Let the battle commence."

Proctor left the platform and stepped to the open flap of the tent. He had borrowed a small table from somewhere and on the top was a steel moneybox.

"Put your money in the box, gentlemen and ladies," Proctor yelled. "Fifty cents a skull, and it would be cheap at half that price to see the fight of the century."

Matt watched the excited crowd shuffle into a semblance of a line and one by one drop coins into the box. He was joined by Mayor Kelley, who stepped beside him. The man was beaming like the cat that ate the canary, a fat stogie glowing between his teeth.

"Hand over fist, Marshal, hand over fist," Kelley said. "Just look at the money pouring in, and the town will get its share." He indicated the tent with the chewed end of his cigar. "I'm even renting that to Proctor for ten dollars a day, and another ten for the seating. It's time we turned a profit on that damned stuff."

Matt nodded absently. The tent had belonged to a preacher who had held a revival meeting in town a couple years before. Unfortunately he'd skipped town with the donations and a hot-to-trot soiled dove the cowboys called the Galloping Cow, leaving his wife and seven kids to fend for themselves.

Kelly, at heart a caring man, had paid the woman two hundred dollars for the tent and the wagon and mules that had hauled it, figuring that the tent might come in handy one day.

Now it had, and Mayor Kelley was mighty pleased.

The last of the crowd had filed inside, a noisy, boisterous mix of cowboys, ranchers, soldiers, gamblers, freighters, women of the fancier sort and a surprisingly large gathering of somber bearded farmers and respectable townsmen in black broadcloth.

Matt watched Proctor slam the lid on the moneybox; then the man tucked it under his arm and walked over to the lawmen and the mayor.

"Coming in to watch the fight, gentlemen?" he asked. "Free of charge, of course."

"I wouldn't miss it"—Kelley grinned—"especially since you're covering the hundred dollars I bet on Kennett."

"Indeed, Mayor," Proctor said, his hot eyes following a slim young dove just entering the tent. He tore his gaze from the woman and looked back to the mayor. "And at odds of three to one, no less. And there's plenty more been bet on Mr. Kennett, I assure you. Just to name a few, I'm covering a thousand from Chalk Beeson and five hundred from Mr. Bodkin, the banker. Bat Masterson has bet a thousand on my boy, Ben, but I think a lot more money will be laid down on Kennett when the odds go to five or six to one before the fight is called."

"Is Bat the only one betting on ol' Ben?" Festus asked.

Proctor nodded. "So far, he's the only one. It seems that the imposing and belligerent figure of Mr. Bill Kennett has scared everyone else away." The man bowed slightly, his grin sly as he extended a hand toward the door of the tent. "And now, gentlemen, shall we go observe the fray?"

As Kelley led the way to the tent, Matt grabbed Proctor's elbow and pulled the man aside. "You know," he said, his blue eyes cold, "I'll take it real hard if you're unable to pay off on your bets."

"Don't you worry none about that, Marshal. If Kennett comes up to scratch five times, I'll gladly pay everyone who put money on him." Proctor's smile widened. "But that won't happen. Bill Kennett doesn't stand a chance against my boy."

chapter 4

Winners and Losers

The ring had been set up in the middle of a rectangle of tiered seating, the highest row six feet above the ground.

Proctor ducked under the ropes, then held up his hands for silence. "My lords, ladies and gentlemen," he yelled, "I have an announcement to make."

The crowd turned to look at the man, and when he had the quiet he wanted, he waved a hand toward a slender man in a buckskin jacket, who stood beside him.

"You all know Jim Buck, the stagecoach driver. He will act as referee for the contest."

There were cheers from some, mocking hoots from others.

With a dramatic flourish, Proctor pulled a huge Smith & Wesson .44 from the waistband of his pants and waved it above his head. This was an unexpected turn of events and the crowd grew silent again.

"Ben Hillman," Proctor yelled, "was once a Nubian prince, a mighty warrior from the jungles of darkest Africa." Amid jeers from the crowd, the man continued: "Like many of his kind, Ben can revert to the bloodthirsty savage in the blink of an eye. I warn you all now, right before your horrified gaze, you may see him transform into a wild man with only one thought in his heathenish mind: the desire to maim and kill."

The crowd was up on its feet, cheering wildly, and it took Proctor several minutes before he once again restored quiet. "With this terrifying possibility in mind, I am now giving Jim Buck this"—he paused for effect—"murderous revolver. He has assured me that at the first sign of Ben Hillman reverting to a savage beast, he will shoot him dead on the instant, and Mr. Bill Kennett will be declared the winner of the contest."

"I will do my duty," Buck said, with an admirably straight face.

The crowd roared its approval, and again Proctor held up his hands for silence. "One more thing," he said. "A physician is in attendance, and he will examine both contestants after the fight is over. He assures me he is an expert at setting broken noses and repairing chawed ears."

The answering roar from the crowd was punctuated by yells of encouragement directed at Kennett as the man entered the ring, grinning, pumping his huge fists above his head.

Hillman made his entrance to a chorus of boos and quietly walked to his corner.

Buck shoved Proctor's revolver into his waistband,

motioned both fighters to come to scratch in the center of the ring, then announced: "London prize ring rules will apply throughout. A knockdown is the end of a round. If any part of the body but for the soles of the feet touches the canvas, it is a knockdown and the round is over."

He looked from Kennett to Hillman. "Now, gentlemen, go to your corners, then come to scratch. And may the best man win."

Kennett had stripped to the waist, his suspenders hanging over his pants. His arms and shoulders were hard-muscled and massive, covered in black hair, his scarred fists as big as nail kegs. He was grinning and confident, a man who had killed with his bare hands before this and seemed eager to do it again.

Ben Hillman looked slender and almost short by comparison, his dark skin smooth and hairless, though his shoulders were wide and he was well muscled in the biceps and belly.

It was David fighting Goliath, Matt thought. The only problem was that Ben Hillman didn't have a rock handy to sling at the big rancher's head—and it looked like he'd soon need one.

Both men came to scratch and circled each other, warily keeping their distance.

Suddenly Kennett stepped inside and lanced a powerful right to Hillman's head. Ben slipped the punch, though the bigger man's knuckles scraped across his left cheekbone, drawing a smear of blood.

The crowd roared, and somebody yelled: "You've got him, Bill. Now finish it."

Kennett grinned as he worked closer. He swung another right that missed badly, but followed up with a hard left that exploded on Hillman's chin. Hurt, Ben staggered back a couple steps and Kennett, eager to end the fight, came after him.

Kennett ripped punches into Hillman's body with both hands, pounding the smaller man's ribs. For a moment, Ben took the hits, then lay back on the ropes and covered up. But Kennett was relentless, swinging rights and lefts at Hillman's head, smashing aside his covering fists.

But the big rancher's wild swings were leaving him wide open. Suddenly Hillman came out of his crouch, stood tall and stabbed a powerful left to Kennett's mouth.

Surprised and hurt, Kennett staggered back and Hillman came after him, following up with an arching right to the bigger man's massive jaw.

Kennett's head snapped to his left, spraying blood from his smashed mouth and he slammed against the ropes. Hillman moved forward, his fists up, getting ready to end it—and he walked into a tremendous right from Kennett that crashed between his eyes and dropped him in his tracks.

The crowd roared for Kennett as he raised his arms above his head, grinning from split lips, and swaggered back to his corner and sat on his stool, his amused eyes on Hillman.

Groggily Ben got up on his hands and knees, his head hanging. As the crowd jeered and a few pennies were thrown in his direction, he staggered to his feet and walked back to his corner, blood trickling from his nose.

Matt's eyes moved to Proctor, who was walking among the crowd. He was yelling that he was now offering odds of five to one on Kennett, and he was getting plenty of takers, the thick wad of bills in his hand growing by the second.

Matt studied Proctor, taking measure of the man. Despite his loud, expensive clothes and fine linen, Matt decided that Proctor was a practiced and expert crook. A hog with a gold nose ring is still a hog, and he'd take some watching.

The marshal stepped closer to the ring as Buck consulted his watch, decided a full minute's rest had passed and ordered both men to scratch.

Hillman still seemed unsteady on his feet, and Matt heard Kennett say: "Hillman, I'm going to end it soon, boy. I'm going to smash you to a pulp."

Standing toe-to-toe, the two men went at it, slugging viciously, neither of them taking a step back. Then Kennett gave ground and Hillman followed. He swung a right hook to the bigger man's chin, but Kennett saw it coming and tucked his head into his chest. Hillman's fist crashed into the top of Kennett's skull and Matt heard him cry out in pain as his knuckles hit rock-hard bone.

The crowd heard Hillman's yelp of agony, and there were taunting cheers and yells for Kennett to finish it.

The big rancher grinned, shrugged off a Hillman left to his ribs and swung a roundhouse right that connected with the side of the smaller man's jaw. Hillman was lifted off his feet by the force of the blow, and he slammed onto his back and lay still.

The second round was over.

Somehow Ben got to his feet and staggered back to his stool. His mouth was streaming blood and his chest was rising and falling with every shuddering breath.

"Ten to one on Bill Kennett!" Proctor yelled.

"I'll take some of that," a businessman in the crowd yelled. "Five hundred on the rancher from Texas."

The crowd cheered wildly, but most everyone else had already laid down their bets, and this time there were few takers at the new odds.

Matt saw it then, an exchange of looks between Proctor and Hillman, followed by a nod from the promoter.

Buck again called the fighters to scratch. Confident now, Kennett moved in quickly, to be stopped in his tracks by a hard, straight right from Hillman that landed smack on his mouth.

Spitting blood, Kennett backed off. For the first time, the big rancher looked shaken, as though the tremendous power in Hillman's punch had surprised him. Earlier, Ben Hillman had looked flat-footed and awkward. Now he was up on his toes, a dancing target that was constantly moving and hard to hit.

As Hillman weaved closer, Kennett landed two wicked blows to Ben's body. Hillman absorbed the punches and countered with a right to Kennett's head. Then as the man tried to sidestep, Hillman hit him hard with a left that opened up a wide cut on the rancher's cheekbone.

Kennett's knees turned to rubber, and he sagged back against the ropes. Stepping closer, Hillman pounded a fast flurry of rights and lefts to the big man's head. As Kennett started to fall, his hands dropped and he left his face unprotected. Hillman

swung a tremendous uppercut that landed solidly on
Kennett's chin. The man screamed as his head
snapped back, a sudden scarlet arc of blood erupting
around him. He slid to the canvas and sat, his unfo-
cused eyes looking dazedly at his feet.

The third round was over.

Hillman walked back to his corner, and Kennett
crawled to his stool, his face as gray as death. Jim
Buck stepped beside him, looked into his eyes and
asked: "Bill, are you throwing in the towel?"

Matt saw defeat in the man's glazed stare, but Kennett had sand, and he shook his head. "Damn you,
I'll come to scratch," he said.

The crowd roared its approval as the new round
began. Then Hillman immediately smashed Kennett
with another straight right. The rancher staggered
back, his fists dropping, and Ben hit him again, a left
hook that opened up another deep cut, this time
above Kennett's right eye.

Scarlet fingers of blood streamed down the big
man's face, and he shook his head to clear his vision,
splotches of red spattering the onlookers nearest
the ring.

Hillman was relentless. He shrugged off a pawing
left from Kennett, then hit him with another smashing right. As the rancher started to fall, Hillman
moved closer and threw a looping left to the man's
chin that sounded like an ax hitting a pine log.

As the crowd roared its fury, Kennett went down
on his belly and lay still.

Buck stepped quickly beside the fallen rancher, got
down on one knee and examined him briefly. He
shook his head and rose to his feet.

"He's out cold!" he yelled to the crowd. He glanced at his watch. "Bill Kennett has sixty seconds to come to scratch or the fight is over."

The crowd yelled encouragement to Kennett, urging him to get up. But it was over. After the minute had passed, Buck stepped beside Hillman and raised his arm. "The winner and still champeen!" he yelled.

Proctor climbed into the ring to a chorus of boos and held up his hands for silence. "We have a qualified physician in attendance," he yelled above the din. "Dr. Galen Adams will now examine both fighters."

Matt was surprised. He hadn't noticed Doc in the crowd until now. To angry jeers, the wiry physician stooped under the top rope and kneeled beside Kennett, who still hadn't moved.

"I'd say Mr. Proctor has made a killing here today, my hundred dollars included."

Matt turned and saw Mayor Kelley standing at his elbow, looking glum.

The marshal smiled. "Mayor, I've always told you that the quickest way to double your money is to fold it over and put it back in your pocket."

Kelley shook his head. "Matt," he said, "what you just said doesn't make losing any easier."

As the crowd filed past him, most of them looking as dejected as the mayor, Matt saw that Doc had Kennett in a sitting position and was talking to him. He helped the man get onto his stool and began to wipe blood from his face.

Doc turned and saw Hillman about to leave the ring, but his yell stopped him. "You too, young man. I want to take a look at you."

Hillman flashed a white grin. "I'm all right." He nodded to Kennett. "He's the one who lost the fight."

"I know," Doc said. "But, nevertheless, I want to take a look at you."

"Do as he says, Ben." Proctor grinned. "Remember, the doctor knows best."

Hillman shrugged and strolled back to his corner, his hands on the rope on either side of him, waiting.

Bat Masterson, dapper in a dark gray suit and matching bowler, stepped beside Kelley. "How did you do, Mayor?" he asked.

Kelley glanced at the wad of bills Masterson was counting and growled: "I bet on the wrong fighter."

Masterson shook his head. "You should have talked to me first, Mayor. I saw Hillman fight Jem Mace, so I knew where the smart money should go."

Morosely, Kelley watched Masterson slide his winnings into his billfold. "Next time I will," he said.

Masterson touched his hat to Kelley and then to Matt. "Then I'll bid you good day, gentlemen. The gaming tables await."

The mayor watched Masterson leave, then said to Matt: "You know, I'm beginning to take a real dislike to that man."

Matt didn't answer. He was watching Doc, who had placed an ivory stethoscope tube against Hillman's chest and was listening intently.

Doc was scowling . . . as though the young fighter's heart was whispering some bad news.

chapter 5

Proctor Gets a Warning

"Ol' Bill Kennett will be all right in a few days," Festus said as he poured himself coffee. "He's got a couple of broken ribs and a sore jaw, but apart from that, he's just fine and dandy."

Matt watched as his deputy stepped to his desk and perched on a corner. "Good scrap though, wasn't it, Matthew? Ben Hillman sure cut Bill's suspenders for him."

"How's Kennett taking it?" Matt asked.

Festus shrugged. "As well as he takes anything that don't go his way. He's already talking to Proctor about a rematch, a five-thousand-dollar purse, winner take all. He says next time he'll punch first and keep punching until Ben drops."

"And what does Kennett think Hillman will be doing all that time?"

"Well, see, ol' Bill reckons he underestimated Ben first time around, and he says when they meet again he'll be more on his guard, like."

Matt nodded, his face grim. "Only there won't be a next time."

Festus looked shocked. "Matthew, I don't get your drift."

"It's easy enough to get, Festus. There's nobody in Dodge can stand up to Ben Hillman in the ring. Bill Kennett is a big man, and tough as they come, but he ended up with two broken ribs. What happens when some cowboy gets likkered up and decides he wants to crawl Hillman's hump?" Before Festus could answer, the marshal answered his own question. "He gets killed or crippled—that's what happens."

"Who?"

Exasperation fleeting across his face, Matt snapped: "Damn it all, Festus. The cowboy, of course."

Festus nodded, as understanding slowly dawned on him. "It could happen, I guess. Ol' Ben hits real hard, an' that's a natural fact."

"Sure, it could happen. But it won't, because I'm shutting Proctor down."

Festus' face worked as he thought that through. "What about the mayor, Matthew? He sets store by Proctor."

"He did." Matt smiled. "But since he lost a hundred dollars on the fight, I'd say his admiration for the man has begun to wear mighty thin."

The marshal rose to his feet. "I'm going to talk to Proctor right now. Have you seen him?"

Festus nodded. "Yeah, last I saw him he was over to the Long Branch, trying to drum up opponents for Ben."

As Matt stepped outside, night had come to Dodge, and the lamps were blazing along Front

Street, casting shifting blue shadows in the alleys, splashing the fronts of the saloons and other buildings with pale orange light. Out on the plains, the coyotes were talking, and a boisterous wind tugged at the marshal's shirt and hat as he crossed the street.

The Long Branch was roaring full, crowded with hard-drinking cattlemen, and a piano gallantly competed to be heard above the ceaseless din. The doors were open to catch the evening breeze and help clear the fog of smoke that hung in the air.

Kitty Russell was helping out behind the bar, and Matt smiled and nodded to her before his eyes swept the room, searching for Proctor.

"Matt!" Kitty said, as she beckoned him over.

The marshal stepped to the bar, wary men clearing a space for him, and Kitty said, smiling: "You're wearing your official lawman's face, Matt. That means you're looking for someone."

"Does it show that much?"

Kitty's smile widened as she shrugged her beautiful naked shoulders. "It shows. As soon as I saw you walk in, I knew you were not here to pay a social call."

The marshal grinned. "Do you always read me that well?"

"Most times. Now you've relaxed a little, I can tell what you're thinking right now by the way you're looking at me."

"And what am I thinking?"

"That you like how I look this evening."

"Guilty as charged," Matt said. "You look wonderful tonight, Kitty."

The woman made a show of fluttering her eyelashes. "Well, thank you, kind sir. Now can I get you a drink?"

Matt shook his head, his eyes again scanning the crowd. "No, but you can tell me where G. P. Proctor is."

"He's sitting at a table over in the far corner with Mayor Kelley and a few others."

Matt touched his hat brim. "Obliged, Kitty."

"Sure you don't want that drink?"

"Maybe later," Matt said.

Kitty smiled. "I'll hold you to that."

The tall marshal made his way through the throng, stepping around couples who were dancing with more enthusiasm than skill, the cowboys booted and spurred, wide sombreros pushed to the back of their heads, the girls in silk dresses of vivid scarlet, yellow and blue.

The room smelled of sweat, cigar smoke, bourbon whiskey and cheap perfume, mingled with the ever-present earthy tang of the cattle pens down by the crowded stockyards.

Sitting with his back to the wall, Proctor was in earnest conversation with Mayor Kelley. Opposite them sat a skinny young puncher with a nose that had been broken at one time. He was sharing a bottle with an older man in dusty range clothes, who looked up belligerently at Matt as he reached the table.

"Look out," this man said, a sneer etching itself on his thin mouth. "Johnny law is here."

Matt ignored the man and nodded to Kelley. "Evening, Mayor."

"Evening, Matt." Kelley smiled. "And to what do we owe this unexpected pleasure?"

"Town business, Mayor." Then, he decided to get right to the point, and his eyes shifted to Proctor: "I'm here to tell you that I'm closing you down."

Kelley looked shocked and opened his mouth to speak, but Proctor cut him off, his eyes suddenly unfriendly. "Harsh words, Marshal, and most unkindly spoken. Why would you shut me down?"

"Proctor, I'll spell it out for you. Bill Kennett is laid up with a couple of broken ribs, and I don't want to see somebody else get hurt, maybe badly. There isn't a man in Dodge who can stack up against a professional prizefighter like Ben Hillman. You know it, and I know it."

"But, Matt, think of the town, the revenue," Kelley objected. "Our share of the gate money today alone was close to one hundred dollars."

"Is a hundred dollars worth somebody's life, Mayor?" Matt asked.

Kelley sat in silence for a few moments, then said: "Well, perhaps not."

"Mayor, we have an agreement," Proctor said, his face flushed.

Kelley shook his head. "We have nothing in writing."

"No, but I thought we had an agreement between gentlemen," Proctor said, putting heavy emphasis on the word *gentlemen.*

Kelley was ill at ease and it showed. "I know, G. P., but if Matt is concerned about someone being hurt . . ."

"I am concerned, very concerned," Matt said. "Somebody could get killed in that ring."

The man with the sneer rose to his feet. He was almost as tall as Matt, with challenging black eyes and a gun low on his thigh, an affectation among would-be hardcases that the marshal had seen much of over the past couple years.

"And I say my saddle pard over there"—he nodded to the young puncher, who sat blinking like an owl as the whiskey worked on him—"I say he can clean this Ben Hillman's plow."

"He wouldn't even come close," Matt said. His eyes turned to Proctor again. "As of tonight, I'm closing you down. And I want you and Hillman out of Dodge by this time tomorrow."

"Listen, you. I've got a pile of money riding on this fight," the tall man said. "Nobody is closing down nobody until Tom Danby here gets in the ring tomorrow."

Matt ignored the man and turned to go. "You heard what I told you, Proctor. Make sure you heed it."

But the tall man grabbed Matt's arm and pushed closer, his wet teeth bared in a snarl. "My name is Husky Wilson. That mean anything to you?"

Matt glanced down at the man's hand on his arm, then lifted his eyes to Wilson's face. "Not a damn thing."

"Well, it should. It means that where I come from hick lawmen call me sir."

"Take your hand off my arm," Matt said, his voice low but cold and flat.

Wilson had been drinking, and he didn't read the warning signs, nor did he notice the sudden hush that had fallen over the saloon.

"I said, take your hand off my arm," Matt repeated.

Wilson just grinned, and his fingers squeezed hard

into Matt's biceps. "You didn't say please, and you didn't say sir."

Matt's fist traveled less than six inches, but it crashed into Wilson's chin with tremendous power. The man's eyes rolled in his head, and he rushed to join his shadow on the floor.

Without raising his voice, Matt looked at Proctor. "Remember what I told you." He nodded to Kelley. "Evening, Mayor."

Then he bent and grabbed Wilson by the back of his shirt and dragged him across the floor of the saloon, through the doors and into the street. Matt pulled Wilson into the marshal's office and relieved him of his gun before throwing him into a cell.

He was hanging Wilson's gun belt on the rack when the door opened and Ben Hillman stepped inside.

chapter 6

The Spawn of Hell

"Hope I haven't arrived at a bad time, Marshal," Hillman said. "G. P. just told me about your run-in with Husky Wilson."

Matt nodded. "Mr. Wilson is sleeping peacefully."

Hillman flashed a quick grin, then said: "G. P. told me something else."

"And that's why you're here. Did Proctor send you?"

"No, I came all on my own."

Matt showed the man to a seat by his desk and then sat himself. He looked across at Hillman, waiting for the man to talk.

Except for skinned knuckles, Hillman showed few signs of his fight with Kennett. But he seemed uncomfortable, as though he was weighing each word before he dared utter it.

Finally Hillman took a deep breath and said: "Marshal, I need another fight with Bill Kennett. He's asked G. P. if he's willing to match five thousand dollars, winner take all, and G. P. said he would."

Matt shook his head. "I won't let it happen, Ben. I know you carried Kennett for a couple of rounds until Proctor got the odds he wanted. Then you beat him to within an inch of his life. Kennett is a bull-headed man, and he has sand, but he's not too smart. He doesn't realize that next time he could get killed."

"Marshal, I need my share of that prize money," Hillman said, his eyes pleading. "I can take it easy on Kennett, make sure I don't beat him too badly."

"Why do you need the money?" Matt asked. His gaze ran over Hillman's clothing. "You're wearing a fifty-dollar suit and a plug hat that probably cost three times what I paid for my Stetson."

"G. P. bought me these duds," Hillman said. "I don't want money for fancy clothes. . . . It's . . . it's for something else." The man hesitated. "Someone else."

"A woman?"

Hillman nodded. "Yes, a woman. My sister, Arrah."

Matt waited. He reckoned all the talking would now be done by Ben Hillman.

"Marshal," the man said after a long silence, "just eighteen months ago, I was a buffalo soldier sergeant in the Tenth Cavalry. I served under Colonel Shafter throughout his campaign against the Comanche on the Staked Plains." Hillman's smile was slight. "In one fight, I collected a strap-iron arrowhead in my left thigh and, after that, a medal.

"When the campaign was over, a letter from home finally reached me. By then it was three months old.

It was hard to read because my ma had cried so much the writing was blurred. But I could make out the important part: Arrah had run away from the family farm with a man called Mitch Haythorn."

"Haythorn?" Matt was surprised.

"You know him?"

"He's a gambler and sometime pimp. He's real good with a gun, and I'm told he's a dangerous man to cross."

"I deserted the day I got the letter," Hillman said. "Later I hooked up with Proctor."

"How did you meet him?" Matt asked.

"He had a boxing booth set up in a small town on the Red and was offering fifty dollars to anyone who could go five rounds with his fighter. I needed the money, so I fought the man and won. Right afterward, G. P. offered me the fighter's job." Hillman shrugged. "I had to earn my keep while I searched for Arrah, so I accepted his offer."

Hillman leaned across the desk. "Marshal, a white man traveling with a beautiful black woman doesn't escape notice, and my search eventually led me here. I know that Mitch Haythorn and Arrah are somewhere in Dodge. I intend to take my sister from Haythorn and send her east, where she can make a new start."

"Not back to the farm?" Matt asked.

Hillman shook his head. "She wouldn't go, and I don't blame her none. It's no life for a young woman, living on a hardscrabble hundred sixty acres that will make her old before her time. The farm grows nothing but rocks, weeds and heartbreak, and our ma and pa still have a passel of young'uns to feed."

Understanding came to Matt. "And that's why you want the fight with Bill Kennett. How much did Proctor say he'd pay you?"

"Two thousand dollars. That's enough for me to put Arrah on a train east and give her money to support her while she finds honest work. After that, I'll surrender to the Army and take whatever punishment I got coming to me."

Matt took a few moments to sort out his thoughts, then said carefully, "Ben, Mitch Haythorn arrived in Dodge a few weeks ago. He brought five women with him, one a fine-looking black girl."

"Arrah!" Hillman exclaimed. "Where is she?"

"Last I heard, all of Haythorn's women are working the line down by the tracks."

Hillman looked like he'd been slapped. "Then I'm going after her."

The young man sprang to his feet, but Matt's voice froze him in place. "Ben, you go after Mitch Haythorn with threats and he'll kill you. He's good with a gun, and he's already bedded down three or four hardcases who had big reputations. He's not the kind of man to take a step back from anyone, and he's best left alone."

"But I have to get Arrah away from him, Marshal."

"Then let me talk to him." Matt touched the star on his vest. "Haythorn has always respected this. He'll give me a fair hearing."

"Will he let Arrah go?"

Matt shrugged. "Mitch Haythorn can't hold a woman against her will. I'd say what happens next is up to your sister."

"Then we'll try it your way, Marshal. But if you

fail, I'll take her away by force if I have to." Hillman hesitated, his dark eyes searching Matt's face. "You know, I didn't carry Bill Kennett for two rounds like you said. He's a tough man and he hits hard. I only picked up the pace because I realized if I didn't he might beat me."

"Why are you telling me this?"

"Because I need the fight. I need the two thousand dollars for Arrah." Hillman's voice was pleading. "Marshal, you know what happens to cow town doves. They end up dead from disease or opium. I don't want that to happen to my sister."

"Some do, some don't," Matt said mildly. His eyes lifted to Hillman. "You gave Bill Kennett two broken ribs. He's in no shape to fight you again."

Hillman smiled and shook his head. "A couple of broken ribs mean nothing to a man like Kennett. They won't even slow him down." The young fighter brought his hands together like he was about to pray. "Marshal Dillon, I'm begging you—don't close us down until I fight Kennett again."

"All right," Matt said. "I'll study on it some and give you my answer later. In the meantime, no more fights. I don't want some fool cowboy killed in that ring."

"I promise, Marshal," Hillman said. "No more fights until I meet Bill Kennett."

"If you meet Bill Kennett," Matt said.

After a few inquiries around town, Matt tracked down Mitch Haythorn in Chalk Beeson's Saratoga Saloon. Beeson had spared no expense fixing up his place, which boasted leather club chairs, plush Persian rugs, ornate chandeliers and a gold-flecked mirror brought all the way from New Orleans by steamboat and wagon.

Beeson catered to a better class of clientele, mostly ranchers, cattle buyers and the town businessmen. His bonded bourbon and fine liqueurs were served in sparkling glasses of Waterford crystal, but French champagne and iced oysters were always readily available.

His hostesses were of the better sort, prettier and less hard-eyed than run-of-the-mill saloon girls, and sexual assignations were handled with considerable discretion. The house gamblers were said to be straight up and honest, including the gregarious Bat Masterson, who often presided over the blackjack table.

A Mr. Lawson, whose poignant rendition of "The Lakes of Killarney" was much requested and never failed to bring a tear to every eye in the house, provided entertainment nightly.

The Saratoga was the natural habitat of a man like Haythorn, and Matt found him at the poker table, a growing stack of chips in front of him.

But what caught the marshal's attention was the stunningly beautiful black girl standing behind Haythorn, her hand on his shoulder. She wore a yellow dress of watered silk, the neckline cut low to reveal her generous curves, and every now and then she bent her head, her glossy lips moving, to whisper into Haythorn's ear, the man responding with a smile.

The woman had to be Arrah Hillman, Matt decided, and judging by the way she looked at Haythorn, it didn't seem as though she was pining for the farm—or anywhere else for that matter.

Matt stepped closer to the table and Haythorn's eyes rose to his.

"Evening, Marshal." The man smiled. "A social call, I trust."

"You could say that," Matt responded. "I'd like a word with you."

"Anything you say." Haythorn looked around, saw one of the house gamblers standing at the bar and called out: "Chance, play this hand for me, will you?"

Haythorn rose and the man called Chance took his seat and picked up his cards. "At the bar, Marshal," Haythorn said. "Is that quite convenient?"

"It will do," Matt said.

Mitch Haythorn was a tall, slim man dressed in the frockcoat and starched and frilled shirt of the frontier gambler. He was handsome in a dark, flashy way, his teeth very even and white under a pencil-thin black mustache, and he affected the accent and manners of a Southern gentleman, a pretension pioneered by Doc Holliday and quickly picked up by others of his kind.

Matt studied Haythorn but saw no obvious gun. The man would have his short-barreled Colt tucked away somewhere, in a shoulder holster maybe or a leather-lined pocket.

"What can I do for you, Marshal?" Haythorn asked. "You know I'm always happy to cooperate with the law." He hesitated; then his eyebrows rose in a question. "Drink?"

Matt shook his head. His glance fell briefly on

Arrah as she stepped behind Haythorn, standing very close to the man as though giving him her support.

"I'm here to talk about Arrah," Matt said. His eyes moved to the woman again. "I take it you're Arrah Hillman?"

The girl nodded. "I am."

"Your brother is in town," Matt said. "He wants to talk to you."

"You mean Ben?" Arrah's melodious voice rose in surprise.

"He's here with a man by the name of G. P. Proctor. Ben is working for Proctor as a prizefighter, taking on all comers."

The woman's face registered even more shock. "I heard there was a young black boy fighting over to the boxing booth, but I never thought for one minute it was Ben. The last I heard from him he was in the Army."

"He was," Matt said. "But he deserted from the Tenth Cavalry eighteen months ago."

"Why?" Arrah asked. "Ben doesn't want to go back to farming any more than I do."

Matt decided to lay it on the line. "Arrah, Ben deserted because he wanted to find you. He plans to send you back east, where you can make a decent life for yourself."

"Ah, now we come to the crux of the matter," Haythorn said. He smiled, carefully placed a thin black cheroot between his teeth and turned his head slightly. "Arrah, it seems your brother wants to save you from a fate worse than death."

"I don't need saving," the girl snapped. "I want to stay with you, Mitch."

The gambler thumbed a match into flame and lit his cigar. He removed the cheroot from his mouth, contemplated the glowing end for a few moments, nodded his satisfaction, then said: "My dear, in the ugly business we are in, money talks louder than words." His eyes lifted to Matt's. "Marshal, take a look at Arrah, at the jewels around her lovely neck, at the gown she's wearing. She has a closetful of others that are just as expensive. I'd say, up to this point, that I have two thousand dollars invested in this young lady. Now, if brother Ben can come up with that amount of cash, we'll talk."

Tears sprang into Arrah's eyes. "Mitch, you . . . you'd sell me for money."

Haythorn shook his head. "My dear, that was the whole idea, remember, to sell you for money."

"But I . . . I thought you loved me."

"Arrah, a man passes time with a dove," Haythorn said. "He doesn't love her."

The girl stood for a few moments, stunned. Then she sobbed and buried her face in her hands before she turned and ran to the far end of the bar. Immediately a couple saloon girls, wise in the ways of men, rushed to her, cooing comfort, their accusing eyes slanting to Haythorn.

A small anger was building in Matt. He hated to see any woman mistreated, and he fervently wanted to punch Haythorn in the mouth. But he forced himself to remain calm. If he hit the man now, all he'd do would make a bad situation worse and solve nothing.

Keeping his voice even, the marshal said: "Haythorn, you can't sell a woman. Not in my town, you can't."

The gambler smiled and shook his head. "Then let's not use the word sell, Marshal. Arrah will cry for ten minutes, then come back to me. She always does. But if brother Ben wants me to cut her adrift for keeps, he knows where to find me. The only thing is, he better have the two thousand ready."

Haythorn looked closely at the tall, grim-faced lawman. "I can see disapproval in your eyes, Marshal. Suddenly they're blue and ice cold, like the eyes of a hanging judge." He smiled. "But don't judge me too harshly. I'm in a hard, all too often dangerous business where there's little room for sentiment. A hearts-and-flowers man who handles cards and women goes broke or he ends up on the saloon floor with a bullet in his belly and sawdust in his beard."

Matt shook his head. "I'm not judging you, Haythorn. I was only wondering what kind of hell spawns a man like you."

Haythorn laughed out loud, genuinely amused. "Marshal, my father was a riverboat gambler, my mother a saloon girl, and three days after I was born, they abandoned me. I was raised by a sharecropper who beat the living tar out of me every single day of my life until one morning I was big enough and mean enough to break both his arms." The man's grin faded to a shadow of a smile. "That's the hell that spawned me. I've been making a living with cards and a gun since I was fourteen and now I give the devil his due, but as for everyone else, I owe them nothing."

Matt had met men like Haythorn before, men with holes in their chests where their hearts should have been, the empty space filled with self-loathing and contempt for the entire human race. The big marshal was all done talking. Nothing he could say would reach Haythorn in any case.

"I'll speak to Ben Hillman," he said. "He'll want to see his sister, and I'll take it real personal if anything bad happens to him."

Haythorn's smile was back. "Rest assured that brother Ben can visit Arrah anytime, Marshal. We have a room at the Dodge House, and he'll suffer no harm from me"—he shrugged—"unless he comes at me with a gun, of course. Under those circumstances I offer no guarantees."

chapter 7

A Morning of Bad News

When Matt Dillon left the Saratoga, the hour was late. Darkness had gathered in the alleys and a horned moon rode high in the sky, nudging aside the crowding stars.

The marshal stood on the boardwalk in a rectangle of yellow light from the saloon window, unsure about what to do next. Should he talk to Hillman now? He decided against doing that. Arrah might still be upset and if Ben found her in that state he'd be sure to angrily confront Haythorn, and that could well end in a shooting.

He decided to leave off telling Ben until the next day. By then his sister would have had time to regain her composure.

His mind made up, Matt turned toward his office. He would check on Husky Wilson and then catch a couple hours of sleep before making his final round of the saloons.

The boardwalk ended at an alley between the telegraph office and Newly O'Brien's gun shop, and Matt stepped down to the dusty street. The alley was angled in deep shadow, and the marshal glanced casually into its inky depths as he walked past. But he stopped in his tracks as a empty bottle clinked. Was someone there?

That question was answered a moment later as a kitten ran out of the alley right toward him. The little animal looked up and saw the human at the last moment, and Matt took a step to his left to avoid a collision.

That move saved his life.

A split second later the roar of a heavy rifle hammered apart the night, and a bullet split the air close to Matt's head, buzzing like a spiteful hornet.

The marshal drew and fired at the spot where he'd seen the orange flash of the gun. He thumbed off two more fast shots, dusting to the right and left of the rifleman's position.

In the ringing silence that followed, Matt crouched low and stepped into the alley, keeping well to the shadows. He stopped, listening into the night, but heard nothing.

Behind him, out in the street, a man's drunken voice yelled: "Hey, what's all the shooting about?"

Matt moved deeper into the alley, aware that his softly chiming spurs were betraying his every step. He moved his Colt to his left hand, wiped the palm of his suddenly sweating gun hand on his pants and again grasped his gun in his right.

"Come out with your hands up," he said into the darkness. "Or do you want me to drill you square?"

The sudden drumbeat of a running horse was his

mocking answer. The bushwhacker was making his escape and now there would be no chance of catching him.

Matt punched empty shells from his Colt and reloaded, suspicion lying thick upon him. He'd been around buffalo hunters often enough to distinguish the distinctive statements of various large-caliber rifles.

And he was sure by its bark that the man who'd tried to kill him had been using a Sharps .50-70.

Streamers of jade and scarlet streaked the sky as Matt made his way to his office the next morning. Festus was already there and had the coffee boiling. "Mornin', Matthew," the deputy said. "I was up at first light and scouted around the back of the alley like you tole me. But I didn't see anything." He scratched his hairy cheek. "I went on foot since Ruth didn't like it much, my gettin' her up so early I mean. Matthew, never argue with mules or cooks since they have no sense of humor. I learned that a long time ago."

Matt smiled. "I really didn't think you would find anything. I figure whoever shot at me was smart enough to cover his tracks pretty well."

"You suspicion anybody?" Festus asked.

Matt shook his head, for the time being deciding to keep his thoughts to himself. "I'm studying on it, Festus," he said. "Maybe later I'll start to put it together."

The marshal caught his deputy's sidelong glance. Festus knew he was holding something back, and he opened his mouth to speak but he finally decided to let it go. When the time was right, Matt would let that particular cat out of the bag.

A cup of coffee at his elbow, the marshal caught up on paperwork for an hour, then buckled on his gun belt and stepped outside.

The gaudy sky had faded to pale blue, and the rising sun was washing out the shadows from the alleys. In the hard glare of morning, the buildings along Front Street looked tired and faded, their ill-fitting pine planks warped and ashy gray. Dodge was showing her age, like a weary old dowager who shuns the day but welcomes the darkness and the tender mercy of candlelight.

Cattle were bawling down by the railroad tracks and hooves drummed on loading ramps. A train whistle shrieked, splitting the air with sound. It shrieked again, then fell silent.

Matt moved to the edge of the boardwalk. Freight and express wagons were beginning to crowd the street and a few farming families were in town for supplies.

The marshal watched riders coming from a long ways off, the wagon trailing behind them streaming ribbons of dust from its wheels. When they reached the far end of Front Street, he recognized the Shaklee clan, Barnabas in the lead, sitting a rangy buckskin.

Matt eased his Colt in the holster as the Shaklees rode closer. Barnabas wore his clerical collar and a black suit that seemed to have been made for a much shorter man. His low-crowned, flat-brimmed hat was pulled down over his eyes, and he carried a Bible in the crook of his right arm.

His five sons rode behind him, ragged, unshaven

and dirty, and Mordecai's wife held the reins of the
wagon, the other women sitting in the bed.

As Barnabas drew abreast of Matt, he swept his
hat from his bald head and made an exaggerated
bow across the saddle horn. "Good morning, Marshal Dillon," he called out. "A grand morning to be
alive, is it not?"

Behind him one of Barnabas' sons sniggered and
the others made no attempt to hide their impudent
gap-toothed grins.

Matt did not answer, and then the wagon rolled
past, the eyes of the Shaklee women measuring him
from head to toe. One of the women cupped her
hand around the ear of a hard-faced brunette and
whispered a few words, grinning. The brunette listened, then laughed out loud, a harsh, humorless
cackle, and Barnabas turned in the saddle and looked
back at her, his face like thunder.

Matt stepped from the boardwalk and watched the
Shaklee procession until Barnabas' led the way into
Texas Street and they were lost from sight.

Anxiety tugged at the marshal. That the Shaklees
were in Dodge was bad news—but worse was Matt's
sense of foreboding that they were bringing hell
with them.

Later Matt checked on the Shaklees, reluctant to
let them out of his sight for too long. The clan was
camped about a half mile outside town, under a
small trellis bridge that carried a railroad spur over
a dry wash running off the Arkansas.

The marshal sat his horse, studying the lay of the
land around him. The Shaklee camp was situated un-

comfortably close to the whitewashed houses over on the respectable side of Dodge, and Matt decided that at the first hint of trouble he would run the clan out of there.

Matt was returning to his office when Doc Adams stepped out of his surgery and beckoned him over. "Can you spare a minute for a word?"

"For you, Doc, anytime."

He swung out of the saddle and left his horse with the reins trailing and followed Doc into his office. Matt took a seat in a high-backed cane chair by Doc's desk. The man came right to the point. "Matt, don't let Ben Hillman fight Bill Kennett."

"He seems to have his heart set on it, Doc," Matt said.

"It's his heart I'm talking about," Doc said, the irritation that was always close to his surface showing in his eyes.

Matt shook his head. "I don't understand."

"Then I'll spell it out for you. I listened to Ben's heart after his first fight with Kennett. It was a routine thing doctors do, but Ben is a young, fit man and I didn't expect to find anything wrong."

"Your face tells me you did."

"Yes, Matt, I found something wrong, seriously wrong. I won't go into the medical jargon, but Ben Hillman has a dangerously rapid and irregular heartbeat, and it can be brought on by strenuous exercise like a prizefight." Doc sat on the corner of his desk and his eyes found Matt's. "Now Ben could live many years if he takes it easy." The physician's face was suddenly bleak. "But another fight, especially with a grizzly bear like Bill Kennett, could kill him."

"You mean he could die in the ring?" Matt asked, suddenly alarmed.

"Die?" Doc nodded. "Yes, damn it, he could die, and real quick. His heart could start to palpitate rapidly and he might well drop to the canvas and never get up again."

Matt considered that. Then he told Doc about Arrah Hillman and her brother's plans for the Kennett fight prize money.

"He'll take this news hard, Doc," the Marshal concluded. "Ben sets store by his sister, and he wants to see her lead a better life."

"I think," Doc said, again obviously teetering on the thin edge of irritation, "that when you tell Ben that a punch from Kennett could kill him, it might soften the blow." He smiled slightly. "So to speak."

Matt nodded. "I guess you're right, Doc. I'll talk to him and tell him what you said."

The marshal rose to his feet and Doc said: "Matt, a heart condition like Ben has is not to be taken lightly. Sure, he might be able to save his sister from the clutches of Mitch Haythorn, but he'll have to be prepared to lay down his life for her." Doc shook his head. "Seems to me, that's a mighty high price for any man to pay to redeem a fallen woman."

chapter 8

A Dowry for Miss Arrah

Matt was in his office before sunup. He set the coffee on the stove to boil, then walked back to the cells. "Wilson," he hollered, "wake up. I'm letting you out of here."

Husky Wilson turned sullen eyes to Matt, then rolled off his bunk and got to his feet. The marshal clanked the key in the lock and ushered the man into the front office.

"Your gun belt is on the rack, Wilson," Matt said. "Take it. Then get your pony and ride out of Dodge."

"And if I don't?" Wilson sneered.

"Then I'll just toss you in a cell again, only this time I'll throw away the key."

Wilson opened his mouth to speak, but saw the ice in the big lawman's eyes and decided against it. He took his holstered Colt and gun belt from the rack and stepped toward the door. Then he turned and said: "You didn't give me a fair shake, Dillon. If we'd been using guns, I would have killed you."

The marshal's smile was thin. "Not on your best day, Wilson, you no-good tinhorn." He nodded toward the door. "Now you git, and don't let me catch you in Dodge ten minutes from now."

"This ain't over, lawman," Wilson said, his face ugly. "It ain't over by a long shot."

Matt clenched his fists and moved toward the man, but Wilson gulped, hastily opened the door and was gone, his boot heels thudding rapidly on the boardwalk.

The marshal shook his head and to himself said aloud: "Some folks just never learn."

The sun was climbing toward its highest point in the sky as Matt crossed dusty Front Street and headed for the boxing booth. Proctor had set up cots for Hillman and him in a partitioned area to the rear of the tent, after the man decided that hotel rooms would cut into his profit margin.

Matt stopped in the middle of the street to let a heavy beer wagon piled high with barrels trundle past, its team of huge Percherons straining into their collars. A couple young punchers rode past, blanket rolls tied behind their saddles. They were heading back for Texas with nothing in their pockets besides lint, but had stashed away enough memories of exciting, glittering Dodge to last them until next year's spring roundup.

Matt pushed open the flap of the tent and ducked inside. Ben Hillman and Proctor were at ringside, in earnest conversation, and a bored woman in a skirt and low-cut Mexican blouse sprawled on one of the tiered seats, a cheroot curling blue smoke in her hand.

The look the woman directed at Matt was challenging and hostile. He recognized her as Stella Shaklee, who had been abused by her husband at the camp by Mulberry Creek, and he wondered how she had found her way to the boxing booth so fast.

Had Barnabas sent her? And if so, why?

Matt had no time to ponder those questions because Ben Hillman walked quickly toward him, smiling. "Have you decided about the fight yet, Marshal?" he asked.

The tall lawman shook his head. "Ben, I've got news for you, and there's nary a word of it good." His eyes moved to Proctor. "You should hear this too."

Proctor nodded, then said to the woman: "Stella, you run along now." He stepped beside her and shoved some bills into her hand. "I'll see you tonight."

The woman rose to her feet and glanced at the money. "I can hardly wait," she said.

Stella Shaklee sauntered past Matt, waving the money at him, her wide hips swaying an invitation. The woman brushed him with her shoulder as she passed, an impudent smile on her scarlet lips.

Proctor watched her go and smiled at the marshal. "Fine big girl that. And still fresh, on account of how she just got into town."

Matt ignored the man and turned to Hillman, who was asking a question: "Marshal, if you're not here to talk about the fight, did you find my sister?"

"I did find her, but I'm also here to talk about the fight with Bill Kennett."

"What about it?" Proctor asked, suspicion in his eyes. "You're not closing it down?"

"Is that the bad news you have for me, Marshal?" Hillman said.

"Ben, I had a talk with Dr. Adams," Matt said. "He was the man who examined you after your fight with Kennett."

Hillman nodded. "I remember. He didn't find anything wrong with me."

"He did, Ben. He found something seriously wrong"—Matt tapped his chest with the fingertips of his right hand—"here."

"What are you talking about?" Proctor demanded. "Cut to the chase, man."

"Ben, your pump is bad," Matt said, laying it on the line. "Doc says you have a dangerously fast heartbeat and another fight could kill you."

Hillman looked like he'd been slapped. "There's nothing wrong with my heart. Sure, I feel a bit dizzy sometimes but—"

"Ben, I trust Doc Adams. If he says you could die right here in this ring, then I believe him."

"Damn it all, Marshal, that's only the opinion of a cow town quack," Proctor snapped. "Ben is right. There's nothing wrong with his pump."

"Proctor," Matt said evenly, fighting down a sudden flare of anger, "Doc Adams is a fine physician. He knows what he's talking about."

Hillman stepped away and found a seat. He buried his face in his hands, and for a few long minutes, he sat in silence. Then his eyes lifted to Matt's and he said: "I'll take my chances, Marshal. I owe that much to Arrah."

"You also owe it to yourself to live, Ben. Doc Adams says if you give up prizefighting you could live for many years." Matt stepped beside Hillman and placed his hand on his shoulder. "Ben, you could work things out with the Army. After an Army doctor examines you, they could assign you desk duties, maybe."

Hillman's smile was slight. "If they don't shoot me for desertion, you mean."

"Hell, nobody's getting shot for desertion," Proctor said. "Ben, a few more years and we can clean up, you and me. You can retire a rich man and forget you ever were in the damned Army." He turned on Matt. "We can move the fight out of Dodge. You couldn't stop it then."

"Yes, I could," Matt said. "Proctor, I'm a United States marshal. My jurisdiction extends beyond Dodge to every state and territory in the Union. I can shut you down no matter where you go."

Defeated, Proctor's shoulders slumped. He raised bleak eyes to Matt. "Then why not let Ben decide? When they pinned a star on your chest, Marshal Dillon, they made you a lawman. They didn't make you God Almighty."

Matt turned that over in his mind, then said to Ben: "All right, you want to risk your life for your sister. You told me you want to talk to her, and now is as good a time as any. Let's hear what she has to say about you dying for her."

"Where is she?" Hillman asked, his brown eyes suddenly alight.

"She's at the Dodge House with Mitch Haythorn. We'll go there. A word of warning though, Ben. Don't push Haythorn too hard. He's a dangerous man, real fast with the gun, and he's got a temper as quick as his draw."

"I just want to talk to Arrah," Ben said. "I'll cause no trouble."

"So be it," Matt said. He turned on Proctor. "You stay here. I suspect that you and Mitch Haythorn are two of a kind, but he might just shoot you out of spite."

Arrah and Haythorn had finished lunch and were lingering over coffee when Matt and Hillman stepped into the Dodge House dining room.

Haythorn saw them first and he rose to his feet, his eyes wary.

Sensing the man's unease, Arrah turned her head to follow his gaze—and let out a startled little yelp of amazement when she saw her brother.

Arrah leapt to her feet and ran into Hillman's arms. "Ben," she sobbed, her head on his shoulder, "it's been so long."

Hillman pushed Arrah away to arm's length, grinning. "Let me look at you," he said. "Arrah, you're a grown woman. Where did that skinny little girl in pigtails go?"

"She's still here, Ben," Arrah whispered, smiling through tears. "I haven't changed so much."

Matt and Haythorn traded nods. Then the gambler said: "If I'd known we were having a family reunion, I would have delayed lunch so we could all sit around the table."

"Ben," Matt said, "this is Mitch Haythorn."

Haythorn smiled and stuck out his hand. "As you can probably tell from the tone of the marshal's voice, he doesn't like me much." Ben ignored the proffered hand and Haythorn's face changed as he let it drop. "And so it seems, neither do you."

Protectively sliding his arm around Arrah's slender waist, Hillman looked at Haythorn belligerently and said: "I'm taking Arrah away from here. From Dodge, and most of all from you."

"Ah"—Haythorn smiled—"the loving brother speaks." He waved a hand to the vacant chairs at the table. "Then why don't we sit and discuss matters?" The gambler's smile grew wider and mocking. "There is the thorny question of the dowry."

"Dowry? What the hell are you talking about, Haythorn?" Ben asked.

"Why the two thousand dollars I have invested in dear Arrah. It will cost you that much for me to cut her loose."

"Mitch!" the woman cried out. "I don't want to leave you."

Haythorn shook his head. "My dear, remember what I told you. Business is business. A dove is a valuable commodity around these parts, and your price is two thousand." He smiled. "Cash on the barrelhead."

For a moment Ben Hillman stood stunned. Then a roar of fury erupted from his throat. He ran at Haythorn with his right fist cocked, death in his eyes.

The gambler was fast. He reached inside his coat and suddenly a nickel-plated Colt was in his hand and moving up level with Hillman's belly.

Matt was faster. He drew with lightning speed and Haythorn froze as he felt the cold blue muzzle of Matt's gun press against his temple.

"Lay it on the table, Mitch," the marshal whispered, his voice even. "Or I swear, I'll scatter your brains."

It had all happened so quickly, that Ben Hillman barely had time to react. He stopped at the table, uncertain what to do next. He was a man well used to guns, but not to gunfighters, and the speed of the clash between Matt and Haythorn had shocked him.

"Fast, Marshal." Haythorn smiled. He laid his Colt carefully on the table in front of him. "I don't think I've ever seen faster."

Matt's own smile was grim. "And me not even half trying too," he said.

Hillman looked from one man to the other, then eased a step forward. "I'm taking my sister, Haythorn," he said. "I'm taking her now."

The gambler nodded. "Arrah," he said, "come to me."

For a moment or two, the woman seemed as uncertain as her brother had been earlier. Then she picked up her skirt with one hand and ran to Haythorn's side.

"Mitch, are you all right?" she asked.

"I'm fine." He rubbed his temple, where Matt's gun had pressed. "Slight headache, is all." His eyes moved to Hillman. "Why don't you ask her? Ask her to leave with you."

"Arrah?" Hillman said, a world of question in that one whispered word.

The woman shook her head. "Ben, you're my brother and I love you, but my place is here with Mitch."

Haythorn sat and Arrah placed her hand on his shoulder. He studiously pushed his Colt away from him with his left hand and said: "She'll only leave if I tell her to leave," he said. "And the price for that, Mr. Hillman, has just gone up. It's now two thousand five hundred dollars."

Matt saw the anger in Hillman's face as Ben said, "Arrah, this man doesn't care for you. Leave him and come with me. You can go east, start a new life."

"He's my man, Ben. Good or bad, right or wrong, he's still my man and I love him. I can't leave him."

"Then God help you, Arrah," Ben said. "Maybe all I can do now is stay around long enough to pick up the pieces after he's done with you."

Matt realized that there was nothing to be gained by drawing this thing out any longer. "Ben," he said, "wait for me outside."

Hillman opened his mouth to speak, thought better of it, then turned on his heel and rushed out of the door.

After the man was gone, Haythorn's eyes lifted to Matt. "You have some final words to say to me, Marshal?"

"No words, final or otherwise. I reckon this is now between Ben and Arrah." He picked up Haythorn's gun, thumbed the hammer to half cock and swung open the loading gate. He held the Colt upright, rotated the cylinder and let its five shells thud one by one onto the table. Then he handed the revolver butt first to Haythorn.

"Think I'd shoot you in the back as you leave?" the gambler asked, his face flushed with indignation.

Matt's thin smile was slow in coming. "I don't think you would, Mitch. I know you would."

chapter 9

Gunfire in the Darkness

The day shaded into night, and over Dodge the stars were appearing and there would be an early moon. A fretful wind blowing off the prairie rustled around the town buildings and banged loose doors open and shut, making alarmed dogs bark and men restless. Dust lifted off the streets in brief yellow veils only to be shredded by the breeze and scattered; gritty particles worked their way into every nook and cranny, settling thick on floors and furniture.

The reflector lamps were lit along the boardwalks, dancing puddles of orange and yellow light splashing into the streets like wet paint.

Every saloon in town was filled to bursting. Roaring men drank deep as women's laughter cascaded around them like tinsel . . . tawdry, loud and fake.

"Town's on a tear tonight, Matthew." Festus Haggen grinned as he peered out the window of the marshal's office. "Three more herds come in today, one of them all Herefords."

Matt looked up from his paperwork, laid his pen in the inkwell and nodded. "Sign of the times, Festus. The way the cattle buyers talk, the day of the Texas longhorn might soon be over."

"More beef on a Hereford anyhow," Festus said. "A longhorn steer ain't nothin' but horn, bone and bad attitude."

The deputy glanced at the railroad clock on the wall. "It's almost ten. Maybe it's time I headed across the tracks an' let them lace-curtain folks over there see a tin star."

Matt nodded. "You do that, Festus. The way those boys are drinking, some rooster might load up on bumblebee whiskey and take it into his head to hoorah the rich side of town for a change."

The marshal again bowed his head over the letter he was writing, a reply to an angry missive from the railroad company demanding better protection for its employees after one of its engineers was roughed up and dumped in a horse trough outside the Alamo Saloon. That the man had been caught with an extra ace slipped into a sock was not mentioned.

As the deputy stepped to the door, Matt's voice stopped him. "Festus, step careful out there," he said. "Be a bit nicer to the Texans than is called for, but don't take guff from anybody."

"I'll remember that, Matthew." The deputy grinned. "Though by an' large me and Texans tend to get along jes' fine."

Twenty minutes later, as he was signing his name to his letter, Matt heard the gunshots.

There were two, close together, and they'd come from across the tracks.

*   *   *

A lawman with sense doesn't run pell-mell into danger. He walks, taking his time to scan the terrain ahead. And Matt Dillon was a sensible man. His spurs ringing on the boardwalk, he walked toward the tracks, his restless eyes probing into alleys and vacant lots, where mysterious shadows angled.

Like many Western towns, Dodge City was divided into two sections. Falling rapidly behind him was the older part of town, a sprawling collection of saloons, dance halls, bawdy houses, stores and shanties. The only reason for the town's existence was the warren of cattle pens and feed sheds that backed up to the railroad tracks. It was here that ranchers held their herds while awaiting buyers and shipment east. There was no church or school in this part of Dodge, and the hard-drinking cattlemen did not miss either.

Across the railroad tracks, where Matt was headed, was the lace-curtain side of town, situated a good piece from the smells and flies of the holding pens. Here were the homes of the merchants who had moved into Dodge as the town grew, whitewashed buildings of timber with vegetable gardens, carriage houses and servants' quarters.

The tracks that Matt now stepped over separated one world from the next, a barrier of thin iron between cattle, cowboys and courtesans on one hand and class, wealth and position on the other.

The gunshots suggested that someone from the wild part of town had crossed that Deadline—in Dodge, the worst of all transgressions and one that was severely punished.

Once he'd cleared the tracks, Matt stood and let

the darkness crowd around him as he listened into the night. Where was Festus?

"Marshal, over there!"

Matt's eyes probed the gloom, and he saw a man leaning out of a house window about thirty yards to his right. The man was jabbing a finger in the direction of a large gingerbread house, the barn behind it a looming shadow.

The marshal waved to the man and moved toward the house. Around him lamps were being lit in darkened houses, rectangles of yellow light angling across the ground, and people in night attire were stepping out onto their porches, watching him.

Matt felt a niggle of irritation. If bullets started flying . . .

"Stop right there, pardner, or I'll drill yah."

It was Festus' voice.

"Festus, it's me, Matt."

"Matthew?" A moment's silence, then: "Come on ahead."

The marshal followed the sound of his deputy's voice. He found Festus standing by a side window of the house, shards of broken glass and a dead man at his feet. Festus still held his Colt in his right hand.

"What happened?" Matt asked.

It took Festus a while to collect himself. Finally he holstered his gun and said: "I was passin' this way as I began my rounds. Then I heard glass break, and it sounded like it was coming from this house. Matthew, I knowed the house was empty 'cause the couple who live here left for Boston town a week or so back. The wife's sister is right poorly, so they tole me to keep an eye on the place while they went to visit her. They're a nice couple, older people, and Mr. Ferguson—that's the man's name—well, he does some accounting for cattle buyers an'—"

"You heard glass break, Festus," Matt interrupted. "Then what happened?"

"Then I seen this ranny here"—the deputy looked down at the dead man—"climbing out of the window." He stepped to a burlap sack lying on the ground and nudged it with the toe of his boot, making it clank. "He was carrying this."

Matt was aware of people drawing closer, their faces pale in the darkness. "What happened next?"

"Well, I tole him to stay right where he was an' hold up his hands. But he cursed a blue streak an' drew down on me." Festus' eyes sought Matt's in the gloom. "Matthew, a man as slow as this one had no right to be drawin' down on anybody."

"You shot him?"

"I surely did." It's not an easy thing to kill a man, and Festus was chalk white to his lips. "Matthew, I went for my gun and fired. Hit him square. He got one shot off, but by then he was already dead on his feet and he missed."

Matt dropped to a knee beside the dead man and turned him over on his back.

Festus was good with a gun, an easy man to underestimate. His bullet had hit the burglar in the middle of the chest, and the burglar must have been dead when he hit the ground.

But Matt was troubled, because he'd seen this man before and he knew nothing good would come of his death.

It was Mordecai Shaklee.

"Recognize him, Matthew?" Festus asked as he squatted beside the marshal, reading his eyes.

"Yeah, his name is Shaklee, and he rode into town this morning with his pa and four brothers and their women." Matt's chin jutted in the direction of the east. "They're camped along the tracks a ways, under the trellis bridge over the wash."

Back in the Tennessee hills, Festus had been born to the feud, and he knew the ways of vengeful kinfolk. His voice had an uneasy edge to it as he asked: "Matthew, you reckon them Shaklees will take the death of this one real hard?"

His face like stone, Matt got to his feet, then put a hand under his deputy's arm and helped him rise. "Festus, unless I can somehow head it off, I think we could be in a heap of trouble," he said.

"Think they'll come after me?" Festus asked.

"I can't say, not for sure. But in the meantime I don't want you going anywhere in Dodge alone. From now on, you sleep in the office, and if you leave for any reason, I'll be with you."

"How many brothers, Matthew?"

"Four. And their pa, and I believe he's the worst of them."

Festus swallowed hard and shook his head. "A man pulls the trigger, he just don't know what he's gettin' himself into."

"You did your duty, Festus," Matt said. "In your shoes I would have done exactly the same."

The deputy said: "I reckon you would, Matthew. But it sure don't make killin' a man any easier."

"No, it doesn't, Festus." Matt nodded, his lips thin. "No, it doesn't."

chapter 10

Dodge the Devil

Matt Dillon knew that what had to be done would not wait.

He picked up the burlap sack that Shaklee had carried and looked inside. It held silver plate, several pieces of expensive jewelry, a gold watch and a finely engraved Tranter revolver in a walnut presentation box.

Matt carried the sack with him as he and Festus crossed the tracks and headed back to his office. He left the sack in a locked jail cell; then, figuring his deputy would be safe for that night, he led Festus to the Long Branch and told Kitty to give him whatever he wanted.

"Trouble, Matt?" Kitty asked, her lovely face concerned as she poured the deputy a drink.

The big marshal nodded. "Could be. Festus killed a man tonight—a man who has some mighty mean kinfolk. I'm going to talk to them, or at least try."

"Matt," Kitty said, alarmed, "be careful. At least take Newly O'Brien and Quint Asper with you."

"No, I should come with you, Matthew," Festus protested. "If them Shaklees get to feudin', it's me they'll come after."

"Nobody's coming with me and, Festus, you're staying right here," Matt said. He glanced around at the crowded saloon. "You'll be safe at the Long Branch until I get back."

Kitty opened her mouth to speak again, but Matt swung away from the bar and rushed outside. Right then the last thing he needed was a woman fussing over him.

Matt walked to the livery stable, saddled his horse and bridled Festus' mule, and for once Ruth didn't act up, perhaps sensing his urgency. The marshal swung into the leather, then led the mule down Front Street and across the tracks.

He draped Shaklee's body across Ruth's back and caught up her reins again.

It was time to talk to Barnabas.

The night falling close and midnight blue around him, Matt followed the railroad tracks east. The vast arch of the sky was ablaze with stars so near the marshal figured a man could reach up, grab a handful and let them trickle through his fingers like diamonds. The horned moon rode high, surrounded by a lilac halo, and the wind had dropped to a whisper. In the distance the coyotes began to talk, and Matt's bay tossed its head in irritation, the bit jangling.

When he was close enough to see firelight reflected on the iron beams of the trellis bridge, Matt slid his Winchester from the scabbard and levered a round into the chamber.

Now he had it to do.

He hailed the camp when he was still a ways off, but did not draw rein on his horse. Careful to keep his eyes away from the fire, which could blind him momentarily when he looked away, Matt rode into the camp, taking stock of his surroundings.

Barnabas Shaklee and his sons had been sitting around the fire. Now they rose warily to their feet. A couple of the men wore belt guns, but Shaklee's hands were empty, hanging at his sides. There was no sign of the women. They were either in the back of the wagon or in town.

It took a few moments before Barnabas saw the burden on the mule. His eyes lifted to Matt and he said: "Why do you bring a dead man into our camp?"

Matt motioned with the muzzle of the rifle without moving the butt from his thigh. "He's yours, Shaklee. It's Moredcai."

Shaklee's expression did not change. He nodded toward the mule and said: "Joshua, Aaron, go see." He watched his sons step toward the mule, then asked: "What happened to him?"

One of his sons answered the question, calling out: "He's been shot, Pa. There's blood all over him."

Matt made a half turn in the saddle. "You two, take him down from there. Then get back beside your pa where I can see you."

"Who did this thing?" Shaklee asked. The firelight stained the right side of his face red but his eyes were lost in shadow.

"He was caught stealing valuables from a house across the Deadline," Matt answered. "He went for his gun."

"Who did this thing?" Shaklee asked again.

"My deputy," Matt said, knowing that he'd just thrown the fat on the fire.

Mordecai was a tall man and heavy, and Shaklee's sons staggered as they carried his body beside their father and laid it at his feet. Barnabas glanced at his dead son; then his eyes again lifted to the marshal. "Mordecai was good with a gun," he said. "Fast on the draw."

Matt nodded. "Where you come from, maybe. Not around here." Micajah and Simeon had joined their father and brothers, and Matt was facing a half circle of hostile faces. "I brought him to you because I figured you'd want to lay him out and see him buried properly," the lawman said.

"This deputy of your'n, what is his name?" Barnabas asked.

By now the killing of Mordecai would already be common knowledge in Dodge, and Matt saw no reason not to answer the man's question. "Deputy Marshal Festus Haggen. Mordecai gave him no choice."

Barnabas slowly repeated the name, as though he wished to brand it on his memory forever. Then he said: "Marshal, you give Deputy Marshal Festus Haggen a message from me and my sons. Tell him we demand an eye for an eye, a tooth for a tooth. Yea, the slayer himself shall be slain and the dark powers of hell shall be arrayed against him to carry him unto his damnation."

"Shaklee, Festus Haggen has been able to dodge the devil before," Matt said. "Go against him and I guarantee you'll leave more dead sons on the street." The tall lawman's cold eyes swept the faces in front of him. "Besides, if anything happens to Festus, I'll take it real personal. Depend on it. I'll come looking for you."

"The boasts of the wicked are as dust in the wind," Shaklee said.

"Want me to take him, Pa?" Joshua, a crazy recklessness in his eyes, was looking at Matt, grinning. The man wore a Colt on his hip and he seemed eager to go for it.

The marshal's voice was flat and as hard as iron as he swung down his rifle and pointed it right at Joshua's belly. "Boy, try to shuck that Black-Eyed Susan and I'll blow your navel clean through your backbone."

"Joshua, let it be," Barnabas snapped. "He's a trained killer and he'll gun you for sure. Be certain the righteous shall soon smite the oppressor hip and thigh." He turned to his son. "But, damn you, boy, in our own way and our own time."

"Shaklee," Matt said, "one step out of line and I'll run you out of Dodge and clean out of Kansas. The only thing stopping me from doing it right now is that you have a burying to do."

It was an empty threat and Matt knew it. He would not let the Shaklee clan out of his sight until he could find enough evidence to arrest them for the murder of the young cowboy Samuel McDermott. He was also sure that Barnabas had tried to kill him, and that too was a hanging offense in Dodge.

Barnabas opened his mouth to speak, but the wagon creaked and rocked and a blond woman stepped into the circle of the firelight. Her eyes took in what was happening at a glance, then dropped to

Mordecai's body. She turned her head and yelled: "Stella!"

"What the hell do you want?" a voice from inside the wagon answered. "I'm asleep."

"Better come see this," the blonde hollered. "It's your man. It's Mordecai."

The wagon creaked on its springs again, and the woman called Stella appeared, long hair falling over her face. Even from where he sat, Matt smelled the whiskey on her.

Stella looked to the other woman, her bloodshot eyes puzzled. The blonde nodded toward the body. "There. It's Mordecai. He's dead."

For a few moments, Stella stood there stunned; then she let out a shrill shriek and dropped to her knees beside the dead man. Stella wailed and tore at her hair, and one by one the other women appeared from the wagon, crowded around the body and joined in her lamentations.

"Go now," Barnabas said as he stepped closer to Matt. "Leave us be to mourn our dead."

Matt saw hatred in Shaklee's eyes, that and madness. The marshal had suspected the man was dangerous in the extreme, and now, with the death of his son, he would be even more so.

From now on, every moment of the day and night, Matt knew that he and Festus would have to watch their backs.

chapter 11

Mitch Haythorn
Kills a Man

The night following his meeting with Barnabas
Shaklee, Matt's routine paperwork was again interrupted by gunshots. The marshal laid down his
pen and stepped to the door, in time to see a boy
running down the boardwalk toward him.

"Marshal," the kid yelled, "Mr. Haggen said for
you to come right smartly!"

"Where?" Matt demanded.

"The Dodge House."

"Do you know what happened, boy?"

"I should say." The boy grinned. "Mitch Haythorn
just killed a man."

Matt spun the boy a coin, then took his hat from
the rack and settled it on his head. He was already
walking along the boardwalk as he buckled his gun
around his hips.

A crowd had gathered at the mouth of the alley
between the hotel and Jamison's hardware store, and
Matt spotted Haythorn off to one side, standing aloof

from the rest, a thin cigar between his teeth curling smoke.

The marshal glanced at Haythorn, who bowed from the waist and grinned, and stepped toward Festus, who was standing with a woman in his arms, her face buried in his shoulder. As he got closer, Matt recognized the woman as Arrah Hillman.

"Evening, Matthew," Festus said, talking over the top of the woman's head. "Ol' Mitch just bedded down a feller."

Arrah turned a tearstained face to Matt, and for the first time, he noticed that her dress was torn at the shoulder, and she had an angry welt on her left cheek.

"What happened, Festus?" Matt asked.

Arrah disengaged herself from Festus and ran to Haythorn, who took her in his arms and gently stroked her back.

"The feller attacked Miss Arrah," Festus said. "He started to drag her into the alley. Then, as Mitch tells it, he stepped out of the hotel for a cigar and heard the young lady's screams. He said he came into the alley and saw the man struggling with Miss Arrah. He says the man drew down on him, but he was faster and cut his suspenders for him."

"Show me the man," Matt said.

He followed Festus into the alley, which was deep in shadow. The deputy stopped, thumbed a match alight, then took a knee beside the dead kidnapper. "Do you know him, Matthew? I sure don't."

Matt studied the man's face in the shifting glare of the match. He was young and bearded and dressed in a threadbare brown suit and collarless shirt. When

Festus struck another match, the marshal noticed a battered brown derby lying close to the body.

The man's suit and hat were of good quality; he looked like someone who had once been fairly prosperous but recently had fallen on hard times. Dodge was full of such men, anonymous drifters reduced to poverty by gambling, drink or just sheer bad luck.

"No, I don't know him, Festus," Matt said. He nodded toward the people crowded around the entrance to the alley. "See if anybody here recognizes him."

"I already did," Festus said. "I showed this ranny to everybody around, an' a puncher claimed he saw him spending money at the Saratoga earlier this evenin', but that's all he knows."

"What does Arrah Hillman say?"

Festus scratched his cheek. "Well, Matthew, she says that she an' Mitch had a quarrel."

Matt nodded. "They seem to do a lot of that."

"An' then she left the hotel. Says she was plannin' to walk around some until her temper cooled." Festus shook his head and grinned. "I guess ol' Mitch doesn't know that there's two theories to arguin' with a woman, an' neither one works."

"Then what happened, Festus?" Matt asked.

"Why, then, a man ran out o' nowhere, she says, grabbed her and dragged her into the alley."

"Did he try to molest her?"

"He sure didn't, Matthew. Lookee here." Festus thumbed another match into flame and held it over a dirty striped pillowcase lying on the ground. "She says he slapped her around some, then tried to shove that over her head and shoulders. Right about then

Mitch showed up, saw what was happenin' an' plugged the feller.''

Matt kneeled beside the dead man. ''Bring another match over here, Festus,'' he said.

The deputy struck the match and Matt searched the dead man. He found a few dollars in his pocket, but no gun.

''I thought you said he drew down on Haythorn?'' he said.

''That's what Mitch said, Matthew. He said the man was reachin' inside his coat for a gun, so he shot him.''

Matt rose to his feet. ''Let's go talk to Arrah and Haythorn,'' he said.

He and Festus elbowed their way through the growing, excited crowd, and walked up to Haythorn, who was still comforting the woman. They separated when they saw the two lawmen.

''Festus told me what happened, Miss Hillman,'' Matt said. ''He says the man slapped you, then tried to put a pillowcase over your head.''

Arrah nodded, her eyes bright with tears. ''He told me he wasn't going to hurt me. But he said he needed me for a friend of his.''

''Did he say who this friend was?''

The woman shook her head. ''No, he didn't. But he told me his friend would treat me real good.''

Matt stood deep in thought for a few moments, then said: ''He must have been watching the hotel, waiting on his chance. I'd guess it came a lot earlier than he expected.''

''I don't let Arrah go anywhere in Dodge without

an escort," Haythorn said. "The man must have realized that, surely."

"But you leave Arrah alone at the hotel sometimes," Matt said. "He could have known that. Maybe he figured to wait until you left and then try to get into Arrah's room."

A wild thought raced through Matt's head. He hesitated, then decided to give it voice. "Haythorn, have you taken on any new girls recently?"

The man shrugged. "A couple. They just got into town."

"Do they have names?"

"Sure they have names. Ellie and Stella Shaklee. I think maybe they're sisters." He raised an eyebrow. "Does it really matter?"

"Maybe and maybe not. Those two women are not sisters. They're married to the sons of a man named Barnabas Shaklee. Shaklee claims to be some kind of preacher. Do you know him?"

Haythorn smiled. "Preachers are outside my usual circle of acquaintances, Marshal."

"I know him." Arrah's statement was so unexpected that every head turned to her. "Early this morning, he came to collect money from Ellie and Stella. I'd gone down to the New York Hat Shop to pick up a new hat I'd ordered—"

"And very expensive it looks on you, too, my dear," Haythorn said, a wry smile touching the corners of his mouth.

Arrah ignored the remark and continued. "Shaklee saw me in the street and introduced himself as a reverend. He ordered the other women back to their camp. Then he told me he was burying a son today. I gave the man my sympathy, but then he said a wounded soul can only be healed by lying in lust with a fancy woman."

Arrah hesitated and Matt prompted her. "And what happened next?"

"Then he asked me how much I charged. I walked away from him then, but he called after me. He said I was an uppity black dove, and one day very soon he'd cut me down to size with a horsewhip."

Haythorn's face was like thunder. "By God, I'll put a bullet in that man's belly."

Matt let that go and said: "I thought you told me you never let Arrah go anywhere unescorted?"

"Marshal"—the gambler spread his hands wide—"who would expect a woman to be accosted just after sunup when every puncher and ne'er-do-well in Dodge is asleep?"

Matt waved a hand toward the alley. "Haythorn, you told Festus the man went for a gun and you shot him." The lawman's eyes sought the gambler's in the gloom. "I searched him. He doesn't have a gun."

"It was dark in there." Haythorn shrugged. "When you see a man's hand go inside his coat, you assume he's pulling a gun. I really didn't have time to think it through." The man smiled. "You considering charging me with his killing?"

"I could," Matt answered. "But there isn't a jury in the West would convict of murder a man who was only coming to the aid of a lady in distress."

"Then I'm free to go?"

Before Matt could answer, Percy Crump hopped

beside him. His vulture eyes went to the tall lawman. "I heard there is a deceased, Marshal. Shot down in his prime, I'm told."

Matt nodded. "In the alley, Percy. He's as dead as he'll ever be, and nobody seems to know who he is. He's also broke, just a couple of dollars in his pocket."

"Then my bill will go to the mayor's office, as usual?"

"Wait," Haythorn said. He fished in his vest pocket and spun a gold double eagle to Crump. "Bury him decent," he said. "Give him a headstone and say he was shot by Mitch Haythorn."

"You always bury your dead, Haythorn?" Matt asked.

"When I can." The gambler smiled. "And I always order the headstone. A man in my line of work needs the publicity."

Mordecai Shaklee's funeral procession rolled past the marshal's office on its way to boot hill early the following morning.

Barnabas rode in the lead, wearing his clergyman's collar, his Bible held against his chest. His eyes were fixed on the way ahead, neither turning to the left nor right. His four surviving sons rode behind him, all of them wearing guns.

The wagon, its canvas cover removed, carried the body. Stella and Ellie sat in the driver's seat. The other women walked, crying and wailing, in the dust kicked up by the rear wheels.

Matt and Festus watched the wagon roll by, Mordecai's body jolting back and forth as the wheels hit sunbaked ruts in the street. But what caught the lawmen's attention was the crudely painted, wooden sign nailed to the wagon bed, the letters six inches high:

MURDERED IN THE
STREETS OF DODGE

Festus had removed his hat as the procession passed, and now he settled it back on his head. "Matthew, I didn't murder that feller," he said, his eyes troubled. "Ol' Barnabas knows he drawed down on me first."

Matt, lean, tough and watchful, nodded. "He knows all right, Festus. But he lives by his own code—a code that demands an eye for an eye, a tooth for a tooth."

Festus' right eyebrow crawled up his forehead like a hairy caterpillar. "Think he'll come after me tonight, maybe?"

"Festus, I'd guess we can depend on it," Matt said.

chapter 12

A Cutthroat Strikes

Night fell on Dodge, and down by the tracks, the cattle were milling around in their pens, jammed in so close their horns clashed as they bawled their misery. A locomotive clanked and hissed, and railroaders yelled to one another, holding up lanterns against the darkness.

But none of these sounds carried to Front Street, where the roaring saloons were in full swing, competing pianos loudly cascading notes into the bustling clamor of the evening.

Matt made his way back to his office after spending the best part of an hour attempting to reassure a widow woman across the tracks that the Peeping Tom she'd seen at her kitchen window was probably just a stray cat.

"Well, Marshal," the woman had concluded as she showed Matt to the door, "if you do find that it was a man, send him here to talk to me. I want him to explain himself."

"I'll do that," Matt had said. "I'll send him right over."

The woman had seemed pleased by this arrangement, saying that she must immediately change out of her drab housedress and get to fixing her hair.

"Lordy," she said, "I can't meet a gentleman caller looking like this."

The marshal was no sooner back in his office than the door opened, and a small, timid mouse of a man in a broadcloth suit and plug hat stepped inside. Matt decided his visitor had the look of a drummer, a notion that was confirmed when the man announced: "Marshal, my name is Thaddeus J. Brumley. I travel in ladies' corsets and other sundries for the fairer sex."

"Pleased to make your acquaintance, Mr. Brumley," Matt said. "What can I do for you?"

The man looked uncomfortable. "Well, see, that's the thing. Maybe nothing. Maybe I'm concerned without cause."

The big marshal smiled to set the man at ease. "Why don't you tell me what's happened and let me decide?"

"But . . . but maybe nothing's happened," Brumley said. "That's the thing of it."

"From the beginning, Mr. Brumley," Matt prompted, his prolonged smile beginning to slip. He waved the man into a chair. "Be pleased to sit."

Brumley took a chair, cast nervous baby blue eyes around the office, then said: "Mine is a lonely profession, Marshal. I mean, months away from home, constantly on the go from town to town, no loved ones near."

"A lonely profession indeed," Matt said sympathetically. He waited.

"Well, naturally, I was drawn into a friendship with another commercial traveler. His name is Jonathan Cheshire, and like me, he specializes in ladies' intimate apparel of the more . . . ah . . . delicate sort. Well, earlier this evening, Mr. Cheshire and I were indulging in a few drinks at the Lone Star Saloon when he told me he had to step outside to use the facility provided for bodily relief."

"And then?" Matt asked.

"Well, he never came back. He'd just ordered another round of drinks and his rum punch is still sitting on the bar."

"Maybe he met a woman," Matt suggested.

Brumley vehemently shook his head. "Marshal, like me Mr. Cheshire is a happily married man. He'd never dream of doing such a dreadful thing."

Matt knew plenty of happily married men who regularly succumbed to temptation and did the dreadful thing, but he let that go. "I'll walk with you to the Lone Star, Mr. Brumley," he said. "Your friend may be back at the bar by the time we get there."

Matt towered over the diminutive drummer as they walked along the boardwalk to the saloon. For his part, Brumley seemed pleased to be seen in the company of such a famous lawman. He puffed out his chest and smiled and tipped his hat to everyone they passed, eagerly sharing in the marshal's reflected glory.

The Lone Star was crowded, and Matt had to elbow his way to the bar, clearing a path for Brumley. "See, Marshal," the man said when they finally reached their destination. "Mr. Cheshire's drink is still here."

Matt nodded. "I'll take a look out back."

"I'll come with you," Brumley said quickly. His face fell. "Geez, I wish I had a gun."

Matt, the excited drummer in tow, made his way to the rear of the bar, exchanging nods and greetings with drinking men as he passed.

Outside, the darkness hung close. Matt made out the bulk of a three-holer outhouse, the last word in modern luxury, but the door hung open on its hinges and no one was inside.

"Dear, dear, where could Mr. Cheshire have gotten to?" Brumley asked.

Matt still suspected the man had gone in search of a female companion, but he stopped and looked around, his eyes probing the darkness. "Well, I don't think he's out here," he said.

The marshal moved to his right, toward the high wall of a warehouse. A large freight wagon, its tongue lifted, stood behind the building and beyond that were a small stable and corral.

He stepped in the direction of the corral—and almost tripped over a dead man.

Matt dropped to a knee and Brumley did the same behind him. The marshal found a match in his pocket and thumbed it into flame. Sudden yellow light splashed on the face of the dead man. His mouth was set in a grotesque grin, his throat cut from ear to ear.

Brumley sprang to his feet, and after a few moments, Matt heard him retching convulsively, interspersed with gasps of "My God. Oh, my God."

Matt searched the dead man. He found no wallet

or watch. Then he saw that the little finger of his left hand had been severed, presumably to get at a ring.

Rising to his feet, the marshal stepped closer to Brumley, but maintained his distance. "Is that him?" he asked. "Is that Cheshire?"

The little drummer nodded. "It's him," he wheezed. "My God, Marshal, who would do such a thing?"

"Did he have a wallet and a watch?" Matt asked, ignoring the man's question.

"I don't know."

"Try to remember. Did he have a wallet?"

Brumley stood and wiped his mouth with the back of his hand. "Yes . . . yes, I remember. He had a wallet and he wore a watch. It was a yellow watch on a chain, but I don't know if it was gold or not."

"Gold or brass, he was murdered for it," Matt said. "That and his wallet and the ring he wore on his finger."

"Oh, his poor wife and children," Brumley groaned. "Poor Mrs. Cheshire."

"Step inside and drink a brandy," Matt said. "I'm going to take a look around out here."

Brumley nodded, his eyes red, glazed with shock. He turned and stumbled into the rear door of the saloon, and Matt stepped back to the dead man.

There was little to be learned. The area was strewn with empty bottles. Cowboys and others regularly used it as a shortcut to the saloon, so the dusty ground was covered by hundreds of footprints.

In the end all Matt knew was that Mr. Jonathan Cheshire, a drummer who sold ladies' intimate apparel, had been savagely murdered by a man who wanted to rob him.

There were dozens of such men in Dodge.

*   *   *

Matt waited until Percy Crump had performed his melancholy duty and removed the dead man. Percy seemed almost jolly, like a hungry buzzard that had just found a week-old buffalo carcass.

And why not? Like every other merchant in town, the undertaker was prospering.

When Matt returned to his office, he found Ben Hillman waiting for him. The young man got right to the point. "Marshal," he said, "I need the fight with Bill Kennett now more than ever. You've got to let it go ahead."

The marshal hung his hat and gun belt on the rack and crossed to his desk. He settled himself in his chair before he spoke. "I take it you want to pay Mitch Haythorn his two thousand five hundred."

Hillman moved, as lithe and lean as a cougar, and sat on the corner of Matt's desk. "Arrah won't leave him, not of her own free will—that much I've learned. He'll have to shut her out of his life, tell her to go."

"But he wants money to do that."

"Exactly, Marshal. And the only way I can earn that much money is to fight Kennett again."

Suddenly weary, Matt met Hillman's eyes. "Ben, Proctor told me that when they pinned this badge on me, it didn't make me God. He was right about that. I'm not God, just a lawman who does his best to do his duty as he sees it.

"You're a grown man, Ben, and I've got no right to make your decisions for you. I figure if I stop the fight you'll just set it up in some other town. I can't be everywhere at once. At least here in Dodge we have a first-class doctor if things go bad."

Hillman smiled. "Then I can tell G. P. that you're not shutting us down?"

"You can tell him that." Matt's probing eyes lifted to the young fighter. "You're laying your life on the line. You know that, don't you?"

"I know that," Hillman answered. "Marshal, Arrah and me, we're black people living in a white man's world. When we were kids, we never had much, didn't expect much, but it never stopped us dreaming. My sister wants to be a fine lady one day, with a big house and a carriage and servants, like the fine folks across the tracks here in Dodge.

"Well, I can't give her those things, but if I get her away from Haythorn, maybe she'll have a chance."

"And that's worth dying for?"

"It is to me. Marshal, I was raised hard, went to bed hungry more times than not, but Arrah was the one beautiful thing in my life, like a rose growing in a weed patch. I believe that rose is worth saving. I don't want to see it torn up by the roots and thrown away."

Matt nodded. "A man does what he has to do, I guess. I won't stand in your way."

Hillman rose to his feet. "I don't believe the doctor that another fight could kill me. I feel just fine."

"Ben, Doc Adams isn't much of one for empty talk. When he says a thing, believe him."

"Then I'll just have to take my chances," Hillman said.

"Your funeral," Matt said, smiling to take the sting out of it.

Hillman laughed. "Marshal, trust me. Bill Kennett won't bed me down."

"I wish I could be sure of that, Ben," Matt said.

After much soul-searching, the marshal had made his decision. Now, as he watched Hillman leave, he wondered if it had been the right one.

chapter 13

A Ripper Strikes

Proctor, perhaps fearing that Matt would change his mind about the fight, arranged for the bout to take place in three days.

"I spoke to Bill Kennett, and he says that will be enough time for his ribs to mend some," Festus said the next morning as he and Matt drank coffee in the marshal's office. "He's primed, Matthew. When ol' Bill talks about Ben Hillman, he grits his teeth like he could bite the sights off'n a six-gun."

Matt shrugged. "Kennett lost the first fight fair and square."

"Bill don't see it that way. He says Ben had something in his right hand, a roll of dimes maybe. He says he's goin' to get the referee to examine Ben's fists afore they come up to scratch." Festus rubbed his unshaven cheek, his eyes thoughtful. "That's what he says all right."

Matt was about to reply but a shout from outside stopped him.

"You in the jail! Show yourselves and be damned to ye!"

It was Barnabas Shaklee's voice.

Matt rose from the desk and strapped on his gun. He heard Festus snap shut the Greener after checking the loads; then the two lawmen stepped onto the boardwalk.

Shaklee sat his horse in front of the marshal's office under a red-streaked sky. He wore his clerical collar and was carrying his Bible. He appeared to be unarmed.

The man's eyes were wild and his gray hair streamed long in the wind. "Vengeance is mine, I shall repay," he yelled. "The righteous shall cast down the wicked and thrust them into the everlasting fire." He pointed a trembling finger at Festus. "Vile Herod, slayer of the innocents, soon ye shall be felled by a thunderbolt and hurled into the bottomless pit."

Shaklee fought his horse for a moment as it tossed its head, battling the bit. "Then the dusky whore of Babylon shall be made clean by the whip and the branding iron," he screamed at the top of his lungs. "She will be shown the path of righteousness and only then will the just take her to bed."

"Never did cotton much to preachers, Matt."

The marshal turned to see Doc Holliday at his elbow, Bat Masterson beside him. The gamblers were dressed in frockcoats, boiled white shirts and string ties; they were obviously on their way to the Long Branch for their morning bourbon and cigars.

Matt nodded to the two men and his eyes swung

back to Shaklee. "Clear the street, Shaklee," he said. "Or I'll arrest you for disturbing the peace."

"Matt, want me to put a bullet in his belly?" Holliday asked, his pale face eager as he slipped a hand inside his coat. "It would be no trouble at all."

"Leave him be," Matt said, his dislike of Holliday apparent. His cold eyes again lifted to Shaklee. "I won't tell you a second time."

A small crowd had gathered on the boardwalk and Shaklee's mad, bloodshot eyes swept along them. "I will go now, but I want all of you to bear witness to my prophecy, for the destruction of Babylon and all its vile whoredom is close at hand."

Before Matt could act, Shaklee swung his horse away from the office and spurred the animal into a gallop, dust kicking up behind him.

"Matt, you should have let Doc plug that damned preacher," Masterson said. "He's a crazy man and he means to cause you no end of trouble."

"I'll deal with him, Bat," the marshal said. "Now you and Doc go about your business."

Bat touched his plug hat to Matt, and the big lawman watched him and Doc Holliday cross the street and step inside the Long Branch before he and Festus went back into the office.

The deputy was silent as he poured himself coffee, his face thoughtful. Finally Matt said: "There's something sticking in your craw, Festus. What is it?"

"Matthew, who is that Herod feller ol' Barnabas was talkin' about, him that kills innocents an' sich? Is he some kind of outlaw down in the Territory, maybe?"

The marshal smiled. "Festus, King Herod was a bad ruler back in the Bible days. He massacred a whole passel of children, trying to get the baby Jesus."

"But I've never killed no babies," Festus said.

"I know. But in Shaklee's book, you're just as bad as Herod, and maybe worse."

The deputy shook his head. "That ol' boy sure knows how to hate, don't he?"

Matt nodded. "I'd say he works on it considerable."

That night there was another murder in Dodge.

A saloon girl who called herself Fanny Noble was found dead in an empty stall at the livery stable. She'd been stripped naked and mutilated, but whether before or after she'd been strangled to death, Matt could not tell.

The marshal asked Doc Adams to examine the body, but the physician could add little to what was already horrifyingly obvious.

"She's been dead for no more than two hours," Doc said. "I'd say she was lured here. She was then stabbed and strangled."

"Any way to identify a suspect, Doc?" Matt asked, clutching at straws.

Doc shook his head. "This was a big girl. All I can tell is that the man who murdered her was enormously strong, and he may be insane. When he was done, he'd be covered from head to toe in blood."

"Then he couldn't very well have walked through town. Someone would have noticed."

The physician nodded. "He'd have looked like

he'd just come from a slaughterhouse." He picked up the girl's purse, a dainty velvet bag closed at the top with a ribbon. "Empty. Her killer also robbed her of what little she possessed."

"Was that the main motive, Doc? Robbery?"

"I don't think so. A deep-seated hatred of doves or women in general might have been the real motive." The physician shrugged. "The robbery was probably an afterthought."

A perceptive man, Doc studied Matt's face closely in the guttering, uncertain light of the oil lamp the marshal had placed close to the body. "Matt, I see something in your eyes," he said. "Do you have a suspect?"

Matt nodded, thinking of Barnabas Shaklee. The man was certainly insane and he had made no secret of his hatred for prostitutes. "Yes, Doc, I suspect somebody," he said. "For this killing and the murder of a drummer last night. Add to that the shooting of a young cowboy and I believe he may have murdered three people already."

"Anybody I know?"

"A man named Shaklee, calls himself a preacher. He rode into Dodge about a week ago with his sons and their wives."

"Wait a minute, Matt. Didn't Festus kill a man named Shaklee the other night over the Deadline?"

The marshal nodded. "Mordecai Shaklee, one of the sons."

"Caught him breaking into a house, I believe."

"Yes, he did. The man drew on Festus and didn't give him any choice."

Matt saw the worry in Doc's eyes as the physician

said: "This is a bad business. The man who did this is crazy, and he'll kill again."

"I could arrest Shaklee, but I've got no reason to hold him," Matt said. "All I'd do is get him off the street for a day or two."

"And all you'd do is postpone the next murder for a while," Doc said gloomily.

When Percy Crump arrived, Doc gave him a cold nod, only too aware that their professions were very much in opposition to each other.

But even Percy, who had seen violent death in all its forms, was appalled by the savagery of the killing. "This poor girl met a terrible end, just terrible," he said, shaking his head. "Look at her face, Marshal. She was terrified."

But Matt had seen enough. "Just carry her out of here, Percy, and for God's sake, get her decent."

The undertaker nodded. "Yes, Marshal, I'll carry her out. But get her decent? I'm afraid that's impossible, even for me."

Matt Dillon was not a drinking man. But when he returned to his office, he found the bottle of whiskey he kept in a drawer for visitors and poured himself a stiff shot. He followed it by another, and slowly the horror of the evening became less vivid in his memory.

He knew Barnabas Shaklee was the only man who could have committed the crime, but he did not have a single shred of proof.

Doc said the killer would look like he'd just come from a slaughterhouse. How could a man in blood-saturated clothes have escaped notice?

He could have driven a wagon, or had someone drive it for him while he hid in the back. But who would be party to such a crime? One of Shaklee's sons? That was possible, but unlikely. Someone else then?

Matt shook his head. Probably Shaklee had driven himself. It would be easy enough to climb behind the seat and handle the reins from there. Later he could have disposed of his bloodstained clothes, washed and changed into others he'd stashed in the wagon.

Come first light Matt planned to take a look at the wagon and scout around for evidence of badly bloodstained clothing.

The sound of the office door opening brought Matt back to the present. Mayor Kelley stepped inside, wearing a canvas duster and a worried frown. "I just heard, Matt," he said. "A nasty business." Kelley dropped into the chair opposite Matt, his measuring eyes moving from Matt's face to the bottle on the desk. "That bad, huh?"

"Bad enough," Matt answered. Then, sparing none of the details, he told the mayor just how bad it had been.

By the time the marshal stopped speaking, Kelley's face was ashen. He reached out an unsteady hand, grabbed the bottle and poured whiskey into the glass. He tossed off the bourbon, shuddered as the raw alcohol hit his stomach, then gasped: "I'll never be able to tell all that to Mrs. Kelley. The poor woman would be all atremble in an instant." The mayor's eyes probed Matt's face. "Do you suspect anyone, Matt?"

The marshal shrugged, unwilling as yet to tip his

hand to Kelley, a notorious gossip. "I'm working on it, Mayor. I believe the same man murdered a drummer last night and was responsible for the death of the young cowboy with the silver ring on his finger."

"McDermott," Kelley said absently. "His name was McDermott." He leaned forward in his chair. "Matt, find this killer. If he strikes again, we could have a mass exodus from Dodge and that—"

"Would be bad for business." The marshal finished it for him.

"Exactly." Kelley rose wearily to his feet. "Matt, if you need any help, any help at all, just let me know."

"I'll do that, Mayor. And thanks for the offer."

Kelley walked to the door, put his hand on the handle and stopped. He turned, his eyes scared, and said: "Marshal Dillon, may all the saints in heaven protect and preserve you and all of us."

"Thanks," Matt said. "I can use all the preserving and protecting I can get."

chapter 14

"I'll See You Hang"

At daybreak the coyotes were still yammering on the plains as Matt and Festus, a driving wind at their backs, followed the Arkansas east. Just ahead of them lay the Shaklee encampment and the wagon the marshal planned to search. Festus carried the Greener across his saddle horn and Matt held his Winchester upright on his thigh.

The river was low at this time of the year, sluggishly flowing around sandbanks, where trapped tree trunks washed down by the spring runoff raised skeletal gray branches to the lemon sky.

The rising sun was felling through the leaves of the cottonwoods when the two lawmen rounded a bend of the river and saw a woman dipping a bucket into the water. She recognized them, rose to her feet and shaded her eyes with a hand, watching them come. Matt was close enough to hear her yell: "The law's comin'!"

A man stepped out of the shelter of the bridge, a

rifle slanted across his chest. He was joined by another, and they stood waiting and tense until Matt and Festus rode up on them.

"Morning," Matt said. He motioned toward the wagon. "Mind if I take a look at that?"

"There's womenfolk in there," one of the men said. He had close-set eyes and wet yellow teeth, and Matt remembered that this was the son Barnabas Shaklee called Aaron. Without taking his sullen eyes off the two lawmen, the man turned his head and yelled: "Pa!"

Barnabas appeared, hooking a suspender over the shoulder of a white vest that Matt noticed was remarkably clean. "Damn it, boy, what's all the hollering about?" Shaklee asked.

Aaron did not answer, but merely inclined his head toward the mounted lawmen.

Shaklee's eyes followed the motion, and when he saw Matt and Festus, they immediately turned murderous. "What do you two want?" he demanded.

"I want to take a look inside your wagon, Shaklee," Matt said. He swung his Winchester on Aaron, who had been fingering his rifle, a wild look in his eyes. "And if your boy doesn't drop that gun right now, I'll shoot at the top button of his shirt. And I don't usually miss."

Aaron Shaklee threw a despairing look at his father and dropped the rifle like it had suddenly become red-hot. "I'm out of it," he yelled.

"The Philistines are upon us but the glory of the Lord shall be our sword and buckler," Shaklee yelled. "The day of reckoning is close at hand."

Matt swung out of the saddle, and without turning, he said: "Watch my back, Festus."

"Got you covered, Matthew," the deputy said, his eyes beady on Barnabas.

"Now I want to look in that wagon, Shaklee," Matt said.

His eyes suddenly sly, Shaklee said: "Now why would you want to do such a thing? To see our womenfolk naked, maybe?"

"Get them out of there," Matt said. He raised his rifle until the muzzle was level with Shaklee's belly. "I'm all through fooling around with you, Shaklee. Now move!"

The man shrugged. "I got nothing to hide."

Matt following close behind him, Shaklee walked to the wagon. He stood at the closed canvas and yelled: "Stella, you and them others make room in that there cat wagon."

"Barnabas, it's way too early in the morning," a woman's voice answered. "Go cool off in the river."

A chorus of giggles followed, but Shaklee scowled and said: "The law is here and they want to search the wagon. Now climb out and let them look."

As the wagon shook and women swore, Shaklee's four sons stood behind their father. A couple of them were wearing belt guns, a fact not lost on Festus. He rode his mule closer, then held his scattergun ready across his chest.

Four women tumbled out of the back of the wagon, casting annoyed looks in Matt's direction. "It's all yours, lawman," Stella said. "But don't you go pawing around our unmentionables, now."

The woman laughed and Matt's lips tightened as he walked to the wagon and looked inside. He moved away clothing and blankets and checked out the pine floorboards. They were clean, as though they'd been recently scrubbed. The wagon seat told the same story. It too was free of anything that even suggested a bloodstain.

Disappointment tugging at him, Matt walked back to where Festus sat his mule. "Find what you were looking for, Marshal?" Barnabas asked, his voice and grin mocking.

A small anger flared in Matt. "Shaklee, where were you last night? Say, around ten o'clock?"

"Why, right here, Marshal." Shaklee waved a hand to the others. "Tell him. Wasn't I right here?"

"He was here," replied a half dozen voices.

"Then all of you are damned liars," Matt said.

"Those are hard words for any man to take." Micajah Shaklee, a sour-faced man with a deep knife scar down his left cheek, took a step toward Matt. Micajah was wearing a gun and behind him the marshal heard a creak as Festus moved in the saddle, covering the man with the Greener.

For a moment Matt thought Micajah would go for his gun, but Barnabas' voice ended it. "Let it be, Micajah," he said. "Dillon is looking for any excuse to kill us."

"You listen to your pappy, boy," Festus said quietly. "Make a move toward that pistol and I'll cut you in half with this here scattergun."

Micajah, suddenly looking sick, backed off, and Matt's eyes, cold and accusing, swung on Barnabas. Wanting to see how the man reacted, he said:

"Shaklee, let's make this official. I believe you murdered a woman last night and a drummer the night before. I also believe you shot and killed a young puncher because you wanted the ring he wore. Now I can't prove any of this as yet, but I will eventually. And then I'll see you hang."

Barnabas Shaklee's face showed only rage. "And the wicked shall spread their calumnies but they will not prevail. Yea, though I walk through the shadow of the valley of death, I shall be spared, for the Lord is with me."

"You heard what I told you, Shaklee," Matt said, his voice tightening. "I aim to see you swing at the end of a rope."

Matt turned and walked to his horse. He stepped into the leather and motioned Festus to follow him. The two lawmen backed their mounts for a distance, then swung to the west.

Matt glanced over his shoulder to make sure they were not being followed, and got an unpleasant surprise.

A man had emerged from hiding and Barnabas Shaklee was standing beside him, his arm around his neck. Both of them were looking after the lawmen, grinning.

The man was Husky Wilson.

chapter 15

Matt Gives Kitty
a Warning

The morning had brightened into early afternoon when Matt and Festus returned to the livery stable and put up their mounts.

Festus draped his mule's bridle over the stall partition, then turned to Matt and asked: "How do you rate our chances of getting the evidence to hang ol' Barnabas, Matthew?"

"Slim to none, and slim is already saddling up to leave town," Matt answered, his face bleak. "If I could catch Shaklee in the act, that would put the nail in his coffin. But he covers his tracks real well."

"You reckon the murders will stop now he knows you're on to him, Matthew?"

"I don't think so. Barnabas Shaklee is crazy, and it's his madness that drives him to kill." Matt shook his head. "What I can't understand is why his sons and their wives cover for him. They must know by now what he did to that girl last night."

"Maybe they don't know, Matthew. Could be somebody else is helping him."

Matt immediately thought of Husky Wilson. The man fancied himself a fast gun, but was that the end of it? Was Wilson's mind just as warped and evil as Shaklee's? It was a possibility that could explain much.

Matt had told the gunman never to show his face in Dodge again, but under the cloak of darkness, he and Shaklee could scuttle around town unseen, like cockroaches.

Then so be it. The marshal decided that from now until he had Shaklee locked up in his jail, he would also haunt the shadows—and if luck was on his side, maybe he'd get a chance to stomp Shaklee and Wilson like the vermin they were.

The two lawmen left the livery and Matt returned to his office while Festus went to investigate a complaint about the theft of a paint pony from the hitching rail of the Alamo.

Matt had just gotten started on his endless round of paperwork, from acknowledging the receipt of information on new additions to federal and state law to inquiries from lawmen regarding the whereabouts of wanted criminals.

Just as the clock on the wall joined its hands at noon, Kitty Russell stepped into the office, carrying a basket covered with a blue-and-white-checked cloth.

She walked to Matt's desk and laid the basket in front of him. "When did you last eat, Matt?" she asked.

The tall marshal grinned. "You know, now that I'm studying on it, I don't rightly remember."

"Then I'm taking care of that right now."

Kitty wore a pink gingham morning dress, her hair pulled back from her face, tied with a ribbon of the same color. She looked fresh and pretty and Matt's breath caught in his throat, as it always did when he saw her.

The woman removed the cover from the basket and looked inside. "Roast beef, sliced thin the way you like it, soda bread, butter, an apple pie and a bottle of pretty good claret. Sound all right to you?"

"Sounds wonderful, Kitty."

"Then dig in, Marshal."

After he'd finished eating, Matt sat back in his chair and sighed. "Kitty, those were right tasty vittles."

"I like a man with a good appetite, and you never disappoint me, Matt."

The marshal smiled. "Maybe it's because you're such a good cook."

Kitty laughed with genuine amusement. "You know me better than that. Except for the claret, I bought everything at Ma Smalley's restaurant. Cooking and me have never exactly been on speaking terms."

Matt raised his wineglass. "Then here's to Ma Smalley, for her wonderful roast beef and pie, and to Miss Kitty Russell, the provider of the feast."

Kitty gave a little curtsy and began to put the leftover food into the basket. She stopped, her face suddenly serious. "I heard what happened to Fanny Noble last night, Matt. I took it real hard."

"It's a bad business all right, Kitty. And the killer is still out there."

"She was a real nice girl. Fanny always talked about quitting the profession and marrying a rancher. She said she wanted to live in a house in the shade of a mesa with an oak tree outside her bedroom window. And chickens. She wanted chickens so she could collect brown eggs in the morning."

Kitty's eyes were bleak but she breathed deep and gathered strength. "Somebody took all that away from her."

Matt nodded. He didn't speak for long moments, then said what he had to say. "Kitty, I don't want you to be alone at night. Have Sam Noonan or one of your other bartenders walk you to your room, and don't venture outside after dark for any reason."

"I'll be careful, Matt," Kitty said. She reached into her purse, took out a .40 caliber derringer and looked directly into the marshal's eyes. "I've been carrying this ever since I heard about Fanny."

"It will do the job." Matt smiled. "Get close before you shoot and aim for the belly. That will shock a man into staying right where he's at."

"I was taught by one of the best, remember?" Kitty said as she dropped the tiny gun back into her purse.

"It was time well spent. Just don't forget all the things I told you back then. Take your time and you'll only need to pull the trigger once."

"Matt, do you think the Moonlight Ripper will strike again?" Kitty asked.

"Is that what they're calling him now, the Moonlight Ripper?"

"Heard it this morning at Ma Smalley's. People

were talking about Fanny's murder over breakfast, and they said it could only be the work of a madman." She gave a delicious little shudder. "The work of the Moonlight Ripper."

Matt shook his head. This was all he needed. A name like that was enough to start a panic, and since just about every grown man in town was suspect, some innocent people could get shot by mistake.

"Well, do you think he'll strike again?" Kitty asked, a frown gathering between her eyes.

"He will. I'm sure of it. That's why I don't want you to be alone."

Kitty gathered up the basket and hung it over her arm. "Trust me, Matt. I won't be alone. I'll always have my gun close. I don't plan on leaving anything to chance, not with the Moonlight Ripper on the loose."

The marshal groaned. Things in Dodge were rapidly going downhill . . . and he could see no end in sight—unless he could find enough evidence to arrest Barnabas Shaklee and keep the man locked up permanently.

The wind off the plains picked up by late afternoon, driving hot and dry, smelling only of dryness and dust. Down by the Santa Fe tracks, boxcars were being loaded with cattle and other herds were arriving at the stock pens. Either they'd been late getting started from Texas or had been held up on the trail by some misfortune. And there were plenty of possibilities to choose from: drought, flood, stampede, rustlers or Indians and sometimes a couple of them all at once.

Suddenly restless, the sighing wind calling out to him, Matt left the office and stepped onto the boardwalk. Part of the red, white and blue bunting draped over the false front of the Long Branch had torn loose and was flapping like a warship's pennant in a storm and nearby the batwing doors of John McCoy's beer garden rattled nervously together, their hinges screeching.

The wind picked up the dust along Front Street, lifting ragged yellow curtains high into the air before dropping them again with a faint hiss. A poster blown from the door of the Comique Theater bowled along the boardwalk and fluttered against Matt's legs. The marshal kicked it free, and it rose into the air like a wounded dove and flapped over the roof of the office.

After a freight wagon loaded with sawn timber trundled past, Matt glanced along the street to the boxing booth. He decided now would be a good time to pay a visit to Ben Hillman and learn how things stood between him and Mitch Haythorn.

He couldn't let the matter slide. Haythorn was a dangerous man and whenever possible best left alone.

The tent was flapping in the gusting wind as Matt stepped inside. Hillman was in the ring shadow boxing, and the big marshal was struck by how gracefully the man danced on his toes, his fists so lightning fast their movement was blurred.

Proctor, wearing a loud pearl gray suit, stood at ringside, smiling as he looked up at his fighter—and his left arm was around the waist of Stella Shaklee. The woman's back was turned to Matt, but he noticed that she was wearing a new dress of red silk, cut too tight and too low, but expensive by the look of it.

It seemed that Stella was prospering and had not grieved too long for her dead husband.

Proctor turned and saw Matt; his face broke into a grin. "Welcome, Marshal," the man said. He waved his free hand toward Hillman. "How does my boy look?"

"Pretty good," Matt admitted. "He's moving real smooth and fast."

"Damn right he is." Proctor beamed. He looked up at Hillman. "Ben, come down here."

Hillman nodded to Matt and climbed out of the ring. Proctor placed his palm on his fighter's naked chest and said: "Feel that, Marshal. My boy Ben's ticker is steady as a drum, and I'd say doing no more than forty beats to the minute."

"I'll take your word for it," Matt said.

"I'm feeling good, Marshal," Hillman said, grinning, "stronger than I've felt in months."

Matt was aware that Stella Shaklee was regarding him with raw, open hostility, something that Proctor, who could read sign like a bronco Apache, also noticed because he said quickly: "Stella, my dear, you run along back to the hotel. Wait for me there."

It seemed to Matt that Proctor had made Stella his kept woman, and no doubt Barnabas was getting his cut of the money.

Stella threw the tall marshal a sullen glance and moved to step away from Proctor. But she turned suddenly and kissed the man passionately, her mouth moving on his. At first Proctor seemed taken aback, but then he returned her kiss with equal passion, and when finally their lips parted, Proctor's face was flushed and he was breathing hard.

His voice tight, the man said: "Now please go back to the hotel, Stella." He smiled. "I won't be long."

As the woman walked to the tent exit, Proctor watched her go, his eyes on her swaying hips hot with desire. But they held something else— something vaguely disturbing that Matt caught for a fleeting moment but could not decipher.

He struggled with the meaning of that look for a while, then let it go. Given the nature of the Shaklee clan, Proctor's relationship with Stella could only be a complicated one, and right then he didn't care to delve into it too deeply.

Ben Hillman was of more immediate concern.

"Have you spoken to Mitch Haythorn?" he asked the fighter.

Hillman shook his head. "I reckon there's nothing more to be said until I have his twenty-five hundred dollars." The man's black eyes held a hint of humor. "I haven't called him out if that's what you mean."

Matt allowed himself a smile. "Don't ever do that, Ben. Haythorn is too good with a gun."

"Yet Ben tells me you shaded him at the Dodge House, Marshal," Proctor said.

The marshal nodded. "I said he was good. I didn't say he was better than me."

There was no brag in that statement, and both Proctor and Hillman recognized and accepted it as such. Among Western men, when talk turned to gunfighters, Matt Dillon's name was mentioned with the best. A named man had no need to boast and very few of them did.

"While I'm on the subject of Mitch Haythorn," Matt was talking to Proctor, "he told me that Stella Shaklee was one of his new girls."

"She was," Proctor said evenly.

"Then how did—"

"Money talks, Marshal," the man interrupted quickly. "And when money talks, Mitch listens."

Later, as Matt retraced his steps back to his office, he again tried to interpret what he'd seen in Proctor's eyes as he looked at Stella Shaklee. Had it been dislike? No, not that. Something else then?

Now Matt recalled that it had been a cool, calculating look, as though the man was sizing Stella up for something. A wife? That was hardly likely. Then what?

Matt shook his head. He was like a man trying to grab a handful of mist, and it was getting him nowhere. He'd just confused lust with something else and that was all there was to it.

Still, as he stepped into his office, he again recalled the strange look in Proctor's eyes, and its significance still nagged at him.

chapter 16

Shooting at Shadows

"So ol' Ben looks mighty good, huh, Matthew?" Festus asked.

"He seemed fine to me, moving real fast and easy," Matt answered.

"Could be Doc Adams is wrong about Ben's pump."

"Maybe, but I've never known Doc to be wrong before. He told me once that good judgment comes from experience and a lot of that comes from bad judgment. I'd say by now Doc's judgment is pretty good. If he says Ben's heart is bad, then I believe him."

Festus' left eyebrow crawled up his forehead. "Then are you goin' to stop the fight, Matthew, like you planned afore?"

"No. It's Ben's choice," Matt said. "I've worried the question like a dog with a bone, but I've decided I still won't intervene."

Festus looked relieved. "It's shaping up to be quite

a scrap. Ol' Bill Kennett is loaded for bear. He says that last time he was licked an' whipped afore he even had time to get good an' mad. Since he has to favor his ribs some, he says this time he'll be the one to end it real quick. Funny thing, even though Ben won last time, all the money in town is being bet on Kennett again."

"Some people never learn, I guess," Matt said.

Darkness was crowding into the office, and Matt thumbed a match into flame and lit the oil lamp above his desk. Immediately pale orange light washed out the shadows from the corners of the room and gleamed on the oil of the stacked rifles in the gun rack.

Festus drained his coffee cup and glanced at the clock. "It's gone ten, Matthew. I've got to be making my rounds across the tracks. Them lace-curtain womenfolk are gettin' mighty boogered over this Ripper business."

"I'll go with you, Festus," Matt said. "I don't want you out there alone at night."

"Matthew, I can handle Barnabas Shaklee," Festus said, a note of irritation in his voice.

Matt smiled. "I know you can, but you can't handle Shaklee, his four sons and Husky Wilson all at once."

"You think this could be the night they'll brace us?"

"Any night can be the night. Tonight, tomorrow night, the night after that. I only know it's coming. Why else would Shaklee keep a gun slick like Wilson around?"

Festus had listened intently to what Matt was saying and he'd accepted his logic, but he wasn't about to agree to being chaperoned.

Drawing his dignity around him like a ragged blanket, he said, spacing out each word: "Matthew, I've been in tight spots afore and I'm still here." He tapped the holstered Colt on his hip. "When put to it, I'm pretty good with this thing, and I don't need you a-holdin' my hand."

Matt opened his mouth to protest, but Festus charged right ahead. "An' besides, the Moonlight Ripper is still out there somewhere, an' the only way we can be in two places at once is to split up an' cover both ends of town."

Matt thought it through. Despite his scruffy hang-dog appearance, Festus had sand and there was not an inch of backup in him. And he was good with a gun, a sight better on the draw and shoot than most. Besides, Barnabas Shaklee might think it wise to lie low for a while after the murder of Fanny Noble.

The big marshal smiled. "All right, Festus, we'll play it your way. But be careful tonight."

Festus nodded, pleased. "Matthew, if'n ol' Barnabas opens the ball, I can take care o' myself. You know I wasn't on the brag when I talked about bein' a fair hand with the iron."

Matt nodded, smiling inwardly. "I know that, Festus. A high-talking man can quick brag himself into burying or buzzard bait. But there ain't much paw or beller to a feller who's sure of himself."

For the second time that night, Festus was pleased. "Damn right, Matthew," he said. "There sure ain't much paw or beller to me."

"That's the truth as ever was," Matt said, rising to

his feet. "Now we best be on our way. Judging by the racket outside, Dodge has found its snap tonight."

Matt's usual habit was to patrol Front and Texas streets and check on the rowdy saloons and dance halls. But, under a pale waxing moon, he left the boardwalk and melted into the darkness of the alleys and the mysterious gloom behind the buildings.

Keeping to the shadows, the marshal reached the northern edge of town, where a few scattered shacks gave way to grassland. Out on the plains, the coyotes were talking and heat lightning flashed to the west, now and then illuminating the hard, lean planes of Matt's face as though he was standing next to a magic lantern.

A predator in search of prey, he had switched from boots and spurs to a pair of soft Cheyenne moccasins. And now, as he retraced his steps toward the center of town, he moved through the night without sound, like a fleeting ghost.

The noise of a door slamming open at the rear of the Lone Star Saloon and Dance Hall froze Matt in place for an instant before he melted back into the shadow cast by a small storage building.

His eyes failed to penetrate the gloom, but there, away from the street, voices carried and he heard a girl giggle, followed by the harder laugh of a man.

"No, Clem, not here," the girl whispered, as silk rustled urgently. "Suppose somebody comes out and sees us?"

The man, his throat tight, said something Matt couldn't hear and the girl giggled again. The marshal calculated that the couple was standing against the rear wall of the saloon, toward the corner of the building, where it met the alley. Matt eased his Colt in the holster and waited. He knew the chances of the man being the Ripper were slim, but he could not walk away from it until he knew for certain.

The girl's voice was muffled as she tried to talk around the man's demanding mouth. "No, Clem Moore, like I told you before, let's get one of the rooms inside. It will only cost you but two dollars."

"Aw, Lorraine," the man protested, "we kin sure enough do it right here for free."

Silk rustled again. "No! If the boss caught me giving it away for free he'd take a dog whip to me. Now let's go inside and get a room." There was a moment's pause; then the woman asked: "Do you have two dollars?"

"I got two dollars, Lorraine, but hell, sweet thang, I thought you loved me fer sure."

"And so do a lot of other cowboys," the girl said. Her voice hardened. "Now are we going inside?"

Matt heard the puncher's low grumble; then a door opened, letting out a torrent of voices, chinking glasses and piano music, and slammed shut again. Suddenly the marshal was surrounded only by an echoing silence. He let his breath out slowly and settled his gun in the holster.

The scene he'd just witnessed, or rather heard, might well be repeated dozens of times around Dodge before sunup. And Matt decided that standing in the dark, eavesdropping on other people's conversations, didn't set right with him.

He was getting nowhere, no closer to the Ripper than he'd been when he started out earlier in the evening. The best thing to do was go back to the office, change into his boots and patrol the boardwalks. His tall, grim presence on the streets might deter the killer from striking again.

His mind made up, Matt walked past the corner of the Lone Star and into the shadowed alley. He emerged on Front Street and had just stepped onto the boardwalk when he heard a rattle of shots.

They were coming from across the tracks—and could only mean that Festus had stumbled into some big trouble.

Over at the Long Branch, a drunk cowboy had just climbed into the saddle of a small mouse-colored mustang. The man swayed a little, then tilted back his head and let out a high-pitched wolf howl.

Matt sprinted across the street, grabbed the startled puncher by the front of his shirt and dragged him out of the saddle. The man hit the ground with a thud as Matt stepped into the leather and swung the pony away from the hitching rail.

"Hey," the cowboy yelled, "that's my hoss!"

Matt didn't answer. He was already galloping down the street toward the tracks, the little pony's pounding hooves trailing long streamers of dust.

Ahead of him, Matt heard more shots, the flat hammer of rifles and the sharper, angrier bark of a six-gun.

Its neck stretched out, the bit in its teeth, the mustang jumped the tracks. Apart from a few rectangles of light showing in the windows of surrounding homes, the marshal found himself hurtling pell-mell into a wall of darkness.

There! Off to his left a rifle flared, flared again, the

roar of the two shots shattering the night into pieces, the echoes falling around Matt like broken glass. He battled the mustang and swung him toward the rifles, his Colt in his hand. As he flew past the sprawling home of Bodkin the banker, he remembered that behind the coach house lay several acres of sandy open ground covered in bunchgrass and thick stands of prickly pear. The shots had come from there.

Matt had already reached the edge of the open area when a shadow loomed up in front of him and a rifle muzzle blossomed orange fire. The marshal felt the mustang jerk from the impact of the bullet; then the little horse went down, throwing Matt over its head.

He slammed into the ground hard, rolled and saw the shadow coming toward him fast. Matt fired, fired again, heard a shriek, then the sound of a man's body hitting the dirt.

From farther out in the darkness, a voice yelled: ''Micajah, are you hit bad?''

Matt didn't hesitate. He fired in the direction of the voice, dusted fast shots to the left and right and was rewarded by a startled yelp.

''Matthew, is that you?''

Matt's eyes peered into the gloom. ''Where are you, Festus?'' he whispered.

''Don't rightly know, Matthew.''

Festus' voice was close, no more than a few yards away, but he was invisible in the darkness.

''Are you wounded?'' Matt asked.

A rifle slammed and stinging gravel kicked into the marshal's face. He got up on one knee, thumbed off a shot at where he had seen the muzzle flare, then dropped to the ground again and rolled. Suddenly he slammed against something hard, a bent knee, and he felt the man, unbalanced, fall away from him.

"Festus?" Matt whispered urgently.

"It's me, Matthew. Don't shoot."

The marshal heard boots scramble as Festus regained his kneeling position. Matt was close enough to see his deputy's face as a blur in the gloom.

"Are you hit?" he asked.

"Bullet burned across my shoulder," Festus whispered. "But it don't seem too bad." He hesitated a moment and said, "Them ol' boys bushwhacked me real good, Matthew. I heard a noise back here and came to take a look-see an' they cut loose on me."

"It's the Shaklees," Matt whispered, "and maybe Husky Wilson. Did you get any of them?"

"Nary a one, Matthew. I've been too busy keepin' my head down."

"Well, I think Micajah is dead for sure," the marshal said. "And I may have winged another one."

A rifle roared from the darkness and a bullet split the air above Matt's head. "They've got the range on us, Festus," he whispered. "We have to move away from here."

Crouching low, Matt angled to his right, making no sound in his moccasins. He covered about a hundred yards, then dropped to a knee. Festus crouched beside him and Matt was grateful that his deputy was not wearing spurs, his mule having no liking for them.

A rifle flared and a shot probed the night. Then, off to the marshal's right, another gun fired. He waited. Before revealing his position, Matt wanted to be sure of his target.

A door slammed open and the outraged voice of banker Bodkin called into the night: "What the devil is going on out there?" A flurry of shots thudded into the man's house and the door hastily slammed shut.

Matt felt Festus' breath close to his ear. "I reckon ol' Bodkin jes' learned that the business end of a Winchester don't pay no interest."

"I'd say he did," the marshal whispered, smiling.

Matt's eyes searched the darkness as a narrow belt of misty cloud cleared the moon and thin silver light touched the open ground around them. Nothing stirred and there was no sound.

"Reckon they've left?" Festus whispered.

Matt shook his head. "They're still out there. I can feel them."

From far off, a saloon piano dropped a tangle of notes into the night and Matt knew that people would already be gathering in Front Street, puzzled by the shooting. He fervently hoped that some rooster full of bottled courage wouldn't decide to investigate closer and stumble into Shaklee lead.

A shadow detached itself from the wall of darkness and slowly moved closer, and for a brief moment, Matt caught the gleam of the moonlight on the barrel of a rifle.

"Matthew," Festus whispered urgently.

"I see him," Matt said. "Let him come."

The marshal held his Colt up and ready. As the shadow drew nearer, it gradually took on solid form, that of a man wearing a long duster and a wide-brimmed hat.

"Micajah," the man whispered. "Are you there?"

Matt held his fire.

The man spoke again. "Micajah, did you get that damned deppity?"

Another form emerged from the night, like the first, wearing a duster. "Micajah is dead, Aaron," this man said. "I think maybe he got Haggen, though."

"Joshua, that damned marshal is around here somewhere," Aaron whispered. "I'm sure I seen Micajah shoot him off'n his horse before Dillon got lead into him."

"Maybe Dillon is dead as well," Joshua said. "Maybe he broke his damn neck."

"That'll be the day," Matt said, rising to his feet. "You two, drop those rifles."

It was pitch-dark, but the distance between the Shaklee brothers and the lawmen was less than twelve feet, close enough to see—and close enough that the Shaklees decided to make a play.

As the Winchester muzzles came up fast, Matt fired at Aaron. Beside him Festus' gun roared. Aaron stumbled back, hit hard, but he was working his rifle. Matt felt a sledgehammer blow low in his belly, and an instant later another slammed into his left thigh. The big marshal staggered, but steadied himself and again fired at Aaron. The man's rifle spun away from him, and he rose up on his toes and pitched forward on his face.

Joshua Shaklee lay on his back, his face turned up to the moon. Beside Matt, Festus' Colt was in his hand, curling blue smoke.

"No!" From out of the darkness, a man ran at the two lawmen. They both fired at the same time and the man went down, shrieking high in his throat.

The rolling echoes of the guns lost themselves along the cottonwoods lining the Arkansas and soon faded into silence. Apart from the groans of a dying man, the night was still. An acrid pall of gray gunsmoke drifted in the air as Festus turned to Matt and asked: "Matthew, are you hit?"

"I'm hit bad, Festus, gut shot."

Matt's left hand dropped to his belly, searching for blood. There was none. Then his fingertips touched the heavy steel buckle of his gun belt. It had been mangled by a bullet. He glanced down at his thigh. His pants were torn where the bullet had grazed him, drawing blood, but it was a superficial wound.

Relieved, Matt understood what had happened. Aaron Shaklee's bullet had hit the gun belt buckle, then ranged downward and burned his thigh. He'd been lucky, very lucky, and he knew it.

"I best go get Doc Adams," Festus said, his voice shaking, the dire plight of a gut-shot man weighing heavy on him.

"No need." Matt grinned. He showed Festus the bent buckle. "Quint Asper forged this for me out of a chunk of iron that fell from the sky, and he made it strong to last. I reckon I owe that blacksmith my life."

In the darkness, Matt saw Festus shake his head. "Matthew," he said, "please don't ever scare me like that again."

"Scared my ownself pretty good," the marshal commented wryly.

Out in the darkness the man who had charged Matt and Festus and had taken two of the lawmen's bullets groaned. The marshal thumbed fresh shells into his Colt, then stepped into the gloom. After a few moments, he made out the shape of a man lying on the ground, his back arched across a clump of coarse bunchgrass.

The man's eyes lifted to Matt and he whispered: "Don't shoot me no more, mister. I'm done."

Matt warily looked over the man's recumbent form. "Where's your gun?" he asked.

"Don't have no gun, Marshal. I was trying to stop it . . . stop the killing."

"Who are you, boy?"

"Simeon Shaklee. I was the youngest of the brothers. Or at least I was until you kilt me."

"Where's your pa?"

Shaklee shook his head, a movement that caused him pain because he gasped and talked through clenched teeth. "Pa ain't here. He told the others to shoot the deputy and bring him back his head." The man tried to rise to a sitting position, but failed and let himself sink to the ground again. "Marshal," he said, "I was trying to end it. You had no call to kill me."

"A man who runs out of the dark into the middle of a gunfight—he takes his chances," Matt said, no give in him. "Deputy Haggen and me, we couldn't take the time to see if you were armed or not."

"I'm twenty-one years old and I'm dying for nothing," Shaklee said, blood scarlet on his lips and chin.

"Boy, you're dying on account of your no-good pa," Festus said, "an' that's the misery of it." He took a knee beside the young man. "Now your time is short. Best you lay quiet an' make your peace with your Maker."

But Simeon Shaklee did not hear. He was dead.

Matt gave the man a final, pitying glance, then holstered his gun and said: "Festus, let's go talk to Barnabas Shaklee."

The deputy nodded, his suddenly determined eyes telling Matt that he knew the night's killing was not yet done.

chapter 17

A Railroader Brings Bad News

The two lawmen walked along the bank of the Arkansas, moonlight touching the rippling water with silver. A restless wind rustled in the leaves of the cottonwoods, and once they saw the dim shape of a deer on the opposite bank, watching them warily until they passed.

After thirty minutes of stumbling along in the dark, Matt made out the iron bulk of the trellis bridge in the wan moonlight. He drew his Colt and Festus did the same. "Get ready," the marshal whispered. "This could be almighty sudden."

Silent in his moccasins, Matt crouched low and walked toward the bridge, Festus just behind him and to his left.

Coyotes were yammering in the darkness as Matt reached a huge old lightning-struck cottonwood and there he stopped, Festus stepping beside him. The marshal's eyes searched the gloom. The dying campfire cast a pale red glow on the sandy walls of the dry wash and the underside of the bridge. But there was no sound and the only thing that moved was the feeble flicker of the campfire flame.

Matt motioned Festus to follow, and he left the cover of the cottonwood, moving closer, tense and alert for any sign of trouble. He was thirty yards from the bridge, then twenty, close enough to see that the Shaklee wagon was gone.

Beside him, Festus rubbed dry lips with the back of his gun hand, the blue barrel of his Colt catching a brief glint of moonlight. "Matthew, there ain't nobody here," he whispered.

Matt nodded. "Seems like." Then, low and urgent: "Step careful, Festus. Barnabas Shaklee is a bushwhacker and he could be hidden along the wash somewhere."

The wash ran almost at a right angle to the Arkansas and the Santa Fe tracks curved well away from the river to cross the trellis bridge. Matt and Festus walked between the rails for the remaining few yards, then scrambled down into the wash.

Every nerve in his body clamoring, Matt scanned the darkness around him, his gun up and ready. He felt Festus shove his back against his own as the deputy covered the opposite direction. Only within the dancing crimson circle of the campfire was there light, and beyond that, a wall of blackness. The smell of dust hung in the air, stronger than the musky odor of the wood smoke.

Something scurried on the bank, dislodging a few small rocks that rolled into the wash, and for an instant, Matt felt a spike of alarm, crouching as his gun swung toward the sound.

He straightened as he realized that all he'd heard was a small animal, maybe a packrat returning to its nest among the prickly pear. A wry smile touched Matt's lips. He was getting way too jumpy in his old age.

At that moment a shadowy figure emerged from the darkness under the bridge and a woman's voice said: "They've all gone, Marshal."

Stella Shaklee came closer and Matt saw that she was wearing a dark velvet cloak over her dress. "Stop right there and show me your hands," he said.

The woman smiled. "You don't trust me?"

"No," Matt answered. "Now show me your hands. I've never shot a woman before but there's always a first time."

Stella did as she was told, holding her hands out in front of her, the fingers spread. "Satisfied?" she asked.

"Where is Barnabas?" the marshal asked.

"Gone," Stella replied. "He's with that tinhorn Husky Wilson. Barnabas told the boys to bushwhack you and the deputy and then to meet him at the Alamo when the killing was done."

"And the women?"

"They pulled out half an hour ago, when they heard the shooting start. They decided they want no part of Barnabas or his sons anymore. I warned the boys that killing a United States marshal would end badly because the law wouldn't rest until they were caught and hanged." Stella shrugged. "They wouldn't listen, but the women did. Barnabas told his sons that after you and your deputy were dead, they'd rob one of the fat Dodge banks and head for the Territory."

Stella stepped into the dull red circle of the firelight. "I tried to stop them, but they wouldn't listen. Only Simeon said he wanted no part of it. Then Barnabas got angry and said I'd turned his boys against him. Then he gave me this." The woman turned her head and showed a livid welt on her cheek. "The blow stunned me, and when I came to, Barnabas and Wilson were gone and the women were packing up the wagon to leave."

"Why did you stay, Miz Stella?" Festus asked.

"Because of G. P. He's my man now and I need to be with him. I only came here because I wanted to pick up a few things. I'd rented a horse but the other women took it and left me afoot." Stella shook her head, her eyes deep in shadow. "I guess I can't blame them none. They can sell the nag somewhere along the trail and buy grub."

"You reckon Barnabas will be at the Alamo?" Matt asked.

"I wouldn't count on it. He must know by this time that the boys will not show, not tonight or any other night." Her eyes sought Matt's in the gloom. "I take it that they're all dead?"

The marshal nodded. "Yes, all of them."

"Even Simeon?"

"He ran at us out of the dark," Matt said. "He should have known better."

"Simeon wasn't right in the head," Stella said, her face like stone. "He was what you call simple."

"Too bad," Matt said. "But even a simple-minded

man should have known." He holstered his Colt. "You better come with us, Stella."

"Am I under arrest?"

"No," Matt said. "But I wouldn't want you stumbling around in the dark. You might lose your way."

The woman shook her head. "I can find my own way, Marshal. I want nothing to do with you or your deputy, either."

Matt shrugged. "Suit yourself, Stella. But you step real careful."

The marshal stared into the surrounding darkness, sensing its mystery and its danger. He shivered, though the night was warm.

There was no sign of Barnabas Shaklee in the crowded Alamo, nor in any of the other saloons. Matt asked around but no one remembered seeing him either.

Disappointment tugging at him, the marshal left Festus to contact Percy Crump while he returned to the office.

Now all of the man's sons were dead, Matt had no doubt Shaklee would seek his revenge. It wasn't his style to meet his enemies in the open, gun to gun. He'd bide his time and get even using a bullet from the darkness.

The man had been dangerous before. Now he was even more so. He would be angry, his madness taking a firmer hold on him, and he might kill again, venting his rage and perverted frustration on another innocent woman.

Matt glanced at the clock. It was almost one, but

there would be little sleep for him or Festus tonight and maybe for many nights to come.

The marshal feared that out there in the shadows, Barnabas Shaklee, the man the town was calling the Moonlight Ripper, could already be stalking a new victim.

At seven thirty-four that morning, as indicated by the clock on the wall, a railroad worker, his face gray, burst through the door of Matt's office. The man stood swaying in the middle of the floor, and words tumbled out of his mouth, coming so fast they tripped over one another. "Marshal, checking the trellis bridge . . . me . . . woman . . . naked . . . blood everywhere . . . coyotes at her maybe . . . come . . . come!"

As the agitated railroader hopped from one foot to the other, Matt set aside his coffee cup, got up from his desk and stepped beside the man. "Take it easy, feller. Now, slowly, what's your name?"

The man gulped and managed: "Tom Woodruff, Marshal. I've worked for the Santa Fe, man and boy, this past eleven year."

Matt nodded, and despite the spiking clamor in his belly, he managed to keep his voice level. "And what did you see at the bridge, Tom?"

The man stood in silence for a few moments, obviously trying to collect himself. Finally he lifted haunted eyes to the tall lawman and, working hard to steady each word, said: "I was checking the trellis bridge over the dry wash at . . . at . . ."

"I know where it is," Matt said. "Go on."

"Well, I went down into the wash to make sure that no bolts had popped from the underside of the bridge anywhere." The railroader shook his head. "They will come loose like that, Marshal. It's the vibrations from the passing trains that does it, you understand."

Reining in his impatience, Matt nodded. "Then what happened?"

"Then I seen this woman lying under the bridge, near the wall of the wash." Woodruff shuddered, then made a visible effort to come to terms with what he'd witnessed. "When I got closer, I saw that she was dead, but her eyes were wide open, scared like. I reckoned she was naked, Marshal, but she was so covered in blood, it was hard to tell. I think the coyotes must have been at her, the way she was torn up an' all."

"Did you see anyone else?"

Woodruff shook his head. "Nary a soul, but it looked like folks had made camp under the bridge until recently. There was a fire and the ashes were still warm."

The man's eyes looked wounded. "Marshal, once out Newton way, I seen a hobo who'd been hit by an eastbound freight. I swear, he wasn't tore up near as bad as that poor woman is."

The railroader had just given words to a thought in Matt's mind: that maybe some woman had wandered onto the tracks and been hit by a cattle train. He put a hand on Woodruff's shoulder. "Tom, will you do something for me?"

"Anything, Marshal, just name it."

"Go get Doc Adams. If he isn't up yet, wake him.

Tell him to hitch up his surrey and meet me at the bridge. Will you do that?"

"Sure thing, Marshal," Woodruff said, pleased to be helping the law.

After the railroader left, Matt roused Festus, who'd been grabbing some shut-eye in one of the cells.

Less than fifteen minutes later, under a broken sky tinged red by the rising sun, the two lawmen were mounted and heading for the trellis bridge.

chapter 18

A Terrible Shock
for Proctor

"Hard to tell, Matthew," Festus said, suddenly looking ill, "but it's definitely Stella Shaklee."

"It's her all right," Matt said. He looked down at the dead woman's badly disfigured face. It looked like someone had taken a knife and tried to cut a grin on her mouth.

In an insane frenzy, her killer had also slashed again and again at her naked body, ripping her skin to shreds. A look of horror was frozen on Stella's face, yet under the open, terrified eyes, she was wearing that hideous grin, the corners of her mouth cut all the way to her eyes.

Festus glanced at the sky, where the early-morning sun was burning off the clouds. Then he shook his head. "It's the work of the Moonlight Ripper again, Matthew. That's for darn sure."

A small anger flared in Matt. "Festus, there's no Moonlight Ripper. There's only a madman by the name of Barnabas Shaklee."

Festus was taken aback by the edge in the marshal's voice. "Sorry, Matthew, but Barnabas or no, that's what folks are calling him."

"And it's always the man who knows the least who repeats it the most," Matt snapped. He saw the injured look in Festus' eyes and said quickly. "Sorry, Festus. I shouldn't have said that. I'm on edge, I guess."

The deputy smiled. "No offense taken, Matthew. Sometimes a man talks 'cause he's got somethin' to say. Other times he'll talk 'cause he's got to say somethin'." He looked down at Stella's bloodstained body. "And I had to say somethin', was all."

And so had Doc Adams.

Even before he set the brake on his surrey, he yelled: "Matt, why in tarnation did you send some lunatic wearing a railroader's hat to pound on my door and wake me up before dawn?"

"Sorry, Doc," Matt said. He jerked a thumb over his shoulder. "We have another murdered woman. Over there."

Doc brushed past Festus and got down on a knee beside Stella Shaklee's body. After a few moments, he rose to his feet, his face grim. "She's been dead for five, six hours, maybe a little longer. And this is the work of the same killer, no doubt about that. She was cut up so badly that she bled to death." Doc's bleak eyes met Matt's. "And she was a long time a-dying."

The physician walked around under the bridge, his eyes on the soft sand at his feet. When he returned, he nodded toward the body. "She knew her killer. Knew him well."

"Why do you say that?" Matt asked.

"Because all this Moonlight Ripper talk has women spooked, and she would have run from him. Look at her dress lying over there. It's been carefully unbuttoned and her undergarments just as carefully laid on top. A killer as savage as this one would have ripped off her clothes. No, she knew the man and willingly got naked for him." Doc sighed deep in his chest. "Then he tore her to pieces."

Matt thought for a few moments, then asked: "Doc, could there have been more than one killer?"

"I don't have any way of telling. But it is possible, I guess."

"Matt, are you thinking Barnabas and Husky Wilson?" Festus asked.

"She knew them both. I doubt she'd have run from them."

"But she said G. P. Proctor was her new man. Why would she get herself all nekkid for ol' Barnabas and a lowlife like Wilson?"

"For money, maybe," Matt answered. "Remember, before she took up with Proctor, Stella was one of Mitch Haythorn's doves. She might have been finding it hard to put all that behind her." The marshal thought things through again, then said: "And there's always the chance she could have been forced to undress at gunpoint. She may have snubbed Barnabas, and he drew a gun on her."

"Either way," said Doc, who had been listening intently, "the main thing is she didn't try to run away. She was wearing buttoned boots with high heels, and as near as I can tell, all her prints are right here around the bridge." He looked up and down the dusty wash. "What was she doing in this godfor-saken place, anyway?"

Using as few words as possible, Matt told Doc about Barnabas Shaklee and how he suspected the man had murdered two women, a cowboy and a corset drummer. He then described the events of the previous evening, the deaths of Shaklee's sons and how Stella had refused to accompany him and Festus back to town.

"Then you think that shortly after you left Shaklee returned and murdered the woman?" Doc asked after Matt had finished talking.

"Seems that way," Matt answered. "He might even have been listening out there in the dark, waiting for us to leave."

Doc rubbed the back of his neck, thinking. Finally he turned to Festus and said: "There's an oilskin slicker in the back of the surrey, Festus. Go get it and we'll wrap the woman in it. I'll take her to that vulture Percy Crump." The physician shook his head. "I shouldn't say that, I guess. Percy will treat her with more care and respect than she ever got from a man in her entire life."

Matt and Festus put up their mounts at the livery and walked along the boardwalk in the direction of the marshal's office. But Matt stopped in midstride when he caught sight of the boxing booth.

"Festus, you go on ahead," he said. "I'll head for the Dodge House and give the news to Proctor before he hears it from someone else."

"Think he'll be real broke up about it, Matthew?"

The marshal shrugged. "I don't know. He seemed

to cotton to Stella, but it might just have been a business arrangement. Either way, I should be the one to tell him."

Dust kicked up from Matt's boots as he crossed Front Street and headed for the hotel. He was almost there when a mule skinner driving a freight wagon loaded with green lumber and nail kegs hailed him.

Matt knew the man slightly, a skinny, bearded oldtimer named Lenny Cassidy, who had once scouted for the Army in the Arizona Territory. "Got somethin' to tell you, Marshal," Cassidy said. "Well, it mought be nothin', or it mought be somethin'."

"Let's hear it, Lenny," Matt said. "I've never known you to be a loose-talking man."

Cassidy nodded and took a stained clay pipe from between his teeth. "Day afore yesstidy, I seen Indian sign north of the big bend of the Cimarron, maybe twenty bucks movin' north, no women with them that I could tell."

"A hunting party?" Matt suggested.

"That would be the nothin' notion, Marshal," the old man said. "The somethin' notion is that them braves were painted for war and plannin' mischief." His teeth made a clicking sound as he put the pipe back in his mouth. "I just thought you should know. Plenty of settlers out that way."

Matt's thanks were lost as Cassidy waved, yelled, "Hi-yah!" and slapped the mules into motion with the reins. The wagon lurched forward and the marshal watched it leave, deep in troubled thought.

The last thing he needed right now was a band of hostiles playing hob on the plains. They had crossed the Cimarron keeping well to the west of Fort Dodge, where there were a couple companies of infantry, and that suggested a war party. The Indians were probably either Blackfoot or Cheyenne, not that it mattered any. One was just as much bad news as the other.

For the moment at least, Matt pushed the Indians to the back of his mind. He would deal with the problem when the time came. Right now there was a crazed killer loose in Dodge and that must take priority.

When Matt reached the hotel, Proctor was standing just outside the front door, smoking his morning cigar. Gone was the loud gray suit he'd been wearing earlier, replaced by businesslike black broadcloth. Now that the prizefight was only a few days away, it seemed that the man was putting up a respectable front, the better to fleece the sheep who were putting their money on Bill Kennett.

"Mornin', Marshal." Proctor grinned. "And a fine morning it is." His expression changed. "Well, it would be fine except that Stella didn't come home last night. I think she must have met up with a feller."

"It's Stella I've come to talk to you about, Proctor," Matt said.

The man's gaze searched the marshal's face. "All I can see in your eyes is bad news," he said. "What happened?"

"There's no easy way to say this, so I'll give it to you straight," Matt said. He was interested to gauge the man's reaction and his depth of feeling for the woman as he added: "Stella is dead. Murdered."

Proctor looked like he'd been slapped. "But when? I mean, how?"

"Last night," Matt said. The man seemed genuinely shocked. "It was the same killer who murdered Fanny Noble and a couple of others." The marshal hesitated a heartbeat and then added: "I don't think I have to paint you a picture."

Proctor took the cigar from his mouth with a trembling hand. "The Moonlight Ripper," he whispered. He shook his head in disbelief. "Poor Stella. Just yesterday we were making plans for the future. We were going to cut Ben loose, then head east, maybe to Boston town, and set up in the whoring business. We planned to start our own brothel, a high-class place all brass rails and red velvet, with Thomas Cole paintings on the wall and the best bonded whiskey and the most beautiful doves in town."

"A praiseworthy ambition," Matt said dryly.

The irony was lost on Proctor. He lifted pained eyes to the tall lawman's face. "Marshal," he said, "you have to find this madman. No matter what it takes, find him and hang him."

Matt let that go and asked: "Proctor, did you love her?"

The man seemed surprised. "Stella? No, Marshal, she was a dove. A man doesn't fall in love with a dove." He thought a moment, then added: "We were partners. She gave me what I wanted and I did the same for her. We used each other for our own desires and made no pretense that our relationship went any deeper than that."

"Would you have gone to Boston with her?"

"Yes, I would. We would really have gotten rich, Stella and me. After that, who knows. We'd probably have gone our separate ways." Proctor looked gray and suddenly older than his years. "Find this Moonlight Ripper, Marshal. And if you need any help, any help at all, you only have to ask."

"I'll bear that in mind," Matt said.

The man's shock was apparent and the marshal was impressed by Proctor's honesty. Matt's thoughts went to Arrah Hillman and Mitch Haythorn, who shared a very similar relationship. The only difference was that Arrah was madly in love with Haythorn and would never voluntarily leave him.

As the day of her brother's fight grew near, Arrah's love for Haythorn could complicate matters . . . especially since the man had the unpleasant habit of untangling his life with a gun.

chapter 19

Troubled Times

The first frightened settlers arrived in Dodge late that afternoon.

A wagon with a husband, wife and three children rolled into town just after three, with wild tales of hundreds of hostiles rampaging across the plains. This story was borne out by later arrivals, who swore to all who would listen that they had barely escaped with their hair.

As Matt expected it would, the stories occasioned a visit from Mayor Kelley, who seemed even more agitated than usual. Kelley seemed to have so much to say he looked like he was about to burst out of his frockcoat, but he started off in a subdued tone.

"Matt, the cowboy who owned the pony that was shot from under you is holding the whole damn town to ransom."

"In what way?" the marshal asked, a slight smile touching his lips, aware of Kelley's flair for exaggeration.

"He says he paid fifty dollars for the nag, and I know and you know it was worth no more than ten."

"So what are you going to do, Mayor?"

"Pay him, of course. He swears he'll get a lawyer if I don't. He's even talking about charging you and Dodge City with horse thievery and the reckless endangerment of personal property." Kelley looked like he wanted to spit. "That's the troubles with punchers. They spend too much damn time in the bunkhouse reading law books."

The clock on the wall ticked slow seconds into the room as Kelley drummed his fingers on Matt's desk. Finally he got to the point.

"I've been talking to the settlers, Matt, and this Indian scare is a bad business. I'm told there are hundreds of bloodthirsty savages roaming the plains, scalping people with tomahawks." The cigar in his mouth cold and forgotten, Kelley wailed: "Jesus, Mary and Joseph preserve us, we could all be murdered in our beds."

"No one has been scalped yet, Mayor," Matt pointed out. "And I believe there's only twenty Indians involved. We don't even know if they're hostile. It could be a hunting party roaming way off their home range. Game is scarce since the buffalo are all gone."

"Did you contact the Army, Matt?"

The marshal nodded. "I sent a telegram to Fort Dodge an hour ago. I haven't had an answer yet."

The mayor sat back in his chair, his face bleak. "Matt, I'd feel a lot better about this if you'd take a ride out and see for yourself what those redskins are up to." He put the edge of his right hand on the desk and waved it back and forth. "Look at me, like poor Mrs. Kelley since she heard about Indians on the warpath, I'm all atremble."

"Mayor, I've got my hands full in Dodge with this"—Matt almost choked on the words—"Moonlight Ripper business. I don't want to leave town for any length of time."

"I understand, Matt. I heard about that Stella Shaklee woman—a terrible thing, just terrible." The mayor squirmed in his chair as though what he was about to say was making him uncomfortable. "So far four murders have happened in and around Dodge. Now there's talk of forming a vigilante committee to patrol the streets to make sure there's not a fifth."

"Who's making the talk?" Matt asked, suddenly irritated.

Kelley shrugged and spread his hands. "Plenty of people, Matt, and not just cowboys. Some of the most respectable citizens in town are talking about it."

"Give me names, Mayor," Matt said, his irritation growing into anger.

The mayor's mind scouted ahead and he didn't like where this conversation was headed, but he said gamely: "Matt, I'm just suggesting you need help, especially now with this Indian uprising."

"Who is talking about vigilantes, Mayor?" Matt insisted.

Kelley sighed. "Banker Bodkin for one. Moss Grimmick, Wilbur Jonas, Newly O'Brien, Howie Uzell and the telegraph agent . . . what's his name?"

"Barney Danches," Matt supplied.

"Yes, him, and quite a few others. Even G. P. Proctor wants in, and he's got no real stake in this town.

Add to that the cowboys and ranchers and you could have fifty, sixty, a hundred armed men patrolling Dodge at night. Matt, why not leave it to the vigilantes while you check on those hostiles? We'll soon catch this Moonlight Ripper maniac."

Matt shook his head. "I won't have it, Mayor. You let loose a bunch of likkered-up cowboys in Dodge, shooting at shadows, and you'll have dead men, and maybe a few women, lying in the streets."

Matt leaned forward in his chair, his face grim and unsmiling. "Mayor Kelley, I've seen what vigilantes can do to a town. Vigilantism takes on a life of its own, and it's not a pleasant thing to see. At first old scores are settled. Then anyone who dresses a little different or talks with a foreign accent or doesn't have white skin becomes a suspect. Innocent men are hanged without a proper trial, railroaded to the gallows. Then the vigilantes pass the jug as they watch him kick and slap each other on the back and tell themselves what a great job they're doing."

The marshal shook his head. "No, Mayor, no vigilantes. Not in my town."

If Kelley was intimidated, he didn't let it show. He was an Irishman and tough as they come, and there was no room for stepping back in him. His face stiff and unsmiling, he rose to his feet.

"Marshal Dillon," he said, "I warn you—if there's one more murder in this town, you won't have any say in the matter. There will be vigilantes whether you want them here or not."

Matt's anger bubbled to the surface. "Mayor, so help me, I'll arrest any man who joins a vigilante committee."

Kelley's smile was bitter. "Then you'd better build a bigger jail, Matt. A whole heap bigger."

Night fell on Dodge and there was still no reply from the Army regarding the Indians.

Matt and Festus patrolled every nook and cranny of Dodge, from the Arkansas north to the town limits, but the lawmen saw no sign of Barnabas Shaklee or Husky Wilson.

The saloons were roaring as they always were during the cattle season, but Matt felt a tension in the air. He saw it in the eyes of men who regarded him with cool calculation, wondering if he had found a clue to the identity of the Ripper, and he heard it in the nervous laughter of the saloon girls.

Even Kitty was affected.

She confined her girls to entertaining only men they knew and none of them were allowed to leave the Long Branch after dark without an armed male escort.

"This Moonlight Ripper thing is getting on the town's nerves," Kitty told Matt as he made a stop at the saloon. "Any stranger who comes in for a drink is looked at with suspicion, if not downright hostility."

"The devil is loose in Dodge—that's for certain," Matt said grudgingly, unwilling to accept that control of the town seemed to be slipping away from him.

More to reassure Kitty than an honest statement of how he felt, he smiled and said: "Don't you worry none, Kitty. I'll find this killer soon."

The woman's beautiful face was troubled. "Matt, there's talk of vigilantes."

"I know. I heard about it."

"Maybe that's the best way to go, Matt. Quint Asper, Newly O'Brien and the rest of them—they're good, steady men."

The marshal shook his head. "I know they are, but I'll tell you what I told the mayor, Kitty—not in my town."

Kitty frowned. "You're being stubborn again."

"Not stubborn, realistic. Where there are vigilantes, there's big trouble."

The woman's laugh was without humor. "Matt, like we don't have big trouble already?"

But out in the street, Matt Dillon's troubles were about to get worse . . . much worse.

chapter 20

The Ripper's
Grim Warning

Of all people, the carrier of bad news was Mitch Haythorn. The gambler walked into the Long Branch with Arrah Hillman on his arm and a grin on his handsome face.

"Marshal," he said, stepping beside Matt, "they told me I'd find you here."

Matt made no attempt to conceal his dislike of the man. "What do you want, Haythorn?" he asked.

The gambler shrugged. "Me, I want nothing. But I think you should go back to your office. There's something you might want to see."

"Spill it, Haythorn," Matt said. "What did you come to tell me?"

"There's a note pinned to your door." Haythorn's smile grew wider. "Even as we speak, I'd hazard a guess that your deputy is still looking at it, scratching his head."

"Festus can't read."

"Obviously."

"What does the note say?"

Haythorn looked around him. "I'd rather not tell you here. In fact, you'd better read it for yourself."

Matt touched his hat to Kitty, who gave him an elegant little curtsy in return, and stepped out of the saloon. Across the street at the marshal's office, a small crowd had already gathered and Matt heard a subdued buzz of excited conversation.

When he stepped up on the boardwalk and elbowed his way through the clustered onlookers, Festus pointed out the note, pinned to the door by a large bowie knife.

"Mitch Haythorn tole me what the words say, Matthew," he said carefully. "But I reckon you'd better read 'em for your ownself."

The note was large, written on the back of a poster from the Comique Theater, and the words were scrawled in crude block letters. Matt read . . . and felt an icy chill deep in his belly.

> BIG BOSS, I AM DOWN ON DOVES AND WON'T STOP RIPPING THEM UNTIL I AM BUCKLED. THE ONE UNDER THE BRIDGE SQUEALED BUT TONIGHT'S WORK HAD TO BE QUIET. LOOK FOR HER IN THE SHACK BEHIND THE FEED STORE. I REMAIN YOUR JOLLY, HAPPY-GO-LUCKY FRIEND,
>   THE MOONLIGHT RIPPER

Matt looked around him at the circle of stunned faces, their unblinking gazes fixed on him, like painted eyes on wooden dolls.

"Hey, Marshal," a man yelled, anger edging his voice, "is this somebody's idea of a joke?"

But Matt didn't answer. He was already walking fast in the direction of Moss Grimmick's feed and tack store.

A narrow alley, about as wide as a broad-shouldered man, separated the store from the land office next door. Beyond Grimmick's, in the other direction, were a tightly packed row of other stores and then the Spencer and Drew Saloon.

Matt decided to take the alley, the shortest route to the scattered shacks and pole corral behind the feed store. Stepping carefully he walked into the alley and emerged at the corral, gun in hand. Moonlight splashed bright on the level ground, but formed deep and mysterious shadows around the shacks and other outbuildings.

The nearest shack to Matt, a flimsy wooden structure with a tar-paper roof, lay thirty feet ahead of him. He walked closer and stopped. The tiny cabin was in darkness, tattered lace curtains hanging lopsided in its single flyblown window. Was this the place?

Walking warily, the marshal sought the door. Then stopped in his tracks. The shadowy silhouette of a tall man was lurching toward him through the darkness.

"Stop right there, or I'll drill you," the marshal yelled.

The man held up, swaying on his feet. "No need for gun-gunplay," he said. "I was going to the out-outhouse and got losht."

Matt saw the man's head turn as he looked around him. "Where . . . where did the sal-saloon go?"

Irritated, the marshal holstered his Colt. "Louie Pheeters, is that you?"

"As . . . as ever was. Who is thish?"

"Marshal Dillon."

"Ah, it's you, Mar-Marshal. I'm so sorry we meet under such diff-diffi-difficult circumstances." Pheeters paused, then said: "I've . . . I've lost the saloon, you see." He clapped his hands together. "Poof! It just van-vanished."

Louie Pheeters held the dubious distinction of being the town drunk, a man who had not spent a sober hour in years, his love of the bottle financed by a regular allowance from a doting maiden aunt who lived back east somewhere.

Matt stepped toward the man. "How long have you been out here, Louie?" he asked.

Pheeters swayed, hiccupped and spread his arms. "Forever. I've been losht forever. See, I went to the out-outhouse and—poof!—the saloon was gone." The man hiccupped. "I've been losht forever and ever."

Matt's eyes sought Pheeter's in the darkness. "Louie, did you see anybody out here?"

"Not a living soul, 'cept you, Mar-Marshal." Pheeters shook his head. "Heard a girl crying." He hiccupped again. "Tummy ache, maybe."

"Where, Louie? Show me."

Pheeters turned, swayed on his feet and pointed to a small shack half hidden in the gloom. "Over there. I-I think she had a tummy ache. Maybe she did."

Matt grabbed Pheeters' arm and led him to the
rear door of the Spencer and Drew Saloon. "In there,
Louie," he said.

The man grinned. "Good . . . good for you, Marshal. You made it re-reapp-reappear again."

"Get inside, Louie," Matt said. "And don't come
out again until daybreak."

The man raised his battered plug hat, then staggered to the door. Matt waited until Pheeters had
safely staggered inside, then drew his gun and
walked to the shack that Louie had pointed out to
him.

This one was even smaller than the first cabin Matt
had investigated. It had a swaybacked roof and a
rusted iron stovepipe jutting through the peak on one
side. There were no curtains in the window, but the
four glass panes, one of them cracked, were covered
in yellowed newspaper.

Matt walked around to the front of the shack. A
red railroader's lantern was hung above the clap-
board door, its flame guttering, several white moths
fluttering around the pale crimson light like tiny
ghosts. The woman who lived here and advertised
her services had chosen her location well. The Spencer and Drew was not one of the busiest saloons in
Dodge, but its very quietness attracted customers of
the better sort, mostly cattle buyers, land speculators
and many of the town's businessmen.

She was maybe a small cut above the girls who
worked the line, ridiculed by the punchers as "soldiers' women," since they were all the poorly paid
troopers could afford.

Matt rapped on the door with his knuckles. "Anybody to home?" he asked.

His question was greeted by silence. Somewhere far off an owl questioned the night, and this close to the edge of town the yammering of coyotes was loud in the quiet.

Matt knocked again, and still getting no answer, he pushed on the door. It swung open, creaking on rusted hinges. The marshal looked inside, but saw only darkness. He searched in a vest pocket, found a match and thumbed it into flame.

Matt Dillon had seen violent death many times before, but nothing had prepared him for the sight that met his eyes in the stark, flaring light of the match. He stumbled back, fighting for breath in a suddenly tight chest, then stepped well away from the shack.

"Oh, my God," he whispered. He tilted his head and looked up at the stars but found no comfort, only cold, indifferent chips of ice glittering in a sea of black. "Oh, my God," he said again, while the stars looked down on him, aloof and uncaring.

chapter 21

Two Killers Loose in Dodge

"She died quickly, Matt," Doc Adams said. "He cut her throat before he"—Doc hesitated, then managed—"did the rest of his cutting."

The shack was small, too small to accommodate Festus and Percy Crump and his assistant at the same time, so the five men stood around the door, silent, too shaken to speak.

The girl was young, no more than twenty, and she'd been mutilated. The killer had then knotted a sheet around her upper chest and hung her from a clothes hook on the wall.

Bright red hair hung over the girl's face, hiding her features, but Matt turned to the others and asked: "Anybody know her?"

Festus and Percy Crump exchanged glances but shuffled their feet in awkward silence.

"She had a name," Matt said, his voice rising with his anger. "Even dead doves have names."

"Take it easy, Matt," Doc said quietly. "There are a lot of women in Dodge."

The marshal bent his head, standing silent, the raw iron smell of blood thick in his nostrils. Finally he raised his head and in a softer voice said: "Festus, go get John Alan. Tell him I want him here fast."

"Sure thing, Matthew," the deputy said quickly, obviously glad to get away from that place of death.

Festus returned a couple minutes later with the Spencer and Drew head bartender. Alan was a quiet-eyed man with still hands and a calm way about him.

Matt met him at the door of the shack. "John," he said, "first prepare yourself for a terrible shock. Then go into the shack and tell me if you know the woman inside."

"I don't need to go inside," Alan said, suddenly wary. "Fran Laurie lives here."

"I need to know positively that it's her," Matt said. "It could help with my investigation."

"Beautiful red hair, but not real pretty," Alan said, looking around like he was seeking a place to hide. "Nice enough girl, though."

"I need to know, John."

The bartender gulped, his eyes troubled. "What will I see in there, Marshal?"

"Something that will haunt you for the rest of your life." Doc, scowling, elbowed his way into the question. "Now get in there and tell us if that's Fran Laurie."

Alan touched his tongue to his top lip and nodded. He stepped inside the door, then immediately staggered out again, his face ashen. "It's—it's her," he gasped. "It's Fran." He lifted haunted eyes to Matt. "What's left of her."

The marshal laid a hand on Alan's shoulder. "Thanks John. I appreciate it."

"Never ask me to do something like that again," the man snapped. He opened his mouth to speak, shut it, then managed, outrage flashing in his eyes, "Just don't ever ask me again, is all."

Matt watched Alan stumble into the night, then turned to Doc as the physician said: "As before, Matt, the man who did this would be covered in blood. He'd be real conspicuous."

"Unless he changed clothes after each murder," Matt said. "Or he might have brought a cloak or a duster and stashed it somewhere. After a murder he could have thrown it on and covered the blood-stains."

Doc nodded, thinking. "It's possible that in the dark, he could go unnoticed, I suppose."

Matt set his teeth on edge. "I swear," he said, "when I find Barnabas Shaklee I'm not going to call him out. I'll just draw down on him and put a bullet in his belly."

"No, you won't, Matt," Doc said. "That's never been your style and I can't see you changing now"— he hesitated—"for any reason."

"I guess you're right," the marshal said, managing a wan smile. "But a man can dream, can't he?" He turned to Crump, standing hunched and expectant beside Festus. "She's all yours, Percy. Treat her right."

The undertaker nodded, his black vulture eyes somber. "That," he said, "will be quite a challenge."

*   *   *

Matt sat at his desk, the lamp hanging over his head casting a circle of pale orange light on the killer's note, gleaming on the blade of the bowie knife. So far they'd told him nothing.

Yet . . . wearily he read the note again, something about the words troubled him, something that didn't quite ring true. They just didn't sound like Shaklee's words. The man would surely have invoked hell and damnation or some other perversion of scripture. That was his style—unless he was trying to cover his tracks.

Festus walked into the office and stepped to the desk. The lamp cast dark shadows in the hollows of his eyes and his bearded face looked drawn and pale. The deputy was tired, Matt realized, just as he himself was starting to wear down.

"What are you thinkin', Matthew?" Festus asked. "When I see your brow wrinkled like it is now, I always know you're studyin' hard on somethin'."

"It's probably nothing," the marshal said. "But I'm troubled by this note. It just doesn't sound like Shaklee."

"Read it to me again, Matthew," Festus said.

As Matt read the note, Festus cradled his chin in a hand, his eyes turned to the ceiling as though he was considering the deeper meaning of each word.

When the marshal was finished, Festus shook his head. "I dunno, Matthew. Ol' Barnabas is a mighty strange feller. It could have been him."

"I guess so," Matt said. "He's the obvious suspect. There's nobody else."

Festus poured himself coffee and stepped back to

the desk. "Matthew, it seems to me that if you really want to know a man, find out what makes him mad."

Matt's eyes lifted to his deputy. "I don't catch your drift."

"Is Barnabas down on doves, like the note says? I'd say he was making himself mighty free with them soiled doves who were married to his sons, though I doubt there was a legal wife in the bunch."

"And he made no secret of the fact that he wanted Arrah Hillman to be his woman," Matt said.

"An' Arrah—"

"Is a dove. I know." Matt finished it.

Festus sipped his coffee, then said: "Matthew, there's somethin' else botherin' me. That drummer who was knifed an' robbed—that just doesn't sound like the Moonlight Ripper. He just don't go in for murdering grown men."

"You think there could be two killers loose in Dodge?"

"I reckon that's the way of it. One of them murders for money. The other kills for . . . well, Matthew, we saw tonight what he kills for."

Matt sat back in his chair, his face thoughtful. "That could be the way of it, Festus." But after a few moments, he shook his head vehemently. "I'm getting tired, I guess. No matter how it shakes, the man you call the Moonlight Ripper is Barnabas Shaklee. I'm certain of it. All right, he may not have murdered the drummer, but he killed Fran Laurie tonight, and two other women."

Festus nodded. "It's good to be certain, Matthew."

Matt's head snapped up and he studied his deputy's face. But Festus had his coffee cup to his mouth and his shadowed eyes revealed nothing.

Matt stood at the edge of the boardwalk under a morning sky streaked with bands of red and jade. The saloons were quiet and the early traffic on Front Street consisted of a noisy tangle of freight and express wagons. There were only a few riders, mostly townspeople from across the tracks, the women sitting sidesaddle, stirrup to stirrup with their somber husbands.

Matt nodded to people he knew and a few he didn't, noticing that smiles were fewer and an occasional glance was accusing, as though he was somehow falling down in his duty by just standing there on the boards.

He knew the reason. The Moonlight Ripper had the whole town on edge and it was beginning to show.

A half dozen determined small boys armed with clubs scuffed their bare feet along the opposite boardwalk, heading for the feed sheds by the tracks. Matt smiled. It seemed that Festus' rat-killing posse had not yet disbanded.

He turned as he heard footsteps heading toward him. It was Barney Danches, the telegraph agent, a piece of yellow paper fluttering in the man's right hand.

"Got your answer from the Army, Marshal," Danches said. "I thought I'd bring it right over."

Matt nodded his thanks, took the paper and read. The wire was short and to the point:

TWO COMPANIES OF INFANTRY WILL TAKE
THE FIELD IN SEVEN DAYS FROM THIS

DATE. STOP. THEY WILL ENGAGE AND DETAIN
ANY HOSTILES FOUND NORTH OF THE AR-
KANSAS. STOP.
YOURS RESPCT., JAS. MCKENZIE (MAJOR),
COMMANDING OFFICER, FORT DODGE

And by then the hostiles would be long gone, Matt
thought. Only the Army would dispatch booted infantry to hunt down mounted Indians in flat-riding
horse country.

"Any answer, Marshal?" Danches asked.

"No, none," Matt answered absently, as he reread
the wire.

Danches touched his cap and left, leaving the marshal to his thoughts.

Since sunup, more settlers had arrived in Dodge
with wild talk of marauding Cheyenne, though none
had actually seen an Indian harm a single white per-
son. The last reported position of the hostiles was
near the South Fork of Buckner Creek, though they
were said to have scouts out as far north as Horse
Thief Canyon, once prime buffalo country.

Matt thought matters through. Given marching
time, the soldiers from Fort Dodge would not be anywhere near the creek for another two weeks, and by
then the Indians would have melted into the plains.

Right now frightened settlers in a town on edge
over the Ripper murders were a complication Matt
didn't need. Mayor Kelley had been right. Maybe it
was time he rode out and took a look for himself.
He could ride to the creek and be back in town before
nightfall when he'd resume his hunt for Barnabas
Shaklee. It was also possible that Shaklee was hiding

out on the long grass himself, and he might cut his sign.

His mind made up, Matt stepped into the office and told Festus his plan.

"You ride high in the saddle out there, Matthew," the deputy warned. "If those are really Cheyenne by the creek, they're Injuns for one man to step around."

"I'll be careful," Matt promised. "In the meantime, keep an eye on things here. I don't expect any trouble to start until after dark, but you never know."

Festus raised a shaggy eyebrow. "You mean Moonlight Ripper trouble by day, Matthew?"

"No," Matt said, shaking his head, "I mean vigilante trouble"—he smiled without humor—"by day."

chapter 22

An Ultimatum from the Cheyenne

The plains around Matt Dillon stretched flat and empty to the horizon. The sun had almost made its climb to the highest point in the sky, and the day was hot, the warm wind blowing off the blue mountains far to the west doing little to cool man or mount.

The marshal was six miles to the southeast of Buckner Creek, crossing grass country streaked by wide bands of red and yellow wildflowers, here and there yucca and prickly pear standing tall among the shy blossoms.

Ahead of him the horizon shimmered in the heat, and every dip and hollow held captive its own mirage, glittering pools of water, cool phantoms that existed only in the eye of the beholder.

Matt held his bay to a steady trot, the only sound the soft footfalls of the horse on the grass and the creak of saddle leather.

The sun was hot on Matt's shoulders as the cottonwoods and willows lining Buckner Creek came into sight. Ahead of him a thin ribbon of smoke tied gray bows in the air and he could see splashes of brown and white among the trees where the Indian ponies grazed.

Drawing rein, Matt studied the creek thoughtfully, pondering his next move.

In the end, he decided he had little choice in the matter. He had to determine if the Indians were hostile or not. Only his assurance to the settlers that the Cheyenne harbored no warlike intent would send them back to their homes.

He would go speak his mind to the Indians—and feel mighty glad that he was riding a fast horse.

The Indians saw him coming from a ways off and rode out to meet him, twenty or so warriors who shook out into a loose skirmish line, rifles slanted across the withers of their ponies.

A cloud shadow raced across the grass as Matt waited, letting the Cheyenne come to him. By nature and inclination a careful man, the marshal felt a knot in his throat. The Cheyenne were so close that if things went bad, which had a way of happening around Indians, he knew he'd be in a heap of trouble.

Maybe the warriors felt that one man represented little danger, or they sensed his unease, because the Cheyenne drew rein and an older warrior with thin gray braids rode out from among them. To his relief, Matt saw that the man carried only a feathered coup stick and no weapon.

The Indian stopped when his pony was nose to

nose with the marshal's bay. The old warrior sat his horse and studied the tall man with the star on his vest, his black eyes wary and measuring.

Matt had no way with the Cheyenne language, so he touched his hat, forced what he hoped was a friendly smile and said: "Howdy."

"Why do you come to us?" the old warrior asked, his lined face stiff.

"The chief speaks English," Matt said. He knew it was an inadequate response, but he was desperately hoping to clear the air a little.

For a few moments the old Cheyenne was silent. Then he said: "Custer, Bear Coat Miles and the rest— they taught the Cheyenne to speak English pretty damn quick." The old warrior's eyes glittered. "Why do you come to us?"

Matt swallowed hard and laid it on the line. "Chief, you got to be moving on." He waved a hand to the east. "Many soldiers are coming."

The old man nodded. "I know, but not too soon. Marching soldiers with packs on their backs take a long time to cross the plains, I think."

"How did you know that?" the marshal asked, surprised.

The Indian shrugged. "It is carried on the wind if a man takes time to listen."

His eyes moving beyond the old man, Matt scanned the line of warriors. They were a mix of the very young and the very old, a good many of the men of fighting age already lost in dozens of nameless battle with the bluecoat soldiers.

The old man rubbed his belly. "We are hungry. South of the Cimarron, our people are also hungry.

Our women and children eat smoke while they wait
for us to bring meat." He shook his head. "There is
no meat. The buffalo are all gone."

"What will you do?" Matt asked.

The old chief's reply was direct. "We will steal
what we can. A milk cow, a plow mule. Winter will
come all too soon and our people cannot survive on
antelope and rabbit. There is no fat on antelope and
rabbit to keep out the cold."

"If you steal from the farmers, they will fight you.
Many of your warriors will die."

"They will die anyway, come the first snows. Better to die in battle like men than to starve to death
like dogs."

"You must move on now," Matt said, knowing he
was pushing into dangerous territory. "You must go
back beyond the Cimarron."

The old man turned and in his native tongue
yelled something to the warriors. They reacted immediately and angrily, yipping war cries, a few bran-
dishing their rifles at Matt.

"There is your answer," the chief shouted. "We
will not leave until we have meat for our women
and children."

Matt realized the situation was fast getting out of
hand. Now the Cheyenne moved forward, surrounding him in a sea of hostile faces. A young warrior, who looked to be about fifteen, punched him
on the shoulder, counting coup. When the others
laughed and jeered, he grinned and again pulled
back his fist. Matt slapped the boy's arm away, and
the young Cheyenne backed up his pony and
reached for his rifle.

The old chief angrily barked a command, and the boy sullenly laid his gun back across the withers of his horse. But his eyes, glittering with hate, never left Matt's face.

"You better go now," the old warrior said. "It is time."

Desperately the marshal tried to retrieve the situation. "Chief," he said quickly, "if I bring the Cheyenne meat, will they return to the Cimarron country?"

A few of the Indians who understood English looked from Matt to the chief, waiting to see how the old man would react.

For long moments the Indian sat his horse in silence. Then he stretched out both hands and spread his fingers, pushing them toward Matt. He repeated the gesture five times more.

"Bring that many cows to this place the day after tomorrow and the Cheyenne will return with them to the Cimarron."

The marshal whistled inwardly. At current prices, sixty head of prime beef represented an outlay to Dodge of at least six hundred dollars—and the parsimonious Mayor Kelley might well balk at that kind of expense.

But right then Matt had no choice. "The cows will be here," he said. "The Cheyenne have my word."

As was the Indian way, none of their languages having a word for farewell, the old chief swung his pony around and motioned for the others to follow.

One by one, the Cheyenne headed back to the creek, except for the young warrior who had counted coup on Matt. Without warning, the boy suddenly threw his rifle to his shoulder, took aim at the marshal's head and pulled the trigger.

The metallic *click!* was loud in the silence.

The boy spat over the side of his pony, then glared at Matt. "No bullets. None of us have bullets. The Cheyenne hunt game with empty rifles."

Then he swung his pony away and galloped after the others.

Matt swallowed hard and shoved his drawn Colt back into the holster. That had been way too close.

"Matt, are you crazy? Sixty head of Texas beeves at railhead prices! Do you know how much that will cost the town?"

"I have a good idea, Mayor," the marshal answered. "But it will get the settlers back on their farms. You know that cowboys and sodbusters are an explosive mix. It's only a matter of time before some puncher or pumpkin roller says a word out of place and gets shot."

Kelley stomped around the marshal's office, his agitation evident by the way he nervously puffed on his cigar. Finally he stopped his perambulations and leaned over Matt's desk.

"Just let it go, Matt. You just told me them Cheyenne have no ammunition for their guns. The Army will soon round them up."

"They have plenty of bows and arrows," Matt said patiently. "And they'll run rings around foot soldiers for weeks. Mayor, there are still plenty of settler families out there on the plains. Ever see what a Cheyenne warrior can do with a bow when he's raiding to feed his wife and young'uns?"

Kelley slumped into the chair opposite Matt, his mind working. "I have to agree that it's dangerous to have sodbusters camped out in Dodge during the cattle season," he said finally. "It's bad for business." He waved a hand. "And we're contending with this Moonlight Ripper business. All we need is some respectable farmer's wife to get cut to collops and we could have the governor's office involved."

"Or a daughter," Matt put in mildly.

"That could be even worse," Kelley said, looking miserable.

"Mayor, the Cheyenne are only a couple of hours' ride from Dodge," Matt said. "If their empty bellies make them desperate and they take to the warpath, the violence could spill over to here." Then, knowing how vivid was Kelley's imagination, he added: "We could have Indians rampaging up and down Front Street."

The mayor looked shaken. "Between the Indians and the Ripper, Mrs. Kelley is all atremble already," he said. "The poor woman would be quite undone and faint clean away if she knew that Cheyenne could soon be hooting and hollering all over town."

A thoughtful silence stretched between the two men. Then Kelley slapped his palm on the desk. "I'll do it!" He glanced at Matt irritably. "Do I have your assurance that the Indians will move on after they get the cattle?"

Matt nodded. "I reckon they'll waste no time in driving those cows to their village south of the Cimarron."

"Who will take them out there to the creek?"

"Festus said he'd do it, him and a couple of punchers who owe him a favor or three."

Rising to his feet, Kelley said: "I'll go purchase the cattle and make the necessary financial arrangements. Long John Poteet just came in with a herd of scrub longhorns, and I'm told he doesn't have a buyer yet. I'm sure he'll sell me the number I need, though he's a grim, hard-bitten man and he'll try to skin me alive."

"I believe you're well able to hold your own when it comes to the dickering, Mayor," Matt said.

"Damn right." Kelley grinned, pleased. He moved toward the door, then stopped. "Matt, make sure that layabout town deputy is ready to move the cattle out at first light tomorrow. I want those redskins across the Arkansas by noon."

After the mayor left, Matt stepped to the window, looked into the street and felt a formless dread clutch at his belly.

Darkness had fallen on Dodge.

chapter 23

Night of the
Bounty Hunter

Matt Dillon buckled on his gun belt, settled his hat on his head and stepped out onto the boardwalk. Festus was on patrol across the tracks, carrying the Greener, an extra Colt in his waistband.

"Just don't get nervous out there, Festus," Matt had warned him, casting an eye over his armory.

"Matthew," the deputy had replied, taking no offense, "nerves is just a case of which end of a six-gun a man happens to be lookin' at."

Now Festus was somewhere out there in the darkness, hunting a vicious killer who came and went like a phantom.

Looking up and down the street, Matt was relieved to see that so far the threatened vigilantism had not yet happened. But wary-eyed men were going armed everywhere and they were keeping their women-folk close.

Mitch Haythorn, confident of his gun skill, had not

given up his evening promenade with Arrah Hillman and he stopped beside Matt on the boardwalk.

The marshal touched his hat to Arrah as Haythorn said: "Beautiful evening, is it not, Marshal?" The man smiled, showing teeth that were very white under his thin mustache. "That is, if one can get past the flies and the smell of cattle."

"Another herd just came in," Matt said. "It's a mite crowded down there by the pens." He glanced at Arrah, admiring her dark, exotic beauty, and smiled. "I declare, Miss Arrah, that your presence adds to the pleasantness of the evening."

"La, Marshal Dillon, I did not know you were such a gallant," Arrah said, fluttering her long lashes.

"The marshal is a man of many parts, my dear," Haythorn said. "It does not pay to underestimate him." He smiled. "As I myself have done in the past."

Suddenly Haythorn was serious. "Marshal, just so you know, I noticed a man skulking around the Dodge House late last night, keeping well to the shadows."

"Did you get a good look at him?" Matt asked, all at once on edge.

Haythorn shook his head. "No, I didn't. He was small, moved well, and was not a puncher—I can tell you that. I drew my gun and went after him but he faded into the night and I lost him."

"Could it have been Barnabas Shaklee?"

"Perhaps," Haythorn said, "except that I've never seen the man so I can't be sure. I told you once before that preachers are outside my usual circle of acquaintances." The gambler hesitated, then said: "We do know that Shaklee has set his sights on Arrah."

"Haythorn," Matt said, "I believe Barnabas Shaklee could be the man who has already murdered three women in Dodge."

Arrah let out a little gasp of horror. "You mean he's the Moonlight Ripper?"

"That's what folks are calling him," Matt said sourly. He glanced at Haythorn. "Don't let Arrah out of your sight, not for a minute, and that goes for the other women who are working for you."

"Marshal, after Stella Shaklee left my employ to become G. P. Proctor's woman, I decided to get out of that business," Haythorn said. "It was never really my style anyway. From now on I'm strictly a gambler by profession."

"I'd say congratulations, but I'm sure you'd detect my insincerity," Matt said.

Haythorn laughed. "Damn it all, Marshal, but I like you, even though you don't like me one little bit."

"I can't deny that," Matt said. "I don't like you or your kind."

"Well, that's honest enough." Haythorn smiled and touched his hat. "And now I'll bid you a good evening."

"Remember what I told you," Matt said to Haythorn's retreating back. "Keep Arrah close and be careful."

"My kind always is, Marshal," the gambler said, smiling over his shoulder.

*   *   *

Matt watched Haythorn and Arrah leave until they were swallowed by the darkness; then he crossed the street to the Long Branch.

Kitty saw him and waved, but the saloon was crowded and she was busy helping Sam Noonan and the other bartenders, and he decided this was not a good time to talk to her. He was about to leave when Proctor stepped in front of him. The man waved a hand toward a corner of the room, where Ben Hillman was sitting at a table with—to Matt's surprise—the big rancher Bill Kennett.

"Care to join us for a few minutes, Marshal?" Proctor asked.

Matt nodded, interested in what Hillman and Kennett could have to say to each other. But before he stepped toward the table, Proctor put a hand on his arm and stopped him.

"Another girl last night," the man said, his face haggard. "Have you made any progress, Marshal?"

Matt shook his head. "So far none to speak of, Proctor. But I'm working on it."

"What I said last night still goes, Marshal. If you need any help, just let me know."

"I'll be sure to ask you if it comes to that," Matt said.

Proctor's eyes looked haunted. "I can't get Stella out of my mind . . . the terrible way she died. I feel so guilty that I wasn't there with her."

A waiter jostled past with a loaded tray of drinks; then Matt said: "If you'd been there, you'd be dead too, Proctor, and that wouldn't have solved a thing. A man shouldn't beat himself up about what might have been."

"You're right, Marshal," Proctor said. "But it's a hard pill to swallow."

"For all of us," Matt said.

Proctor led him to the table and pulled out a chair. Matt sat and Kennett nodded. "Howdy, Marshal. I hear you've got yourself a heap of trouble with this Moonlight Ripper feller."

"It's considerable," the marshal agreed. He changed the subject quickly. "How are the ribs?"

"Fair to middling. That's why I'm here talking to Ben. He just promised me he'll lay off them during the fight."

Matt was surprised. "Handicapping yourself some, aren't you, Ben?"

"Nah." Hillman grinned. "I can beat Kennett easy without busting up his ribs worse than they already are."

"Big talk," the rancher said. "But talkin' ain't fightin'. It's going to be over real quick this time around."

"How often are you boys coming up to scratch?" Matt asked.

"There is no scratch and no rounds," Hillman said. "Kennett wants it that way. After the bell rings, we just keep punching until one of us falls."

"And that will be you, Hillman," the rancher said, grinning.

"Where's the smart money going, Proctor?" Matt asked.

"Right now, it's running about ninety to ten on Bill. And after the word gets around that Ben's agreed to lay off his ribs, I think hardly anybody will bet on my boy, even at a hundred to one." The man smiled. "I'm fixing to clean up, so much so that I've already raised Ben's share of the purse to three thousand."

"More than enough, Marshal," Hillman said, throwing Matt a knowing look.

"I reckon it is, Ben," Matt acknowledged, as Kennett looked from one to the other, his face puzzled. The marshal got to his feet. "Well, good luck to both of you," he said.

Hillman's eyes lifted to the tall lawman. "Everything is going to be just fine, Marshal. I'm feeling strong, real good."

Matt made no reply. He just nodded and stepped away from the table. Proctor immediately got to his feet and followed him.

"Find him, Marshal Dillon," he said. "And after you do, throw him in a cell and give me five minutes alone with him."

Matt's smile was without a trace of humor. "If there's anything left of him after I have my five minutes," he said.

Matt did a round of the town, stopping inside the saloons and dance halls. They were as noisy and rowdy as ever, but the tension in the air was growing, and more than one voice, usually that of a woman, yelled out to him: "Hey, Marshal, have you caught him yet?"

Fear of the Moonlight Ripper was everywhere in town, running down the smooth backs of the saloon girls like the fingers of an icy hand.

Matt walked back to his office, a sense of defeat heavy in him. He made his way along the boardwalk

under a sky lit by a glowing moon that competed
with the flaring streetlamps to light up Dodge and
reveal all of its shabby ugliness.

He was about to step into his office when his eyes
were drawn to a lone horseman plodding up Front
Street on a tired grulla. There was something familiar
about the way the rider sat slump shouldered in the
saddle, and the marshal stopped to watch him.

The man wore a dusty, high-buttoned black coat
and gray pants tucked into scuffed mule-eared boots.
A battered plug hat was tilted low over his eyes and
a beautifully stocked Winchester rode in a scabbard
under his right knee. To the casual observer, the man
would have looked harmless enough, but anyone
who cared to get closer would have sensed the air
of menace that hung around him like a dark fog.
And had they approached closer still and looked into
the man's face, they would have been struck by his
ice blue eyes . . . the cold, unfeeling eyes of the professional killer.

The man's glance slanted to Matt, who was now
standing at the edge of the boardwalk. He swung his
tired horse around and stopped in front of the
marshal.

"You what passes for the law around here?" he
asked, his high, raspy voice contemptuous and
belligerent.

"I can tell your manners haven't improved any,
Petrie," Matt said. "Fair piece off your home range,
aren't you?"

The man leaned forward in the saddle as his eyes
sought to penetrate the gloom. Finally he asked un-
certainly: "Matt Dillon, is that you?"

"Yes, it's me, Petrie, and you're not welcome in my town."

The man called Petrie smiled, showing small pegged teeth. "Man in my line of work seldom is," he said.

"What are you doing in Dodge?" Matt asked.

And Garrison Petrie, bounty hunter, killer of seventeen men, told him.

chapter 24

Wanted, Dead or Alive

"Been a long time, Matt. I never did think I'd ever see you wearing a lawman's star, though."

"A man changes, Petrie," the marshal said. "He rides up on a fork in the trail and takes the road he feels is right for him."

Petrie sat on the corner of Matt's desk and his eyes lifted to the tall lawman's unsmiling face. "You were the best of all of us with the iron. I always said you had real talent way back then. Mighty cool in a fight and sudden on the draw. You still as fast?"

"Fast enough. It took a while, but I learned to take my time and shoot once."

Petrie nodded. "Ain't that always the way of it." He smiled with all the warmth of a coiled rattler. "Carl Bender is gone, you know. Shot by the Rangers down to El Paso a few years back. And Luke Bix— you remember Bix, how he was always combing that long yeller hair of his?"

"I remember," Matt said. "Came halfway down his back, as I recollect."

"Yeah, well ol' Luke was gunned in Cheyenne by Bodie Yates. He ought to have knowed better than to draw down on Yates. Hell, Matt, Bodie is near as good with a gun as you and John Wesley."

Matt had no great desire to make small talk with a lowlife like Petrie, but sometimes a man cared to recall old times and the half-forgotten faces that once meant something to him. "What happened to Luther Smith and the rest of that hard Platte River crowd?" he asked.

Petrie shrugged. "Luther was lifting some cows along the Canadian when all of a sudden something broke inside his chest. Them who were with him say he was dead when he hit the ground. As for the rest of them, some are gone from too much bad whiskey and fancy women, a couple were hung, a few were shot and I don't know what happened to the others." The bounty hunter was silent for a moment, then added: "Good times, Matt, way back then, you and me with Wes, Bender and ol' Bix and them."

"Some of it was good," the marshal said. "Most of it wasn't so good."

Matt's eyes dropped to the wanted dodger in his hands. "You know this was issued in Texas. It doesn't cut any ice in Kansas."

"Matt, you're a United States marshal and the whole damn country is your jurisdiction. You know it's your duty to release the prisoner into my custody." Petrie's small mouth twisted into a cold smile again. "Besides, there's a very rich, very powerful senator in Washington who would take it mighty hard if he heard his son's killer was being protected by a lawman. He just might take a notion to ruin that lawman's career." The bounty hunter's smile grew wider. "Yup, he just might at that."

Feeling trapped, the marshal said, his voice like ice, "Petrie, you've never taken in a prisoner alive."

"Look at the dodger again, Matt. It says dead or alive. The State of Texas don't much care one way or t'other. One thing I learned long ago was to fear the man who's feared of me. A bullet solves that problem. And besides, it cuts down on expenses. A prisoner can eat his weight in groceries on a long trail."

"Petrie," Matt said, "we were talking about way back when. I didn't like you then, and I like you even less now."

"Comes with the job," the bounty hunter said, unfazed. "In my line of work a man don't set up to be liked."

The marshal tossed the wanted poster to Petrie. "Tell me about this," he said.

"It ain't long in the telling." Petrie took the makings from his coat pocket and built a smoke. He thumbed a match into flame, lit his cigarette and said: "It happened down Laredo way about three months ago.

"Your boy Ben Hillman was in the Sideboard Saloon along with a shady character who went by the name G. P. Proctor. Well, a young rancher called Jeremy Larsen objected to a black man getting served at the bar.

"Now Larsen fancied himself as a gunslinger, only trouble was that he'd never killed a man. When Hillman sassed him, Larsen went for his gun, figuring that killing a black wasn't going to land him in any trouble with the law."

"Was Hillman armed?" Matt asked.

"As far as is known, no. Anyhoo, before Larsen could clear leather, Hillman hit out from the shoulder and punched the young feller on the chin. He felled Larsen like an ox, is what them who were in the saloon recalled.

"Trouble was, Hillman hit too hard. Larsen never regained consciousness and died later that night. He had some kind of brain damage, I'm told.

"By all accounts it was a clear case of self-defense, but Proctor wasn't taking any chances. He drawed a Smith and Wesson gun and he and Hillman skedaddled."

"What then?" Matt asked, his eyes cold on Petrie.

"Why, then, the dead boy's pa, United States senator Anthony T. Larsen, used his influence, called in a favor on the judge and had Hillman tried for murder in absentia. Hillman was subsequently found guilty and sentenced to be hanged.

"Then the senator put a two-thousand-dollar bounty on Hillman's head and contacted me. I later tracked Hillman all the way to Dodge."

"How did you know he was here?" Matt asked.

Petrie shrugged. "I didn't. I was following a cold trail until I spoke to a sodbuster about twenty miles south of here. He told me a black man by the name of Hillman was fixing to fight a Texas rancher in Dodge, and that a pile of money was being bet against the black. That farmer said he followed the boxing game some and that, if I wanted to clean up,

I should lay some money on Hillman, who was a lot better than most folks imagined. He said his manager was now giving odds of a hundred to one on his boy."

Petrie shrugged. "And now here I am, as ever was." He smiled. "When I asked him, the pumpkin roller told me the law in Dodge was a hard man by the name of Dillon. I didn't make the connection until I saw you in the street, still a couple of inches taller than a ponderosa pine and as sour faced as ever."

Matt let that comment pass and said: "Petrie, Hillman was railroaded. Anybody can see that."

The bounty hunter shook his head. "That's none of my concern. I just bring 'em in when they're on the run from the law." He picked up the wanted poster. "This here dodger is my bona fides, all legal and correct. But I don't want you to arrest Hillman until after the fight. I'm putting money on that black boy. From all I hear, he's pretty good with his dukes."

His insides stiffening, Matt knew Petrie had him over a barrel. A legal court of law had found Ben Hillman guilty of murder and had sentenced him to hang. As a U.S. marshal, it was his duty to arrest Ben and turn him over to Petrie to be returned to Texas, where justice could take its course.

Only he would never reach there alive.

This thought was confirmed when Petrie rose to his feet, smiled at the marshal and said: "And, Matt, don't feed that black boy after you arrest him. A dead man with a full belly do stink on the trail."

*   *   *

After Petrie left, Matt opened the office door to let out the stench of death that seemed to cling to the bounty hunter.

Petrie had been raised on remote Army posts in the Arizona and New Mexico territories. His mother was a laundress who followed the troops, and when Petrie was born, she didn't know which of the many soldiers she entertained was his father, so she named the boy Garrison, figuring that covered all the possibilities.

He had killed his first man at fifteen, a sutler with a reputation as a bully; then he had stolen a cavalry horse and fled into Texas. He'd punched cattle for a while and then ridden with some wild ones, a teenage Matt Dillon among them. Later he'd hired out as a range detective in Montana, and it was there he'd discovered that bounty hunting was an easy way to make money.

Garrison Petrie was not a gunfighter in the accepted sense of the word. He was a sure-thing killer who did not seek a reputation, preferring to ride into a town, find his man and leave again with as little fuss as possible.

He was good with the Colt, better with the Winchester and an all-round dangerous man. None of his seventeen killings lay heavy on his conscience, and he would have laughed at anyone who suggested that they gave him a single sleepless night.

Now Petrie was in Dodge and later he'd carry out the death sentence on Ben Hillman. And Matt, to his bitter frustration, could do nothing to stop him.

The marshal stepped outside, trying to make up his mind about what to do next.

He knew he would have to talk to Ben Hillman and tell him about Petrie. He'd then have to warn him not to attempt to leave town. If Ben asked him about the nature of the man who had tracked him from Texas, he'd tell him that as well.

Anger is the bastard child of fear, and Ben Hillman would have the right to be angry, knowing that his life was now numbered not in years, but in days.

And precious few of them at that.

chapter 25

Shooting at Shadows

Matt crossed Front Street under the night sky, the restless prairie wind tugging at him as he walked. He checked in at the Long Branch but Hillman and Proctor were already gone.

He found the two men at the boxing booth, where Proctor was again sleeping on a cot. With Stella gone, the man no longer felt an urgent need for the expensive privacy of the Dodge House.

When Matt entered the tent, Ben was sitting on the edge of his cot, reading a newspaper by the light of an oil lamp and Proctor was holding up what looked to be a new broadcloth coat, brushing dust off the back and shoulders.

"A late visit, Marshal," Proctor said, his eyes wary. "There's nothing amiss, I hope."

The marshal shook his head. "I've come to talk to Ben. I guess you should hear this too, Proctor."

"Marshal, if it's about the fight, I—"

"It's not about the fight," Matt interrupted. "It's about a dead man in Laredo."

Hillman and Proctor exchanged glances, and Proctor touched his tongue to his top lip. "How did you hear about that?" he asked.

"A man told me, a man by the name of Garrison Petrie. He's a bounty hunter, probably the best there is in Texas or anywhere else, come to that."

Ben Hillman rose to his feet, dropping the newspaper onto his cot. "Marshal, that man in Laredo, he drew a gun on me. I was only defending myself."

"I know that, Ben. But the court saw it differently."

"Court? What court?" Proctor asked.

Matt ignored the man and said: "Ben, you were tried in absentia, found guilty of murder and sentenced to be hanged. The man you killed was a rich senator's son, and his father put a two-thousand-dollar bounty on your head." Matt paused for a heartbeat, then added: "Dead or alive."

"And this man Petrie is here to collect," Hillman said.

"That's about the size of it," Matt allowed.

A silence followed, the only sound the tent canvas slapping in the wind and the slight wheeze of Proctor's breathing.

Finally Hillman asked: "Where do we go from here, Marshal?"

"I will arrest you after the fight and turn you over to Petrie." Matt put a hand on the man's shoulder. "Ben, I'll see that Mitch Haythorn gets his money and I'll put Arrah on a train east."

"I appreciate that, Marshal," Hillman said. "And

give Arrah the extra money I'm getting for the fight
and tell her to ride the cushions all the way to Phila-
delphia or Boston or wherever else she wants to go."

A gleam of hope flickered in the young boxer's
eyes. "Maybe when I get back to Laredo, I can beat
this thing, tell the law what really happened. Surely
somebody there will listen."

Hillman's gaze searched Matt's face. "Marshal, I
have the feeling there's something you're not telling
me. What are you holding back?"

Matt shook his head, his face stiff. "Garrison Petrie
doesn't deliver his prisoners alive. You're bucking a
stacked deck, Ben."

"You mean he'll kill me?"

"Yes, he will, somewhere along the trail."

Hillman looked like he'd been slapped. "And . . .
and you'll give me up to a man like that?"

"The way I see it, I have no alternative," Matt said.
Then a thought clicked in his brain. "Unless . . ."

"Unless what, Marshal? Let me hear it."

"I can go with you, Ben. I can leave Deputy Haggen in charge here and ride with you and Petrie all
the way to Laredo."

"You . . . you'd do that for me?" Hillman asked,
his surprise evident.

"You, Ben, and anybody else. It took me a little
while to figure it out, but Petrie won't try to kill you
when I'm with him. He's a man who steps right careful as far as the law is concerned, and he knows that
gunning a United States marshal would be the end
of him."

"You're forgetting one thing, Marshal." Proctor

had been busily scribbling in a leather-bound book that looked like a diary, now his eyes lifted to the lawman. "The Moonlight Ripper is still out there."

"I haven't forgotten. Ben's fight is the day after tomorrow. I have until then to find him."

"And if you don't?" Proctor asked.

"I'll cross that bridge when I come to it, Proctor. It's too early to stop and build houses of doubt on it."

Proctor shook his head. "You won't catch the Ripper, Marshal. If you plan on riding with Ben to Texas, you'll be leaving yourself too little time to find him."

As he walked back to his office, passing gaslit, noisy saloons, Matt knew that Proctor had been right. He did have too little time. He was cutting it thin, mighty thin.

Festus was a good lawman, but if another woman was killed, the town would erupt. So far vigilantism had been held in check, but it could rear its ugly, violent head at any moment and Festus would have his hands full. He'd be alone and that was too much to ask of any man.

Even if he caught the Katy and rode the rails back to Dodge, Matt figured he could be gone for weeks, and there might be no town left when he returned. Yet Ben Hillman's life was at stake, as was his opportunity, slim though it was, to clear his name.

Matt had plenty of problems—and no solutions were springing to his mind. It was a worrisome thing.

Matt had been in his office for less than ten minutes, when one of the developments he feared most happened. He heard a flurry of shots; then Sam

Noonan, Kitty Russell's head bartender, brought the bad news.

"Matt, you'd better come see this," Noonan said breathlessly. "Louie Pheeters just got gunned. He's lying behind the Long Branch and Miss Kitty is with him. I've already sent for Doc Adams."

Matt rose to his feet. "Who did it, Sam?"

The bartender was in a state of shock, his face without expression. "Matt, it was a young puncher who come up the trail with one of the King herds. He thought Louie was the Moonlight Ripper and cut loose." He shook his head. "Poor old Louie. He's hurt, Matt, hurt real bad."

The marshal followed Noonan across the street to the shadowed, empty space at the rear of the Long Branch. Kitty was kneeling on the ground, Pheeters' head cradled in her lap. An oil lamp fluttered close by, casting a shifting orange light on the woman's pale face. As he stepped closer, Matt saw that her hands were stained red with blood.

"How is he, Kitty?" Matt asked, as he took a knee beside her.

The woman shook her head. "I don't know, Matt. As far as I can tell, he's been hit by a couple of bullets."

Pheeters' eyes flickered open and rested on Kitty. "Ah, I . . . I was trying to find your place, Miss Kitty. Got lost again, don't you know. I'll have . . . I'll have a brandy flip, if you please."

"Shh, Louis," Kitty whispered. "The doctor is coming."

"And one for him too," Pheeters said, his breath coming in short, pained gasps. "He's a fine chap."

"Louie, how are you feeling?" Matt asked. He saw that the front of the man's shirt was wet with blood.

"Got lost again, Marshal. I was . . . I was wandering around in the dark, thought the front of the saloon was back here, you see." He shook his head. "Dark as pitch it was. I couldn't see a thing." His eyes widened as a memory surfaced in his alcohol-fogged brain. "Dash it all, Marshal. Then somebody shot me. Must've . . . must've took me for a wild Injun, I suppose."

"Move aside, Matt. Let me in there."

The marshal turned and found Doc Adams at his elbow. He rose to his feet and said: "Doc, I'll be in the saloon if you need me."

Doc nodded, but he was busily opening his bag, his attention already fixed on his patient.

Matt stepped into the saloon and found his way barred by a tall, rawboned man with a huge dragoon mustache and mild blue eyes. "Marshal, don't be too hard on the boy," he said. "He feels bad enough about what happened."

"Where is he?" Matt's eyes swept the crowded room, where punchers and saloon girls were gathered in groups, talking in low voices about what had happened.

"Over this way, Marshal," the man said. He was about to step across the floor, when he stopped and stuck out his hand. "By the way, name's Pete Hunt. I'm one of the King Ranch foremen."

Matt shook the man's hand, then Hunt led him to a table in a corner, where a cowboy was sitting, his head bowed, a Colt lying on the table in front of him.

"Billy," Hunt said, "the marshal wants to talk to you."

The puncher lifted his freckled face to Matt, skin peeling off the bridge of his nose. He was no more than a boy, and his bottom lip trembled as he said: "There's my gun, Marshal. I'm giving myself up."

"What's your name, son?" Matt asked. "And how old are you?"

"Billy Reed, out of the border country around McAllen. I'm seventeen and I come up the trail with one of the King herds. This is my third season in Dodge."

"Billy's a good hand, Marshal," Hunt pointed out. "He's not a shirker, always does his share an' then some."

Matt took the boy's gun, shoved it in his waistband, then sat down opposite him, aware of the silent, curious crowd that had begun to gather around the table. "Tell me what happened, Billy," he said.

The boy lifted red eyes to the marshal. "I was starting to feel my whiskey, so I stepped out back for some fresh air. Then I seen this figure creeping around in the dark. I'd heard all the talk about the Moonlight Ripper and what he does to women. I figured it had to be him."

"Did you call him out?" Matt asked.

Reed shook his head. "No, I was too scared, I guess. I just drawed my gun and fired." He tried to smile. "Just my luck, it was the first time in my life I ever hit what I was aiming at."

"Anybody ever tell you to make sure of your target before pulling the trigger?"

"My pa told me that a time or two. I guess I forgot."

"The man you shot is Louie Pheeters," Matt said. "He's drunk just about all of the time and he makes a habit of getting lost in the dark."

"I know," the boy said miserably. "That's what I was told." His chin dropped to his chest and he whispered, "I done shot the wrong man."

Matt turned as Doc Adams stepped up to the table. "He'll be on his feet in a few days, Matt," he said. "It wasn't as bad as it looked. Louie took a bullet in his shoulder and a second grazed his ribs." Doc shook his head. "It seems that the good Lord takes care of fools and drunks."

He looked around the room. "I want some of you men to carry Pheeters to my surgery. I can better cut that bullet out of him there."

A few men stepped forward, and Reed rose to his feet. "Let me help, Doc. I owe the man that much."

"Matt?" Doc asked.

The marshal nodded. "Billy, as soon as you do that, come to my office. I'm locking you up tonight."

"What's the charge, Marshal?" Pete Hunt asked, his face concerned.

Matt thought that question through for a few moments, then answered: "Given the circumstances and the youthfulness of the offender, I'll settle for the reckless discharge of a firearm within the town limits resulting in grievous bodily harm." He paused for a moment, then added: "If Louie had died, the charge would have been murder."

"Jail time or a fine?" Hunt asked.

"A fine," Matt said. "And it will be a stiff one."

Hunt looked relieved. "I'll pay it, Marshal. Billy

Reed is a top hand and a real good kid. He has a fine mother."

How many more good kids with fine mothers would shoot at shadows before this Ripper business was through? Matt asked himself.

He did not care to think of an answer.

chapter 26

Matt Hatches a Plan

Festus left at first light with the small herd destined for the Cheyenne and Matt busied himself with paperwork for most of the morning.

At noon, after a positive medical report from Doc Adams, Judge Amos Brooker set Billy Reed's fine at seventy-five dollars, which was paid by Pete Hunt. The boy immediately saddled his pony and headed for Texas, deciding not to push his luck with Dodge's hard-bitten marshal any further.

The young puncher had refused to take his Colt back, telling Matt that it had caused him nothing but grief and that he reckoned all an honest man needed was a rifle. Matt paid Reed eight dollars for the revolver, the gun to be added to the office armory, and sent a miscellaneous expenses chit to Mayor Kelley for the amount.

It was almost one, as Matt's worry over Festus was growing, when the door opened and Arrah Hillman stepped inside. The woman refused Matt's offer of coffee, accepted a chair and came right to the point.

"Marshal, I spoke to Ben this morning and he told me about that awful man Garrison Petrie," she said. "I told my brother to get out of Dodge right away, but he refused." She sighed. "He still has the idea that he can buy me from Mitch and set me on the path of righteousness."

"Haythorn wants two thousand five hundred dollars to cut you loose, Arrah. You know that."

The woman shook her head. "Mitch won't cut me loose, as you say. He needs me, Marshal. Without me he'd be lost. Sometimes he's like a lonely little boy, needing someone to take him by the hand and show him the way."

That was not even close to Matt's opinion of Haythorn, but he let it go. What Arrah thought of the gunfighting gambler was her concern.

"Did Ben tell you I plan on going to Texas with him and Petrie?" he asked.

Arrah nodded. "He did. And for that, I'm grateful." The woman's beautiful black eyes were troubled. "Marshal Dillon, when y'all reach Laredo, do you think they'll hang my brother?"

"I'll speak up for him," Matt said, sidestepping the question.

But Arrah was relentless. "I asked you, will they hang him?"

"I think," Matt said carefully, "it's a good possibility. I'm told there are some mighty powerful folks who want to see Ben kick at the end of a rope."

Arrah nodded, then stood. "That's all I wanted to know. Thank you for your candor, Marshal."

Matt rose to his feet and shook his head. "I'm sorry I can't give you any better word, Arrah," he said. "But I want you to know that I'll do my best for Ben. I'm a United States marshal and sometimes that means people listen to what I have to say."

"Yes, yes, of course," the woman said, her voice as vague and distant as her eyes. "I know you will."

She turned and left, leaving the scent of wildflowers in the office and a tension that hadn't been there before. Matt tried to shrug it off, worrying again about Festus and his dealings with the Cheyenne.

But his mind kept returning to Arrah. He had a feeling that the woman was planning something. But what? He knew any scheme of hers could only involve Garrison Petrie. Was she going to ask Haythorn to buy off the man with money? If that was her plan, she was doomed to disappointment.

When Petrie took on a job, he always saw it through. It was a point of pride with him. To do otherwise would ruin his professional reputation and his bounty hunting days would be over.

He would not let that happen.

Matt was standing on the boardwalk outside his office when Festus and his two punchers rode into Front Street. The afternoon was hot, the sun a ball of fire in a sky free of cloud, and the deputy's mule was dragging its feet, puffs of dust rising to its knees.

Festus swung out of the saddle and waved to his companions, who were already heading for the Long Branch, the trail thirst on them.

"Have any trouble?" Matt asked as his deputy joined him on the boards.

Festus shook his head. "Nary a bit o' trouble, Matthew. The Cheyenne surrounded the cows like they was golden and headed 'em toward the Arkansas. Them boys didn't even talk to us, just up and left. No, that ain't quite true. One young feller asked Lew Holmes for cartridges an' Lew gave him some forty-fours. That Injun seemed sure enough grateful."

The deputy stretched out his chin and thoughtfully scratched his hairy throat, as though deciding if what he had to impart next was worth the saying. "Matthew, on the way back, we cut some sign. Two riders had camped on a stream runnin' off the Buckner. Now this bein' summer an' all, that stream is more mud than water, so there were tracks aplenty where them two had gotten down into the streambed, maybe one with a coffeepot, the other scoopin' up water for him."

Festus looked uncertain. "Maybe what I'm sayin' don't mean a darn thing, on account of how most gossip ain't worth the repeatin' it gets."

Matt smiled. "Let me hear it anyhow."

"Well, one feller was a tallish man, wearin' boots. T'other was some shorter, but he had shoes on his feet." Festus' eyes shifted to Matt's. "Or maybe them elastic-sided ankle boots crazy ol' Barnabas wears."

As Matt thought this through, Festus' eyes followed a freight wagon as it trundled along the street and stopped outside a hardware store. Finally he said: "Matthew, them two had piled up some wood next to where they'd built their fire and they'd left their coffeepot and blankets. Seems to me they plan on headin' back there tonight."

"Maybe Shaklee and Wilson aim to sneak into

town after dark and kill another woman," Matt said, scowling in thought. "Afterward they could ride back to the creek and keep a cold camp until sunup. They know they'd never be seen out there in the darkness."

"They could have been camped there all along, Matthew," Festus said. "They ride into town, do their cuttin' and head back to the creek again."

Matt nodded. "I knew they had to be camped somewhere close. If there's another murder, we'll saddle up and head for the creek before Barnabas Shaklee gets a chance to wash off the bloodstains."

"Catch him red-handed, you mean."

"Exactly that," Matt said. "Red-handed, just like you say."

He nodded to the deputy's mule. "Festus, feed Ruth a bait of oats and let her rest up. Then right after dark, bring her and my horse here to the office. We'll do that every night until we get the chance to ride out and catch Shaklee and Wilson at the creek."

Doubt shadowed Festus' face. "Matthew, suppose Barnabas is all through with killin' for a spell? What do we do then?"

Matt shook his head. "A man like Shaklee is never through with killing. The urge to kill eats at him like a cancer and all he can do to ease the pain of it is to keep on killing."

The marshal's smile was grim, his eyes cold and hard. "This time if he kills in Dodge we'll hunt him down like the wild animal he is—and destroy him."

chapter 27

Two Shots Half
an Inch Apart

As night fell on Dodge, Matt and Festus were out
in the streets, their saddled mounts tied to the
hitching post outside the marshal's office.

The wind was blowing hard from the north, picking up sand and dust from summer-dry creek beds
and washes, driving a stinging yellow hail through
Dodge.

The sandstorm made men and animals irritable.
All over town dogs barked and out on the plains the
coyotes yipped their wretchedness. Scraps of newspaper, empty cardboard boxes and other debris tumbled along Front Street, rising into the air now and
then to fly briefly like stricken birds. Men and
women walked with their mouths covered, their eyes
red and gritty, feet crunching on sand lying thick on
the boardwalks. The sand sifted into their ears and
choked in their throats and the heedless, howling
wind mocked their misery.

A small herd of antelope, disoriented by the storm,

stumbled into town and, unnoticed, walked all the way along Texas Street before disappearing again into the lashing darkness.

And woe to the unwary pilgrim who stepped into a saloon and left the door open a second longer than was necessary. He had to duck a volley of angry curses and hurtling glasses as the sand spun around him and his stammering apology went unheard and unappreciated.

Matt slid his gun from the holster and shoved it in his pants pocket, where the action would be protected, and kept to his patrol of the dark alleys and back ways. His bandanna covered his mouth and his eyelids seemed to grate when he blinked and he had to fight a small battle for each and every breath.

Would even a madman with a need to kill like Barnabas Shaklee venture into town on such a night?

Matt had his doubts, but he doggedly kept up his tortuous progress around Dodge, exploring every nook and cranny where a killer might hide in the shadows.

He found nothing, the secret, dark places filled only by wind and flinging sand.

Matt regained the boardwalk and stepped back toward the marshal's office. His bay and Festus' mule were standing head down, turned away from the wind.

There would be no chasing after Shaklee this night. A man could get lost out there on the plains in the storm and wander in circles for hours.

Gathering up the reins of the mounts, Matt headed for the livery stable, his head bent against the wind. He heard feet pounding behind him and turned to see Festus, looking like a seedy desperado with a frayed bandanna over his nose and mouth.

"See anything, Matthew?" the deputy yelled over the wind.

"Not a thing. You?"

"Nothing. There's nobody in the street tonight. Seems like everybody is to home or holed up in a saloon."

"Then Shaklee won't be around either."

"If he has any sense in that fool head of his." Festus took his mule's reins and fell in step beside the marshal. "Matthew," he yelled, "when you reckon this sandstorm will blow over?"

"Don't rightly know. Soon I hope. They usually don't last long."

"Can't be soon enough for me."

The livery stable brought welcome shelter from the wind and hammering sand, though its warped pine boards creaked and wisps of hay spun crazily in circles on the dirt floor.

Matt unsaddled his horse and rubbed him down with a piece of sacking, taking special care to clean around the bay's crusted eyes. He led the animal into a stall, forked him some hay, then slung his saddle and bridle over the partition.

Festus stepped beside him and slipped his bandanna from his mouth. "Man sure needs to cut the dust from his throat on a night like this," he said, a hopeful gleam in the eye he'd turned to Matt.

"Then you go ahead and get yourself a drink," Matt said. "There's nothing much going to happen tonight. I reckon this storm is the best peace officer in the West."

"Why don't you step over to the Long Branch, Matthew? You look like you could use a drink your ownself, bein' all dusted over and sich."

"Maybe later, Festus. I'm going to head back to the office for a while and catch an hour or two of shut-eye."

John Wesley Hardin stepped out of the storm, the sand cartwheeling around him, the small, half-reluctant smile on his lips that Matt remembered so well. It was him and big, laughing Jeb Holcombe, still wearing his old buckskin jacket with the Arapaho beadwork down the front and across the shoulders.

Matt tried to rise from his desk, but couldn't move, as though he was paralyzed.

"Come celebrate with us, Matt," Hardin said, smiling wider, showing his white teeth. "Me and Jeb, we've come fast and far and we need a drink, being all dusted over an' sich."

Now Matt could move. He shook his head. "Wes, you shouldn't be walking in Dodge. The law is after you, man."

"You are the law in Dodge, Matt. You won't be taking me in, will you?"

"How you doin', Matt?" Holcombe asked before the marshal could answer.

He stroked his rust red beard. "Been a long time."

"Jeb," Matt said, "why do you walk in Dodge? You're dead these long years, a dozen springtimes ago. Remember, the Apaches caught you down in the Arroyo Baluarte country? They cut you up real bad, Jeb. I know because I was there. I helped bury you in the moonlight, me and Wes and a few others."

Hardin nodded. "Good times, Matt." He smiled. "Good times."

"Matt, Jeb is ripped up some," Hardin said, "but he ain't hardly dead." He turned to Holcombe. "Show him, Jeb."

Holcombe opened his jacket, showing his naked belly and chest, the terrible, gaping wound where he'd been cut deep from crotch to neck still angry red and glistening.

"Good times, Matt," the man said. "When it was me an' you an' Wes an' them."

Hardin drew his gun, fast and smooth from the shoulder holster under his left arm. "Let's celebrate old times, Matt!" he yelled. He laughed and fired his gun into the air.

One shot, then another.

Matt Dillon woke with a start, the memory of his terrifying dream slow to leave him, the hammer of gunshots still echoing along the corridors of his mind.

Outside booted feet pounded on the boardwalk and the office door flung wide open. Festus stood there, panting for breath, the blown sand swirling around him. "Matthew, come quick. There's been another killin'."

"Is it a woman?" Matt asked, his alarm clamoring.

"No," Festus said. "It's Garrison Petrie."

Petrie lay facedown on the floor in his room at the Dodge House. He had been shot twice in the back.

The man was naked from the waist up, his only clothing the bottom half of his long johns. He still clutched a sponge in his right hand and a basin of sandy water lay on the dresser.

The bounty hunter's room was on the first floor of the hotel, and his window was open a couple inches—enough for his killer to have taken aim and fired from outside.

"Large-caliber revolver shots, definitely," Doc Adams said, snapping his bag shut. "And only an inch and a half apart. Whoever did this knew how to use a gun." Doc's eyes went to the dead man, then returned to Matt. "Do you know him?"

"His name is Garrison Petrie. He was a bounty hunter out of Texas and other places."

Doc let his distaste for the dead man show. "Well, someone ended his bounty hunting days for good."

Matt heard a tap on the open door. He turned and saw Mitch Haythorn standing in the hallway, a Colt in his hand. "Heard the commotion and your voice, Marshal," he said. "Thought I better come down and see if you needed a hand."

Haythorn wore a white shirt with a frilled front, the top two buttons undone, and his tan pants were tucked into English riding boots.

"Why didn't you come down as soon as you heard the shots?" Matt asked.

Haythorn shrugged and shoved his gun in his waistband. "I hear shots all the time in Dodge," he said. "I figured it was none of my concern. That is, until I heard you and Doctor Adams down here. I thought it might be more of that Moonlight Ripper business."

Haythorn's eyes dropped to the dead man. "Good Lord, that's Garrison Petrie."

"Arrah tell you about him and his interest in her brother?" Matt asked.

"She did, Marshal. But then I knew Petrie from way back. I met him a time or two across the card tables, once in Fort Worth, another time in Denver. He was a sore loser, but he never gave me any trouble. Petrie had a rule never to shuck a gun unless somebody was paying him to shuck it." Haythorn smiled. "Call him the consummate professional."

"Speaking of guns, let me have that Colt," Matt said.

The gambler's smile slipped a little and his eyes hardened. "Marshal, if anyone but you had made that request I would have treated it as a shooting matter. However"—he took the gun from his waistband with his left hand and extended it to Matt—"under the circumstances, I'm willing to make an exception."

"Haythorn, that just fills me with gratitude," Matt said.

And Haythorn had the good grace to laugh.

"This gun has been fired quite recently," the marshal said. "There's powder residue all over the barrel and cylinder."

"I know," Haythorn said, his face bland. "This Ripper trouble has me concerned for Arrah's safety, so I took her down to the Arkansas this afternoon and taught her how to shoot." He smiled. "She did very well, caught on real fast." He nodded to the Colt in Matt's hands. "I was just about to clean that when all this fuss began."

Matt thumbed back the hammer to half-cock, opened the loading gate and checked the loads. None of the five rounds had been fired. He rotated the cylinder again and eased down the hammer on the empty chamber.

Haythorn raised an eyebrow. "Satisfied, Marshal?"

"For the moment," Matt answered, handing the gun back to Haythorn. "Just don't make any plans to leave town in a hurry."

"I will remain at your disposal, Marshal," the gambler bowed. "And now, if you will excuse me, I must return to my room and my lady."

After Haythorn left, Doc scowled. "I just can't stand that man. He's too smooth by half."

Matt was thoughtful, listening to the wind-driven sand pattering against the window. Finally he said: "Haythorn is smooth all right. He's also good with a gun." His eyes fixed on Doc. "Two shots an inch and a half apart, remember?"

The marshal shook his head as though trying to clear his racing mind. "I keep coming back to the fact that Haythorn claims he fired his gun while he was teaching Arrah Hillman to shoot, a woman he plans on tossing out of his life real soon. He figures she's only worth a couple of thousand dollars to him."

"Doesn't make much sense, does it?" Doc asked. "Why would he care that much about her?"

"That," Matt said, "is what I don't understand. But then again, why would he kill Garrison Petrie? He said himself that he had nothing against the man."

"Unless he's fallen in love with Arrah and wanted to save her brother," Doc said. "It happens, Matt, happens all the time."

The tall lawman nodded. "Maybe so, but I doubt it." Matt groaned. "Right now all I've got is a passel of questions, Doc—and no answers."

chapter 28

A Grim Discovery

Garrison Petrie's murder went almost unnoticed in Dodge, and only Matt and Percy Crump attended his boot hill funeral, the undertaker burying the man at first light while the wakening crows were noisily quarreling in the wild oaks.

The morning of Ben Hillman's fight with Bill Kennett was dawning bright, the sky blue to the horizon. The sandstorm had passed in the night and only a light wind came off the plains and wandered into Dodge, carrying with it the smell of grass and wildflowers.

After he left boot hill, Matt saddled his horse and rode out of town in the direction of Buckner Creek. He scouted the area but saw no sign of Barnabas Shaklee and Husky Wilson. The prairie stretched forever in all directions, and the two men could be holed up anywhere.

It was almost noon when the marshal got back to Dodge, put up his horse and returned to the office.

He'd just poured himself a cup of coffee and taken a seat at his desk when Ben Hillman stepped inside, a worried frown on his face.

"Marshal," the man said, "can I talk to you for a minute?"

Matt shoved a chair toward Hillman with his foot. "Take a seat and talk away. Is it about Petrie?"

Hillman sat, then said: "No, not about him. It's about G. P."

"What about him?"

"He's disappeared. I woke up this morning and discovered that he'd left the tent. That was around six, six thirty. He still hasn't come back." His eyes went to the clock. "It's now gone noon."

"Did you check the livery stable?"

"Yes, I did. His old buckskin horse isn't there."

Matt shrugged. "Maybe he decided to take a morning ride."

Hillman shook his head. "Proctor hates riding, says it chafes him. He'll only ride a horse when it's strictly necessary. We've joked about it. He says only a man with half a brain like me would have become a horse soldier."

"Ben, I'm sure he'll show up eventually. You're fighting Bill Kennett in a few hours, and as your manager, Proctor knows he must be here for that."

"I sure hope so, Marshal. He's carrying a lot of cash, all the money that was bet on the fight."

"How much money is that?"

"I don't know exactly, at least eight thousand, maybe more."

A small concern nagged at Matt. Had Proctor bumped into Shaklee and Wilson? They'd kill a man for a lot less money than Proctor was carrying.

Hillman saw that the marshal was turning things over in his mind and he sought to help. "I looked all over town, but didn't find hide nor hair of him."

Matt nodded. Another possibility was that Proctor had decided to take the betting money and make a run for it. Maybe he wasn't as confident as he seemed that Ben would win the fight. A lot of money had been bet on Kennett, and Proctor could soon see his profits vanish if he had to pay out.

"Ben, tell me what you know about Proctor," said Matt.

"I don't know much. I met him just after I, ah, quit the Army. He was operating a boxing booth in a small cow town on the Red, just some shacks with a scattering of stores and a saloon. Anyway, it was there that he took me on as his fighter." Hillman smiled. "Just as well, because we had to leave that town in a hurry a few days later."

"Oh, why was that?"

"A storekeeper's wife was found murdered in her bedroom and G. P. said since we were strangers in town and I was a colored man they'd try to pin the blame on us. So we saddled up right away and hit the trail north."

Alarm spiking at him, Matt leaned forward in his chair. "Ben, how was that woman killed? Did you hear?"

"She was strangled. That's what they said." Realization dawned on Hillman's face. "Marshal, she wasn't cut up, if that's what you're thinking. I certainly didn't do it, and G. P. was just as shocked as I was when he heard about it. There were saddle tramps in that town and some shady-looking Mexicans up from the Rio Grande. Any one of them could have killed her."

"This woman," Matt persisted, "was she young, old?"

"Real young and real pretty," Hillman said. "She served us once when G. P. and me bought coffee and sugar at her husband's store."

A seed of suspicion had been planted in Matt's mind, but he did not want it to grow out of control. He had no real reason to suspect that G. P. Proctor was the Moonlight Ripper. His flight from the Red River was probably just a case of a man being in the wrong town at the wrong time.

But could he be in cahoots with Shaklee and Wilson?

Matt also dismissed that thought from his mind. He was sure those two had acted alone, and three made a crowd that would surely have attracted attention.

The marshal shook his head, telling himself that, like the cowboy who'd shot Louie Pheeters, he was chasing after shadows.

Barnabas Shaklee was the Ripper. Matt was sure of it.

"Anything else you'd care to add, Ben?" he asked.

"There's not much to add, Marshal. G. P. never talked much about his life. He did tell me one time that his mother died when he was young. He was raised by his father, a gambler who worked the riverboats. When he was fifteen, his pa died of some mysterious illness—he'd never tell me what it was—and from then on, G. P. made his own way."

"Well, I'm sure he'll show up before the fight," Matt said.

"And if he doesn't?"

"Then I'll round up a posse and go looking for him."

"I sure hope it doesn't come to that," Ben said, his face worried. "I set store by that man."

Matt let that pass and said: "How are you feeling, Ben?"

The man smiled. "Good, Marshal, real good. In fact, I'm looking forward to putting Kennett's back on the canvas. After this evening, I don't reckon he'll want to fight me again."

"Well, good luck," Matt said. "And don't worry about Proctor. I'm sure he'll show. Bad pennies always do."

Matt spent the early hours of the afternoon walking around town, his restless eyes searching for any sign of Shaklee and Wilson. He had no doubt that the men were close and planning more killings.

But the hundreds of punchers in town and the businessmen from across the tracks were not making it easy for them. Even at this early hour, every woman he saw had a male escort, the men wearing guns where they could be seen.

The settlers had already pulled out, and for that, the marshal was grateful. Now the wives and daughters of the farmers were out of danger and that was one less thing he had to worry about.

Matt was standing outside the Alamo Saloon, watching the busy wagon and buggy traffic on the street, when Festus' rat posse walked past him, now swollen to a dozen urchins with determined expressions, ferocious clubs in their hands.

"Where are you boys headed?" Matt asked, stopping the band in its tracks.

A freckled towhead with green eyes and a gap in his front teeth was obviously their leader, because he stepped forward as spokesman. "Deputy Haggen says we're to search all over town for rats, make sure none have come up this way from the feed sheds."

Aware that the rest, none of whom stood taller than his knees, were looking at him with a kind of fascinated attention, Matt asked: "You catch any?"

The boy's face fell. "Nary a one. We thought we'd trapped one behind the Comique but it turned out to be an ol' bullfrog that had hopped out of the water tank."

"An that's bad," another boy said, "because Deputy Haggen said you'd give us a penny for every tail we brung you."

Matt studied this boy a little closer. "You're Bob Conlan's son, aren't you?"

The kid nodded. "Yup, Marshal, he's my pa."

"How is he? Last I heard he was ailing."

"Ma got him back on his feet. She said all Pa needed to cure his misery was chicken soup in his belly and mustard poultices on his chest."

"Glad to hear that," Matt said. "Your pa is the best carpenter in town."

"We got to be goin', Marshal," the towhead said quickly. "Deputy Haggen would be mighty upset if he saw us standing here talking instead of rat huntin'."

Matt reached into his pocket and found a dollar. He spun it to the towhead, who caught it deftly. "Rat huntin' is thirsty work," the marshal said. "You boys head on down to Wilbur Jonas' store and buy yourself some soda pops."

The towhead grinned. "Gee, thanks, Marshal." The other boys crowded around him, looking at the dollar like it was a rare and fabulous treasure.

A moment later a dozen pairs of bare feet were pounding down the boardwalk toward the general store, the boys whooping and hollering, delighted at their unexpected stroke of luck.

Matt was still grinning when he turned at the sound of a woman's voice.

"Does a lady have to lunch by herself in Dodge, Marshal Dillon?"

Kitty was smiling at him, looking beautiful in an afternoon dress of green taffeta, the bustle very large, the latest style all the fashionable belles in town were wearing.

"It would be my pleasure, Miss Russell." Matt grinned. "I was just thinking of grabbing some grub."

An annoyed little frown wrinkled Kitty's forehead. "Matt, when a man enters a restaurant with a lady, he partakes of lunch." She shook her head at him. "He doesn't grab some grub."

"Sorry." Matt's grin grew wider as he gave the woman his arm. "Then shall we stroll down to Ma's Kitchen and partake?"

"That," Kitty said, "is so much better."

The lunch hour had come and gone and the restaurant was empty when Kitty and Matt entered. They found a table and were scanning the handwritten menus when a bald man in a stained white apron stepped out of the kitchen.

"Everything on there is off, Marshal," he said. He nodded to Kitty and smiled. "Seemed like folks were real hungry today, Miss Kitty."

"You mean you have nothing left for us to eat, Chauncey?" Kitty said, pretending alarm.

Chauncey Webb had been a trail cook for old Charlie Goodnight and was reckoned by all to be one of the best pot rustlers west of the Mississippi.

"Now would I let you go hungry, Miss Kitty, or you either, Marshal?" He smiled. "I've got a real nice joint of roast beef, and the potatoes that was cooked with it, and carrots. You like carrots?"

"Sounds just fine to me," Matt said.

"And to me," Kitty added. "And, Chauncey, some cold buttermilk to drink?"

"Comin' right up," Webb said. "And I saved some apple pie for later."

The food was good and Matt and Kitty ate with an appetite. They had just finished their pie, which Kitty allowed to Webb was the highlight of the meal, when the door swung open and the young towheaded boy stepped inside.

The kid's eyes swept the room and he walked to Matt's table.

"Marshal," he said, "we found something behind the boxing booth while we was huntin' them rats for Deputy Haggen."

Kitty made a disgusted face, as Matt asked: "What is it?"

The boy shrugged. "Dunno. But we think maybe somebody is buried back there."

chapter 29

The Madman's Diary

Matt rose to his feet, wiped his lips with the napkin and laid some money on the table. "Excuse me, Kitty." He smiled. "Duty calls."

"I understand." Her eyes lifted to the marshal. "Be careful, Matt."

Matt nodded, then put his hand on the boy's shoulder. "What's your name, boy?"

"Lonnie Pemberton, Marshal."

"Then show me what you found, Lonnie," he said.

The sun was lowering in a blue sky tinged with pink as Matt and the boy quickly crossed Front Street. There was an impatience in Lonnie that had not been there before, and his freckled face looked pale under his sun-reddened skin.

The boy craned his neck to look up the marshal and said: "It was Tom Cates that found the grave. He saw something sticking up out of the ground and pulled on it."

"A bone?" Matt asked, thinking that Tom had

found the relic of a long dead buffalo or some other animal.

"No, Marshal, it's a coat. It's a man's coat and it's got bloodstains all over it."

Now Lonnie had the marshal's undivided attention. Was the sandy area behind the booth the place where Barnabas Shaklee had disposed of his bloody clothes?

Matt quickened his pace and the boy had to run to keep up. "Round that way, Marshal," Lonnie said, pointing to the side of the tent closest to them.

When the marshal reached the back of the tent, he saw the rest of the boys crowded around a disturbed patch in the sand, close to a clump of bunchgrass, an empty beer bottle tangled in its roots.

Stepping through the boys, Matt saw a coat lying in a heap on the ground, one arm spread out, rust-colored bloodstains to its elbow.

He recognized that coat. It was pearl gray and he'd recently seen G. P. Proctor wearing it. Matt grabbed a club from one of the boys and spread out the coat on the dirt. The entire front and both sleeves were covered in bloodstains.

Digging deeper with the club, the marshal uncovered a shirt, then another and finally a second coat, this one in a loud check. Again he recognized it as a coat worn by Proctor.

Helped by the eager boys, Matt dug deeper, but found nothing else—to the obvious disappointment of Lonnie Pemberton and the others.

"It's just a pile of old clothes," the boy said. "There ain't no body here."

Matt pointed to a kid who looked to be all of eight

or nine. "You," he said, "go into the tent and see if Mr. Hillman is there."

"The boxer?"

"Yes, him. Now go!"

The boy nodded and disappeared around the corner of the booth. Within a few minutes, he returned with Ben Hillman in tow.

"My God, Marshal, it's not G. P., is it?" Hillman asked, looking stricken.

Matt ignored the question and asked one of his own. "Ben, do you recognize these clothes?"

Hillman followed the marshal's eyes to the ground. He got down on one knee and gingerly lifted a corner of the checked coat. After a few moments, he said: "This belongs to G. P." He nodded to the gray coat. "And so does that."

Hillman lifted haunted eyes to Matt. "I . . . I don't understand. What's going on here, Marshal? All these clothes are covered in blood. Is . . . is G. P. dead?"

"Ben, you're sure they're Proctor's coats?"

"Yes, I'm sure. G. P. told me that Stella made him give these old clothes away. She said they were too loud and made him look like some kind of sideshow barker at a one-pony circus." The man thought for a few moments, then said: "He got rid of the gray one first, then the check. And he said he'd also given away his fancy shirts since Stella didn't like them, either."

The seed of suspicion that had been planted in Matt's mind when Hillman had told him about the murder of the storekeeper's wife now took root and grew.

"Ben, did Proctor leave anything in the tent before he left this morning?" he asked.

"I don't think so, Marshal. I didn't really look around."

"Well, let's go do that now," Matt said. He glanced down at the boys, who were looking up at him in rapt attention. "You boys go on home now. It's getting late and your folks will be worried about you."

"Aw," Lonnie said, "we miss out on all the fun." He picked up his club, turned and walked back toward the street, the rest reluctantly trailing after him.

"Now let's go look around the tent," Matt said to Hillman.

The two men searched all corners of the boxing booth but found nothing.

"He's taken everything, Marshal," Hillman said, his eyes concerned, "even his carpetbag. I hadn't noticed that before."

Both the iron and canvas cots were still set up near the ring, since the fight wasn't scheduled until later that night. Matt threw back the blankets of Proctor's cot and found something he hadn't bargained for— the notebook he'd seen the man scribble in was still there.

"Ben, here's something," Matt said, picking up the book.

"Marshal, that's G. P.'s private journal," he said. "I don't think we should be reading that."

"Why would he leave it behind if it meant that much to him?"

Hillman shrugged. "I don't know. He just forgot it, I guess."

"Or he meant us to find it," Matt said.

"But why would he do that?"

"Because he's insane," Matt answered. His eyes found Hillman's. "Ben, I believe I've been wrong all along. Barnabas Shaklee isn't the Moonlight Ripper. It's Proctor. He left the tent at night, did his killing, including the murder of Stella Shaklee, then came back and buried his bloody clothes behind the tent. He told you Stella had ordered him to get rid of his loud coats, but that was a lie."

Hillman shook his head. "That's impossible. I would have heard him come and go."

"Are you a sound sleeper, Ben?"

"Most nights."

"Did Proctor give you anything to drink before you went to bed?"

"Yes, he did. He always gave me a shot of brandy, said it would help me sleep. He said I needed a good night's rest to keep up my strength."

"Ben, on those nights when Proctor's inner demons drove him to kill a woman, he slipped something into your brandy. I don't know what it was, a powder or drops, but it knocked you unconscious. That's why you didn't hear him come and go. You were drugged."

"But why would he murder Stella? He said he thought he was falling in love with her."

Matt shook his head. "I believe a killer like Proctor is incapable of loving any woman. For some reason, he's down on females, especially saloon girls. Stella must have told him she'd be at the railroad trellis bridge the night her brothers tried to kill Festus and me. He went there, waited until we'd left and then ripped her to pieces. When he stalked the three other women, he hid himself in the darkness and watched for his chance. When the time was right, he struck."

Hefting the journal in his hand, the marshal asked: "Now are you sure you don't want me to read this book?"

Hillman's face was like stone, his black eyes tormented. "Read it, Marshal." He bowed his head and squeezed the bridge of his nose with his thumb and middle finger and whispered, "Just . . . just read it."

Matt opened the diary and stepped into a world of shrieking madness. Every entry was written in block letters, like the warning Proctor had pinned to the door of the marshal's office. The very first page gave the reason for the man's deranged loathing of women and might have been written just before he fled Dodge.

BIG BOSS, I SAW MY FATHER, THE MAN I LOVED, BECOME RAVING MAD FROM THE SYPHILIS HE CAUGHT FROM A DISEASED DOVE. I MADE A VOW AT HIS GRAVESIDE THAT I WOULD CUT AT DOVES UNTIL THERE WERE NONE LEFT TO SPREAD THEIR VILE POISONS. AND I WILL KEEP ON CUTTING UNTIL I SWING FOR IT.

On the following pages, going back fifteen years, were detailed descriptions of the murders of twenty-three women in towns all over the West, four in Texas, including the storekeeper's pretty wife, others in the Indian Territory, New Mexico and as far north as Nevada. Proctor dwelled sadistically on his killing of Stella Shaklee, noting that her screams had given him the most satisfaction of all.

A curling sickness in the pit of his stomach, Matt wordlessly passed the journal to Hillman. The man opened the book and read, his wide face revealing more and more horror with every page.

Finally Hillman slammed the journal shut, and his knees suddenly weak, he sank to the edge of his cot. His eyes lifted to Matt. "He never gave any hint of how he felt. I . . . I thought G. P. was one of the sanest men I'd ever met, a hard-nosed businessman who thought of nothing but money and profit."

"He hid it well behind a hearty carnival barker front," Matt said. "But Proctor isn't a businessman or any kind of man, come to that. He's a mad dog and he's filled with so much hatred it will drive him to kill again and go on killing."

Hillman's eyes were bleak. "What happens now, Marshal?"

"I'm going after him. I'll arrest Proctor, bring him back to Dodge and see him hang."

Hillman waved a hand. "You'll never find him out there. He could be riding in any direction, even heading for the mountains."

"I don't believe so," Matt said. "I think he'll strike south for the Indian Territory. Proctor can lose himself there, where the law is thin on the ground, and move on again when the time is right."

Rising to his feet, Hillman said: "After this, there won't be any fight tonight or any other night. I'm through with it, Marshal."

"And Arrah?"

"I don't know. I guess I'll go talk to Haythorn again."

"Ben, wait until I get back to Dodge. Mitch Haythorn is a sudden, dangerous man, and I don't want you meeting him alone."

Hillman nodded. "I'll do that, Marshal. Right now I have to find Bill Kennett and tell him the fight is canceled."

Matt managed a faint smile. "I think maybe Bill will be relieved. He's been telling people his ribs are paining him considerable."

The marshal left the boxing booth and glanced at the sky, flaming red and violet to the horizon, the light around him shading into the pale blue of evening.

He would set out after Proctor at first light tomorrow morning.

But tonight he needed to hire on a first-rate scout.

chapter 30

Manhunt

"**Y**ou're the best tracker in town, Quint. If anybody can find him, you can."

The handsome, hard-muscled blacksmith grinned. "That's only the Indian half of me, Matt. The white half can't track worth a damn."

"I know." Matt smiled in return. "But I'll still pay two dollars a day. That's wages for a whole man."

Quint Asper untied his leather apron and hung it on a pine beam by his cold forge. "Of course I'll track for you, Matt. But I don't want wages. I figure finding Proctor is a service to the community."

"I knew you'd say that, Quint," the marshal said. "Be ready at sunup."

The blacksmith pointed to Matt's mangled belt buckle. "You'd better let me straighten that out for you."

"I will," Matt said, "but I don't want to part with my gun belt until Proctor is in my jail, in the cell next to Barnabas Shaklee and Husky Wilson."

"You think those two were tied up with Proctor?"

The marshal shook his head. "No, but I believe Shaklee murdered a young cowboy on the trail and then killed and robbed a drummer here in Dodge. I don't have proof, but I figure I can get Wilson to rat on Shaklee to save himself from the noose. Hanging one killer out of two isn't bad."

Asper shook his head. "Sure have your work cut out for you, don't you, Matt?"

"Comes with the badge." The marshal waved a hand. "Quint, I'll meet you outside my office at sunup."

"The Indian half of me will be there, Matt. Count on it."

Matt and Asper clattered across the wooden bridge over the Arkansas and headed due south toward the bend of Rattlesnake Creek. Fifty miles ahead lay the border of the Indian Territory, and if Proctor had made it that far, they'd have no chance of catching him.

Asper, wearing a buckskin jacket decorated with blue-and-gray Cheyenne beadwork and a low-crowned and flat-brimmed black hat, constantly leaned out of the saddle, casting around for sign. Matt, a good tracker himself, scanned the plains to the horizon, leaving the close scouting to Asper. The big blacksmith had an ability to read a trail that was born with a man. It was an instinctive skill that was common among Indians but was rare in white men and not easily learned.

After two hours, as the cottonwoods lining the creek came in sight, Asper began to range farther afield, tracking back and forth ahead of Matt like a rider on a switchback trail, his head bent to the grass passing under his stirrups.

The sun had begun its climb into the sky to the east and the morning was already warm, the prairie stretching away from the two riders in all directions, vast, empty and silent. It was a land where a man on the dodge could vanish completely, melting like ice in summer sunlight into the distance, where the seductive mirages shimmered.

Matt saw Asper suddenly draw rein and lift his nose to the talking wind.

"Quint," he yelled, "you on to something?"

"Over here, Matt."

The marshal spurred his horse and pulled alongside Asper. "Do you smell something?"

"Maybe. Wood smoke, I think, but slight, from a dying fire." The blacksmith pointed to the ground just ahead of his paint. "Droppings, from a horse that passed this way some time yesterday. And the grass is still bent where it walked."

"Proctor?"

"Could be. If it was him, I'm guessing he made camp on Rattlesnake Creek and then pulled out early this morning." His brown eyes slanted to the marshal. "Matt, if it is Proctor, he's not too far ahead of us."

"Quint, he had the whole day to ride yesterday. Why didn't he keep on heading for the border?"

Asper smiled. "The white man in me says, how the hell should I know? The Indian says, this is a man who wants to be caught."

"Why do you say that?"

"Because he wants you to kill him, Matt. An insane man who now and then has moments of sanity will look upon his bouts of madness as terrible nightmares. He wakes in terror from each one and does not want to ever sleep again." Asper's eyes held on Matt's. "The only way to end the nightmares is to die and hope his long sleep will no longer be troubled by demons."

The planes of Matt's face hardened. "I want to take Proctor alive and hang him."

Asper shrugged. "No matter. The rope accomplishes the same aim as the bullet. He will be dead, and that's what matters to him."

"You know something, Quint," Matt said. "I think I liked the white man's answer a whole lot better."

They found the ashes of Proctor's fire by the creek, a wisp of smoke trailing from the last of the embers.

"He left here an hour ago, Matt," the blacksmith said. "Maybe less."

The marshal nodded. "Quint, I'll take it from here. You did what I asked you to do, but from now on, there may be shooting to be done and you've no call to get mixed up in gunplay."

"Matt, my ma always told me, 'Run when you're wrong. Shoot when you're right.' Well, I reckon I'm in the right, so if it's all the same to you, I'll stick."

"So be it. But from now on, keep your eyes skinned and your rifle close."

The two men rode across gently rolling country cut through by dry streambeds, tangled stands of prickly pear bunched on their banks. They rode in silence, their eyes scanning the land around them, the only sound the soft creak of leather.

By noon the heat was relentless. Matt had filled his canteen at the creek, but he had drunk often, and it sloshed less than a third full. Ahead of them lay only far-flung emptiness, where nothing moved but the long grass rippling in the wind and the occasional shadow scudding across the plain when a white cloud passed the face of the sun.

Quint Asper broke the silence. "Matt, about half-a-mile ahead of us on your left."

A far-seeing man, the marshal probed the distance. A ruined sod cabin stood beside a solitary cottonwood that had split apart during a winter freeze. The tree was dead, its shattered trunk bone white, and it raised skeletal fingers to the sky.

"What do you think, Matt?" Asper asked, drawing rein.

Matt stopped his bay. "It's probably an old buffalo hunter's shack, and it looks like it hasn't been used in quite a spell."

The roof of the cabin was long gone and its sod walls were broken down, in most places no more than a couple feet high.

"Now, if a man wanted to set up for an ambush, that would be an ideal place," Asper said.

Matt studied the shack more closely. It lay at the top of a shallow rise, but high enough that Proctor could have picketed his horse out of sight on the opposite slope. If the man was hidden behind the low walls, he had an excellent field of fire in all directions, there being little cover but scattered clumps of prickly pear and a few yucca.

As the marshal watched, a jay flew toward the ruin, then suddenly soared away and headed back in the opposite direction.

The bird's startled flight was not lost on Matt, nor had Asper missed its significance. "He's there all right, Matt, laying for us. I reckon he must have seen us coming from a long ways off." He turned his head to the tall lawman. "How do we play this?"

Matt's smile was grim, his chin set and determined. "Quint, they say faint heart never filled a flush." He slid his Winchester from under his knee and racked a round into the chamber. "And I reckon a bunch of kids back in Dodge taught me something."

"What's that?"

"When you need to flush out a rat, go right at it."

Asper grinned and shucked his old brass-framed Henry. As Matt had done, he levered a round into the chamber and then asked: "Any special prayers you want said at your funeral, Marshal Dillon?"

The big marshal laughed. "Yeah. Just say, 'Here lies a jackass of a lawman who thought he had horse sense.'"

He set spurs to his horse and charged for the cabin, Asper pounding close behind him yelling a wild, whooping war cry.

chapter 31

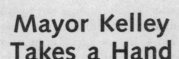

Mayor Kelley
Takes a Hand

G. P. Proctor rose up from behind the ruined wall of the cabin, a Smith & Wesson Russian in his hand. He fired at Matt, missed and triggered a round at Asper.

Matt heard the blacksmith grunt in pain as the bullet hit home. Then the marshal was firing his rifle from the shoulder.

Proctor was hit hard, sudden blood blossoming on the front of his white shirt. The man staggered back a few steps and Matt charged home. He had no time to shove his Winchester back in the scabbard, so he threw it aside and drew his Colt. The work was now at short range and the revolver was a better close-up weapon.

Matt felt the bay bunch under him for a jump and the big horse cleared the ruined cabin's low sod wall. Proctor had retreated to the far wall, and he was firing again, holding his gun at eye level with both hands. A bullet split the air close to Matt's cheek. Then Matt fired and fired again.

Proctor screamed as both of the lawman's bullets found their marks. One smashed into Proctor's left shoulder; the other hit the man's gun. The round deflected off the cylinder, ranged upward and tore away half of Proctor's jaw.

A last, bubbling shriek and the man fell against the low sod wall and hung there, bent over backward, his arms spread wide.

Matt glanced behind him at Asper. The blacksmith was sitting his saddle, holding his right thigh, blood seeping between his fingers.

"Quint, are you hit bad?" Matt yelled.

Asper shook his head. "I don't think so. The bullet hit my thigh and went right on through. I reckon it missed the bone."

"Stay right where you are," Matt hollered.

Asper flashed a tight smile. "I wasn't planning on going anywhere, Matt."

Matt swung out of the saddle and stepped toward Proctor, his gun up and ready. He hooked a boot behind the man's ankles and kicked them away so that Proctor's legs went out from under him and he slid to a sitting position at the base of the wall.

The man's face was a nightmare of blood and splintered bone, but he was still alive and his tongue moved as he tried to speak. Finally he managed: "You done for me at last, big boss."

"I just wish it had been a lot sooner," Matt said.

Scarlet fingers ran down Proctor's chin, and the marshal realized the grotesque expression on the man's face was a grin. "I don't regret it," he said. "I don't regret a damn thing."

"Why did you leave your journal for me to find?" the marshal asked, trying to fit together the last pieces of the puzzle.

"Just for fun, big boss. I thought you'd enjoy reading about what I done to them doves."

Proctor coughed. All the life that was in him was draining away fast. "I could . . . I could have got away clean, but I wanted to cut your suspenders for you before I left. You consort with a known dove, Dillon. I decided long ago that you had to die for that."

A small anger flared in Matt. He thumbed back the hammer of his Colt and pointed the gun at Proctor's head.

"Go ahead, Marshal . . . finish it."

After a moment of struggling with himself, Matt eased down the hammer and holstered the gun. "Proctor, you're a sorry piece of trash," he said.

The man gurgled deep in his throat, choking on his own blood. His eyes lifted to Matt's, and he raised a hand, chopping it back and forth as though he was holding a knife. "Cut . . . cut . . . cut . . ." He grinned.

Behind Matt a rifle roared and the bullet smashed into Proctor's forehead. The marshal turned and saw Quint Asper lowering his smoking gun from his shoulder.

"I think," the blacksmith said, "that man has talked long enough."

The day was shading into night and the lamps along Front Street were already lit when Matt and Asper rode up on the marshal's office.

Matt led Proctor's saddled horse, but they'd left the man's body back at the ruined cabin, agreeing that even coyotes deserved full bellies now and then.

"Quint, you'd better go see Doc Adams about that leg," Matt said.

The blacksmith nodded. "It is paining me considerable."

Matt stuck out his hand. "Thanks for the help, Quint. And I'm sorry you had to get shot on my account."

"It wasn't only on your account, Matt. I was doing it for the town and all those women who died. If ever I wanted to help kill a man, it was Proctor." Asper touched his hat. "I'll be seeing you, Marshal." He kneed his horse into a walk, and then called out over his shoulder: "Don't forget about your buckle."

Matt unsaddled the horses at the livery stable, then returned to his office. He had just poured himself coffee and sat at his desk when Mayor Kelley stepped inside. "Saw you and Quint Asper ride in, Matt," he said. "Mind telling me what's going on?"

Matt took a swig of his coffee and told the mayor about Proctor, sparing none of the details.

After the marshal was through talking, Kelley sat for long moments in stunned silence, then said, his voice a croak: "Matt, do you have any whiskey stashed away? To wet my whistle, like."

Matt smiled, reached into his drawer and produced a bottle and glass. He poured the mayor a stiff drink, which the man downed in a gulp. He extended his glass again and the marshal refilled it.

"I . . . I just can't believe it, Matt. G. P. Proctor was the Moonlight Ripper. Hell, I liked the man."

"Easy enough to make that mistake, Mayor," Matt said evenly. "All Proctor's demons were on the inside, where they were hidden. Only the women he murdered saw them emerge."

"May God rest those poor girls," Kelley said, reaching for his drink.

"We still have three unsolved murders in Dodge, Mayor," Matt said. "The killer of the drummer, the young McDermott kid and Garrison Petrie."

"You suspect—"

"Barnabas Shaklee," Matt interrupted. "At least I believe he murdered the drummer and the young cowboy."

"And the bounty hunter?"

"I don't know as yet, Mayor. But I aim to find out real soon."

Kelley shook his head. "Matt, Shaklee is long gone by this time. You'll never find him."

"I don't think so, Mayor. I think he's holed up close to town, him and a gunman by the name of Husky Wilson."

"But why? If Shaklee knows you're on to him, why would he stay around here?"

"Two reasons. The first is that he wants Festus and me dead for killing his sons. The second, and maybe more important to him, is that he lusts for a woman."

"Plenty of those around here who would be more than willing to accommodate him."

"Not just any woman, Mayor. He wants Arrah Hillman. Shaklee already paid a drifter to kidnap her, but Mitch Haythorn caught the man in the act and killed him."

Kelley nodded. "I heard about that. Didn't know Shaklee was involved, though."

"He's involved all right. Arrah is a beautiful woman, and the way I see it, he's developed an obsession for her, wants to tame her with a whip and make her his wife or something close."

The mayor scowled, his shrewd Irish mind working. "Matt, I just had a thought. If Barnabas Shaklee is obsessed by Miss Hillman, he might have feared that Garrison Petrie would take her away from him."

"I don't catch your drift, Mayor."

"Marshal, by nature I'm a high-talking man, but I'm also a watcher and listener. There was talk around town that you planned on riding with Petrie and Ben Hillman to Texas."

"That's true. I told Ben I would."

"Well, there was other talk. The rumor around the saloons was that Arrah had told Mitch Haythorn she was going along with you. Haythorn said he would accompany her, that Marshal Dillon would need another gun on the trail."

"That, I didn't hear," Matt said, annoyed with himself that he'd missed it.

"Like I said, I'm a listening man. Dodge talks loud, and it could be that Shaklee heard the same rumor and decided he had to get rid of Petrie. He must have known that his chances of getting to Arrah were slim to none with you and Haythorn protecting her."

Matt thought that through, reminding himself that Petrie had been killed by someone who was handy with a gun. Both Shaklee himself or Husky Wilson fit that bill.

"Mayor, what you say makes sense," Matt said finally. "Shaklee is a bushwhacker who wouldn't hesitate to shoot a man in the back. He couldn't take a chance on Petrie losing him his woman, so he snuck up to the Dodge House and gunned him."

"That sounds like the way of it, Matt. But there are still three men standing in his path, you, Haythorn and Festus." Kelley drained his glass. "Step careful, Matt. You step real careful."

chapter 32

Medal for a Hero

After the mayor left the office, Matt had another visitor. It was Ben Hillman. "Marshal, Quint Asper just stopped by the boxing booth and said he had to talk to me. He told me what happened with G. P. Proctor." He shook his head. "I took it hard."

"I wouldn't grieve for a man like Proctor, Ben. He isn't worth it." He waved the man into a chair and asked: "How is Quint?"

"His leg is bandaged, but he says the Doc told him it was a flesh wound and that he'll be fine in a few weeks. Quint says it's paining him some, but he can still get around." Hillman hesitated, then said: "Marshal, when I said I took it hard, I meant the realization that the man I rode a dozen trails with was such a cold-blooded killer. I can wash my hands, as I've done maybe fifty times tonight, but I still can't wash my conscience."

Matt shrugged. "You're not to blame, Ben. As I just told Mayor Kelley, all Proctor's demons were hidden deep inside him. You can't look through a man into his soul like he was made of glass."

Hillman nodded, his face bleak. "I came in to tell you I've reached a decision. After I talk to Haythorn and do what I can for Arrah, I'm heading for Fort Dodge and giving myself up as a deserter. At least that part of my conscience will be clean."

"Ben, that's up to you. But as a lawman I can only tell you that you're doing the right thing." Matt leaned forward in his chair. "How do you think the Army will take it?"

Hillman managed a weak smile. "I didn't desert in the face of the enemy, and they'll take that into consideration. I'm guessing loss of rank and maybe some time in the stockade. Then they'll return me to my regiment." The man's smile faded further. "At least, I'm hoping that's what happens."

"What about that business in Texas?"

"I'll tell them, of course. Maybe the Army will send me back there to face the music, but I doubt it." Hillman reached into his pocket and held something tight in his hand. "I've never shown you this before, Marshal. It's the thing I'm hoping might make the difference." Hillman laid his hand on the desk and opened his fist. A medal dropped onto the scuffed pine.

Matt was silent for long moments, then said: "I've heard about those, never seen one up close until tonight." He picked up the Congressional Medal of Honor and asked: "How did it happen, Ben?"

The young man shrugged. "I once told you that I was with Colonel Shafter during his campaign against the Comanche on the Staked Plains. During one fight I collected an arrow in the thigh, but got it patched up and stayed with the regiment.

"Our officer, a young West Pointer with more sand than sense, managed to get him and me cut off from the rest of our troop. His horse was down, he was badly wounded and we were surrounded by Comanche. I rode among them, fought them off with my rifle and then my Colt and got the lieutenant up on my horse. I told him to hightail it out of there, and then I took up a position among some rocks. I fought it out with the Indians until the regiment arrived."

Hillman picked up the medal. "Afterward Shafter himself patted me on the back and told me I'd done good. A month later they gave me this."

"The Army's highest award for gallantry," Matt said, suddenly looking at Hillman in a new light. "Colonel Shafter was right—you done good."

"Saving that white officer was nothing more than any other Buffalo Soldier would have done." He paused, then shook his head. "Still, when all was said and done, they gave the medal to me. Think it will make a difference, Marshal?"

"I'm sure of it. The Army may reopen the murder case and appoint a lawyer to defend you." Matt smiled. "Or the brass might just say to heck with it and pack you off to some remote post in the New Mexico or Arizona territories."

Rising to his feet, Hillman said: "I guess what's bound to happen will happen. A man can't change his destiny like he changes his socks."

"Ben, meet me tomorrow morning and we'll go

talk to Haythorn. I can't promise you anything, but maybe I can help him see reason." Matt stood. "And there's one more thing. . . ."

The marshal crossed the room and picked up scuffed saddlebags. "These belonged to Proctor and all the betting money he collected is here. See if you can get it back to the right people. Bat Masterson and Doc Holliday will be mighty grateful."

"I'll do that right now," Hillman said. "There must be a scrip in there somewhere with the names of people and how much they bet." The young man settled the saddlebags over his shoulder. "See you in the morning, Marshal."

"Bright and early," Matt said.

After Hillman left, Matt went looking for Festus to warn him to stay close. He stepped into the crowded Long Branch, but Kitty told him she hadn't seen the deputy all night.

"But Quint was in earlier to get a drink, said his wounded leg was paining him," she said. "He told me about Proctor." The woman shuddered. "I'm glad that's over."

"Maybe you should spread the word, Kitty," Matt said.

"I already have. The news is all around town." She looked up at the tall lawman, a frown gathering on her face. "Matt, Quint told me what you did out there, charging right into Proctor's gun. You take too many chances. I don't want to lose you like that."

Matt smiled. "Kitty, caution should not be too cautious. A wise man told me that one time."

"And who was he?"

The marshal shook his head. "Danged if I can recollect. But he was wise. I remember that."

"Just don't do it again, Matt. The way you act sometimes—well, it's a very worrisome thing."

"I'll be more careful in the future, Kitty, I promise. In the meantime, I have to find my missing deputy."

"Try the Alamo," Kitty said, her lips pursing like she'd just tasted something sour. "Sometimes Festus hangs out over there, swapping lies with Doc Holliday and a few other ne'er-do-wells."

"Sounds about right." Matt grinned. "I never could take to Holliday, but for some reason, Festus sets store by him."

"Oh, dear, it couldn't possibly be that Doc is mighty generous when it comes to buying drinks for lawmen who are always broke?" Kitty said, smiling like a cat.

Like the Long Branch, the Alamo was crowded with punchers, ranchers and businessmen of every stripe, from plug-hatted drummers to cattle buyers and real estate agents in elegant broadcloth.

As Matt made his way through the throng, men patted him on the back, congratulating him on tracking down the Moonlight Ripper, and by the time he reached Doc Holliday's gaming table, his cheeks were smeared red from the lipstick and rouge of the celebrating saloon girls.

Holliday's cold blue eyes lifted to Matt as he stepped up to his table. "I'd give you a kiss myself, Marshal," he said dryly, "but that would hardly be appropriate between gentlemen."

"I'll gladly pass on that, Doc," Matt said. He

wiped his cheeks with the back of his hand, getting rid of the makeup.

"What a pity," Doc said. "I thought it quite became you."

Matt let that go and asked: "Have you see Deputy Haggen?"

Holliday nodded. "That stalwart star strutter was here abut fifteen minutes ago, talking to my colleague Mitch Haythorn"—Holliday jerked a thumb over his shoulder—"over there at the poker table in the corner by the stage."

Matt was surprised and slightly alarmed. "Haythorn is here? Is Arrah with him?"

"Marshal, the Alamo is one of Mr. Haythorn's places of business. Why should he not be here? As for the breathtakingly beautiful Miss Hillman, no, she's not with him, more's the pity."

Holliday opened his mouth to speak again, but Matt was already elbowing through the crowd in Haythorn's direction. He found the gambler in the dealer's chair, a tall stack of chips in front of him, with three other players Matt did not recognize. Haythorn, revealing the experienced gunfighter's awareness of any sudden movement around him, immediately lifted his eyes to the advancing lawman.

"Just passing through, Marshal, or can I interest you in a game of chance?"

Matt dispensed with the niceties. "Haythorn, why did you leave Arrah alone?"

"Ah, then that's the purpose of your visit." The gambler laid his cards facedown on the table and smiled. "She's not alone, well, not entirely. Deputy Haggen was here and I asked him to look in on her."

"Why didn't you bring her with you?"

Haythorn shrugged. "Miss Hillman is indisposed. A touch of a headache, I'm afraid." He smiled. "I hear congratulations are in order, Marshal. I wish I'd been able to put a bullet into Proctor's belly myself."

"Haythorn, Barnabas Shaklee and Husky Wilson are staying close to Dodge," Matt said, his patience with the man wearing thin. "Shaklee is a killer and he wants Arrah. You know that."

"Marshal, that's the very reason I hired Festus. He left here sober and clear-eyed, though I'm assured by all that, drunk or sober, he's quite handy with a gun. I'm certain with Deputy Haggen protecting her, Arrah will be quite safe."

"Play cards, Haythorn," growled a grizzled oldster with the look of the diggings about him.

Haythorn's cool eyes angled to the man. "Patience, Mr. Poteet. You'll lose your poke soon enough."

"Then be damned to ye for making a man wait," the old man said.

The other players at the table laughed . . . but their laughter died away into a questioning silence as the crash of gunshots echoed in the distance.

chapter 33

Festus Takes a Bullet

Matt swung away from the table and pushed his way through the crowded saloon. Behind him he heard Haythorn yell: "Marshal, wait for me!"

He ignored the man and walked quickly along the lamplight-splashed boardwalk, his spurs chiming with every pounding step.

The shots had come from the opposite end of town, from the direction of the Dodge House. Was Festus in trouble?

Matt bit his lip and walked faster, easing his Colt in the holster, a sick dread in him. Festus was good with a gun, but Wilson was faster and Shaklee was a back-shooter. No matter how he tried to figure it, the marshal could only come to one conclusion—Festus, good lawman though he was, had been facing a stacked deck.

The Dodge House was ablaze with lights and a crowd was gathered outside the front door as Matt made his way to the hotel.

He was still some yards off when a middle-aged

woman in a nightdress and robe called out: "Hurry, Marshal, there's been a shooting."

Matt elbowed his way through the crowd to the lobby. A man still wearing his nightcap, a candle lamp in his hand, nodded toward the desk: "Behind there, Marshal."

Stepping around the desk, Matt found Howie Uzell lying on his back, another hotel guest bent over him. "He's been hit real bad, Marshal," the man said. "There's blood everywhere."

Matt took a knee beside the clerk. Uzell's face was ashen, his eyeshade slipped to the back of his head. The man had been shot once, low on the left side, and it looked like the bullet was still inside him.

"Has anybody sent for Doc Adams?" Matt asked.

"I don't know, Marshal," the guest said. "It just happened a few minutes ago."

"Then go get him. And make it fast."

A worried expression on his face, the man hurried away.

"Howie, can you hear me?" Matt asked, bending closer to the clerk.

Uzell's eyes fluttered open. "I can hear you," he whispered.

"What happened?"

"They came for Miss Hillman, two men. I was talking to Deputy Haggen here at the desk and they just stepped inside the door and started shooting."

"Where is Festus?"

"I don't know, Marshal." Uzell bit back his pain. "I . . . I heard shooting from out back."

"Howie, just lay there and don't move. Doc Adams is on his way."

"Mar-Marshal Dillon, am I going to die?"

Matt shook his head. "You're hit hard, Howie, but you'll live."

"Find . . . find Deputy Haggen," Uzell whispered.

Matt rose fo his feet, and as people crowded into the lobby, he made his way along the corridor to the back of the hotel. The door was open and he stepped through, drawing his gun.

As his eyes grew accustomed to the sudden darkness the marshal made out two saddled horses standing in the shadows, their heads up as though made nervous by the gunfire.

Matt stepped away from the doorway and his eyes scanned the gloom. Moonlight touched here and there, glinting on the tin roof of a warehouse looming to his right, reflecting like dull iron on its dusty windows.

"Festus," he whispered.

The reply was immediate. "Down here, Matthew, to the left of the door. I'm lyin' in—I don't know what I'm lyin' in, but it surely do smell."

"Keep talking, Festus," Matt said. "I'll follow your voice."

"They shot me, Matthew. But I kept them away from their horses. Winged one of them good. I reckon it was ol' Husky. He took off limpin' an' cussin', fit to be tied."

Matt made out his deputy's prone form lying wedged against the bottom of the hotel wall. He kneeled beside him. "Where are you hit?" he asked.

"Lef' leg, Matthew. It was ol' Barnabas done that. But he couldn't reach his hoss on account of how I kept firing at him and drove him away." Matt saw

Festus' teeth gleam in the gloom as he grinned. "Then them horses got spooked and started into buckin' like you never did see."

Festus grabbed the front of the marshal's shirt. His voice urgent, he said: "Matthew, they got Miss Arrah. They'll be headin' for the livery to steal horses. You'd better go."

"Doc Adams is on his way, old-timer," Matt said, rising to his feet. "In a few minutes, just start hollering."

"I will, but go now, Matthew. Stop them two." Festus eased away from the wall. "Wait, Matthew, what in hell am I lying in here?"

Matt smiled. "I think a skunk must have passed this way a while back."

"Mr. Skunk sure don't trifle when it comes to his perfume," Festus groaned.

A single oil lamp flared on the wall beside the door of the livery stable and the tin rooster on the peak of the roof screeched as it swung this way and that in a tumbling wind. The interior of the stable was in darkness and there was no sound from inside.

Had Shaklee and Wilson made their escape already?

Matt touched his tongue to his dry top lip and frowned in thought. There had been plenty of time for the two men to saddle up and ride out of town. But Arrah was an unknown quantity. If they hadn't tied her up or buffaloed her she might have fought every step of the way, slowing them down.

Did they know he was out there?

Matt smiled. There was one way to find out. He

took up position behind a stack of empty shipping crates and thumbed back the hammer of his Colt. He aimed high, a few inches above the timber framing the top of the door, and squeezed the trigger.

The shot hammered apart the silence of the night and brought an immediate reaction from inside. Matt heard a woman's cry, and a moment later a man ran out of the door and vanished, limping, into the shadowed darkness of the pole corral at the side of the barn.

Matt fired at the man, fired again and, as far as he could tell, scored no hits.

The marshal dropped the empty shells from his gun and quickly reloaded, his eyes searching into the darkness of the stable and the corral.

There was no sound and nothing moved.

"Husky, are you hit?"

It was Shaklee's voice, coming from deep inside the barn.

"No, damn you, Shaklee. I'm not hit."

Matt, his gun up and ready, desperately tried to pin down the voice to a patch of the surrounding darkness. But when the gunman yelled again, he'd already shifted position.

"Shaklee!"

"What is it, Husky?"

"I told you not to try and take her until we were out of town. Now we're trapped like rats."

A cackle of amusement came from the barn, the words that followed shredding in the turbulent wind.

"Husky, sometimes a man can't wait for what's rightfully his'n." There was a few moments' pause. Then Shaklee added, his voice now tight with anger,

"She fought me off once. She won't do it again. I'll take a whip to her until she begs me to bed her. For the whore of Babylon shall know the lash and—"

Matt fired two fast shots into the barn, again aiming high for fear of hitting Arrah. "Shaklee," he whispered to himself, "I've had about all of you I'm going to take."

As he again reloaded from his cartridge belt, Shaklee hollered: "Husky, you still out there?"

"I'm here."

"Who is it? Is it Dillon?"

"Him or maybe Haythorn. One is as damn bad as the other."

"Dillon, is that you out there?"

"I'm here, Shaklee," Matt yelled. "Now come out with your hands in the air, and I'll see you get a fair trial before I hang you."

"On what charge, Marshal?"

"The murder of a young drover and a corset drummer."

"You got no proof of any o' that, Dillon."

"I can prove it."

"Then tell me what proof you have. I say unto you that the righteous shall stand in the place of judgment and shall not be found wanting. His innocence will be revealed to all and his accusers shall be cast down into the pit."

Now it dawned on Matt. Shaklee was playing for time. As he babbled, he was saddling a horse so he could make a break for it. And in the uncertain light, with Arrah up in front of him, he'd be shielded from the marshal's gun.

Matt was not a cussing man, but now he swore

long and fervently under his breath. Barnabas Shaklee had played him for a fool.

He stepped out from behind the crates and sprinted for the side of the barn. A bullet kicked up a V of dust at his feet and another slapped viciously past his head as Wilson fired at him.

Matt didn't slow his pace or shoot back. He was fast running out of time. Only when he reached the corner of the stable did he pull up and walk. He made his way to the rear of the building, stepping warily through inky darkness, feeling his way along the wall for the door.

After a few moments, his fingers touched the handle. Matt pushed the door open, creaking on its rawhide hinges, and stepped inside.

A gun flared a few yards in front of him. The bullet sang its death song past his head and thudded into the timber wall behind him. Matt held his fire. Where in all this murk was Arrah?

Shaklee fired again. This time Matt shot back at the gun flash, dived to the ground, rolled and fired again. He heard a terrible, agonized groan then a crash as Shaklee fell against a stall partition, then hit the ground.

"Arrah?" Matt whispered, his eyes trying to penetrate the darkness.

"Over here, Marshal. To your left."

"Wait, Arrah. Don't move," Matt said. "Stay right where you are."

Shaklee's gun fired and the bullet burned across the thick muscle of Matt's left shoulder.

The marshal triggered a shot, and another. He heard Shaklee scream. Then silence.

Suddenly Arrah was in Matt's arms. The top of the woman's dress was hanging in tatters around her hips, and even in the darkness, the marshal saw the angry welts on her neck and shoulders, where the frenzied Shaklee's fingernails had raked her.

Arrah buried her face at the base of Matt's neck and she sobbed uncontrollably, her tears running warm over his skin. But he pushed the woman away from him.

"Go back into the stall and stay there, Arrah," he whispered. He stared into the darkness where Shaklee lay and said: "I never trust a wolf for dead until he's been skun."

Arrah nodded and stepped back. Only when she had disappeared into the gloom did he walk warily toward Shaklee. Now that he was closer to the door, the oil lamp outside spilled a patch of orange light onto the barn floor. Shaklee's body was still lost in darkness, but his outstretched left hand, palm upward, lay in the light.

Matt took one step, then another, the thudding of his heart loud in his ears. Suddenly Shaklee's hand darted out of the light and the marshal saw the dull gleam of a gun. Matt fired and Shaklee shrieked as the bullet hit him.

The marshal stepped closer. Now he could make out the man's form. Shaklee was sitting, his back wedged against a stall partition. His shirtfront was covered in blood and a thin crimson trickle ran from the corner of his mouth.

Shaklee's eyes had been closed, but now they flew open, bulging with rage and madness in his ashen face.

"Yea, and the seed of the devil shall be slain and be cast down into the fires of hell," he yelled. He desperately tried to bring his gun to bear on the tall, grim marshal looming over him. "The iniquitous shall suffer forever amid the flames as they reap the rewards of their misdeeds. . . ."

Matt fired into the man's chest and Shaklee jerked, then lay still, his open eyes staring into an eternity already stretching away from him.

"Amen," the marshal said, looking down at the dead man without a shred of pity.

Behind Matt, a gun roared. He spun, his Colt coming up fast.

"Take it easy, Marshal," a voice said urgently. "It's me, Mitch Haythorn."

A match flared into life and Haythorn held it high. "See. I told you it was me."

In the brief, guttering light Matt saw a man lying sprawled on his face at Haythorn's feet.

It was Husky Wilson.

Without a word, Haythorn brushed past the marshal. He walked out of the barn and returned with the oil lamp from outside. He stepped beside Matt and let a dancing pool of pale yellow light fall on Wilson's body. A wicked-looking bowie knife was still clutched in the man's dead fist.

"I followed him in here," Haythorn said. "He was about to shove that pig sticker in your kidneys when I drilled him." The gambler shrugged. "It's bad form to shoot a man in the back, I know, but that was the only part of him facing me."

"What took you so long?" Matt asked.

In the lamplight, half of Haythorn's face was

masked in shadow. "I didn't see a real need to hurry. I knew you could take care of yourself."

"A few seconds later and I would have been dead, Haythorn."

"Ah, but then I did hasten a little when I saw that Mr. Wilson here was about to bed you down with his Arkansas toothpick."

Matt shook his head, his eyes hard. "Haythorn, right about now I'm trying to make up my mind on whether to thank you or put a bullet in your belly."

Before the gambler could make a reply, Arrah ran into his arms. Haythorn held her close as he stroked her hair and whispered: "It's all right now, Arrah. It's over and you're safe."

"Mitch," the woman said, "can we go home now?"

"Sure," the gambler said, his teeth white in the gloom. "We can go home now, Arrah. You and me, just like always."

Matt watched the couple leave, Haythorn's arm around Arrah's slender waist, her head on his shoulder.

The marshal stood for a few moments, staring at the ground at his feet, where the light of the oil lamp glowed. Then he walked to the front of the barn and into the arching dome of the night . . . a loneliness in him he could not explain.

chapter 34

Out of the Shadows

Doc Adams perched on the corner of Matt's desk, his face like thunder. "I just don't understand it, Matt. He pretty much suffered the same wound as Quint Asper, no worse, yet Quint is at his forge even as we speak."

The marshal smiled. "Doc, the ladies of Dodge set store by Festus. He's their fallen hero."

"Balderdash! Hero, my foot! He feeds those silly women a pack of lies about fighting Indians and outlaws and they believe every word." Doc jumped to his feet. "Do you know that Mayor Kelley offered Festus the third-best room at the Dodge House, at city expense, mind you, for his"—Doc screwed up his face, as though he'd just tasted something bad—"convalescence?"

"I know, but Mrs. Bodkin wouldn't hear of it. She insisted on setting up a bed in her parlor, so her wounded warrior can get the best of attention." Matt grinned. "I bet right now he's surrounded by pretty belles who are feeding him cake and ice cream."

"Humph," Doc said. "Then I hope he took a bath. He smelled awful."

"I think an angry skunk with a bad aim was to blame for that." Matt's shrewd eyes followed the physician's agitated stomp around the office. "Dr. Adams, I could be wrong, but do I detect a hint of jealousy?"

Doc turned on Matt, and for a moment, he looked like he'd been slapped. Then slowly his face split into a wide grin. "It's that obvious, huh?"

Matt nodded. "Feel the same way my ownself. I never had a bevy of beautiful belles fussing around me anytime I got shot."

"You always had Kitty."

"The last time, after my leg got broke, she stayed for a few minutes, then left a cat to keep me company." Matt's face fell. "An animal that hates me, by the way."

Doc nodded. "I remember that cat, a little calico, wasn't it? Is it still around?"

"Oh, sure," Matt answered. "It's around Dodge somewhere"—he sighed—"plotting my death." The marshal's eyes angled to the clock on the wall. "Doc, I have to get going. I promised Ben Hillman that I'd go with him to speak to Mitch Haythorn about his intentions toward his sister."

As the marshal rose to his feet, Doc said: "Folks were glad you caught the Ripper and settled Shaklee's hash, Matt. But they were sorely disappointed to have missed Hillman's fight with Bill Kennett."

"You should be glad, Doc. You said his ticker wouldn't stand up to it."

"And I was right. I said folks were disappointed. I don't include me in that sentiment. Anyway, Kennett seemed relieved, said his ribs were still paining him, and his winning the fight might have been a mighty uncertain thing. He's a proud man, and I think he figured he was heading for a fall." As Matt settled his hat on his head, then buckled his gun belt, Doc asked: "How is it going with Hillman?"

"He's surrendering himself as a deserter to the Army at Fort Dodge."

"And what will those blockheads do to him?"

Matt shook his head. "I don't know, Doc. But Ben says he's willing to take his chances."

"Then good luck to him. God knows he's going to need it."

When the marshal stepped outside, the morning seemed a little brighter, the air a little cleaner and the birdsong from the live oaks and cottonwoods a little sweeter.

With the deaths of Proctor and Shaklee, a shadow had been lifted from Dodge and a great weight from Matt Dillon's soul.

He stood on the boardwalk waiting for Hillman, the early sun warm on him, and he turned when he heard a woman's voice at his side. "Marshal Dillon?"

Matt turned and touched his hat to a small, care-worn woman in a black dress, gray hair peeking out from under her bonnet. "That would be me." He smiled.

"My name is Sarah McDermott, up from El Paso,

Texas," the woman said. "My son was Samuel McDermott."

For a moment, Matt was taken aback by the sudden appearance of the dead kid's mother, but he said finally, "I'm so sorry, Mrs. McDermott. I'm sure your son was a fine young man."

The woman nodded. "He was, a little wild maybe, but then isn't every boy at his age?"

"I reckon so," the marshal said, thinking back, remembering how it had been.

"I wish death on no man, Marshal," Mrs. McDermott said, "but I want to thank you for bringing his killer to justice. The undertaker, Mr. Crump, told me you killed the man last night and his wicked sons before him."

"Why are you in Dodge?" Matt asked.

"I've come for my son," the woman said. "I'm taking him back to Texas on the three o'clock train. I will not let him lie in foreign soil."

"Is Percy Crump making the arrangements?" Matt asked. "And if there's anything I can do . . ."

"It's all being taken care of by Mr. Crump, Marshal. He's a very nice man."

"Indeed he is," Matt agreed, trying to sound as sincere as possible.

Mrs. McDermott slipped her son's silver ring off a black-gloved finger. "Mayor Kelley returned this to me, Marshal. I want you to have it. It bears the clan crest of our family, the royal arms of Irish kings."

Matt shook his head. "Mrs. McDermott, I can't take your son's ring. It belongs to you and your family."

"Marshal, I do not have a family. With Samuel gone, I have no one. His father died many years ago, and he has no brothers or sisters. I am alone in the world." She shrugged her thin shoulders. "There's no one else."

The woman lifted Matt's big hand and pressed the ring into his palm. "I think you deserve to wear this ring more than anyone."

Tears had gathered in the woman's faded eyes, and Matt knew that if he refused her gift he would hurt her terribly. He managed a smile and slipped the ring onto the little finger of his right hand. "Well, look at that," he said. "It fits perfectly."

"Yes." The woman nodded. "On that finger. My son had small hands, you see."

Ben Hillman crossed Front Street and stepped up onto the boardwalk. He tipped his hat to Mrs. Mc-Dermott and said: "Sorry to interrupt. I know I'm early."

A silence stretched between Matt and the woman. Then she said: "I won't detain you any longer, Marshal. I realize that you have your duties."

Matt nodded. "Good luck, Mrs. McDermott. I'm sorry we had to meet under such sad circumstances."

"Yes, sad, and more than sad." The woman began to walk away, taking slow, tired steps. She bowed her head and whispered: "I'm so very lost."

But Matt didn't know if she'd meant him to hear, and he remained silent.

Arrah and Mitch Haythorn were having breakfast in the Dodge House dining room when Matt entered, Hillman following behind him.

Haythorn rose to his feet, smiled and ushered the

two men into chairs. He was not wearing a gun. Matt refused the gambler's offer of food, but accepted coffee, as did Ben.

After the marshal and Haythorn indulged in a few minutes' small talk about the weather and cattle prices, Matt saw Ben reach into his coat. The young man produced a wad of money, which he shoved across the table to Haythorn.

"This is for you," he said.

Haythorn eyed the bills suspiciously. "What is it?"

"It's the money you bet on my fight with Bill Kennett," Hillman said. "Since the fight is canceled, all bets are off."

Haythorn looked relieved as his eyes moved to Matt. "Did you take this from Proctor?"

The marshal nodded. "Yeah, I reckoned he wouldn't be needing it anymore."

Like a man who had suddenly lost his appetite, Haythorn picked up his fork and pushed scrambled eggs around on his plate. Finally he laid down the fork again and his eyes lifted to Ben. "I guess you've come to talk to me about your sister?"

"I have no money, Haythorn, if that's what you mean. G. P. Proctor saw to that."

"I don't want your money," the gambler said. He turned to Arrah. "I'll let Arrah tell you what we've decided."

The woman's smile was dazzling. "Ben, Mitch and I have decided to stay together."

Matt looked quizzically at the gambler. "A change of heart, Haythorn?"

"You could call it that, Marshal. A man thinks that

he's too set in his ways to change, that he'll never reach marriageable age, and then the right woman comes along and undoes everything."

Matt smiled. "I was always told that calico fever can turn a man's head."

"Well, I realized before it was too late that I wanted Arrah at my side for the rest of my life." His eyes slanted to Ben. "She's not for sale, to anybody, at any price."

Hillman looked at his sister, his face puzzled. "Arrah, does this mean you and Haythorn are getting hitched?"

"Maybe, but that's in the future, when Mitch stacks his chips for the last time and gives up his wandering ways."

"Not so far in the future, Arrah my dear." Haythorn smiled, placing his hand over hers. "Another town, another winning streak, and then we'll talk about it."

Ben shook his head. "Well, if that don't beat all."

"If there's to be a wedding in the future, Marshal," Haythorn said, "no matter where we are, I'd like you to stand up for me as best man."

Matt said the words only for Arrah, who was looking at him expectantly: "I'll be honored."

The woman smiled and her attention fell on her brother. "What about you, Ben? Where do you go from here?"

"To Fort Dodge, Arrah. I'm giving myself up to the Army."

"You don't have to do that, Ben," Haythorn said. "You can always stay with us."

"I'm sure that was kindly meant," Hillman said.

"But, like you and Arrah, I have to do what my heart tells me. And that means clearing my slate with the Army."

Haythorn stuck out his hand. "Well, good luck to you, Ben. And when it's all over, come look us up."

Ben shook hands and then kissed his sister, who had rushed around the table, her eyes stained with tears.

"I'll be all right, Arrah," he said. "Good horse soldiers are in short supply on the frontier."

Matt rose to his feet, and he offered his hand to Haythorn. "I never did thank you for saving my life. I appreciate it."

Haythorn took Matt's hand in his and grinned. "It's the least I could do for my future best man."

The big marshal nodded. "Well, anyhow, thanks again." His eyes hardened. "Now make sure you and Arrah are on the next stage out of town, Haythorn. I don't want your kind in Dodge."

GUNSMOKE
JOSEPH A. WEST

Gunsmoke:
Blizzard of Lead
0-451-21633-4

Gunsmoke:
The Reckless Gun
0-451-21923-6

No other series has this much historical action!

THE TRAILSMAN

Penguin Group (USA) Online

What will you be reading tomorrow?

Tom Clancy, Patricia Cornwell, W.E.B. Griffin,
Nora Roberts, William Gibson, Robin Cook,
Brian Jacques, Catherine Coulter, Stephen King,
Dean Koontz, Ken Follett, Clive Cussler,
Eric Jerome Dickey, John Sandford,
Terry McMillan, Sue Monk Kidd, Amy Tan,
John Berendt…

You'll find them all at
penguin.com

Read excerpts and newsletters,
find tour schedules and reading group guides,
and enter contests.

Subscribe to Penguin Group (USA) newsletters
and get an exclusive inside look
at exciting new titles and the authors you love
long before everyone else does.

PENGUIN GROUP (USA)
us.penguingroup.com